I0549123

Sunset Rising

Book #5 in the Sunset Vampire Series

Jaz Primo

RUTHERFORD LITERARY GROUP

www.rutherfordliterary.com

Novels by Jaz Primo

The Sunset Vampire Series
Sunrise at Sunset: Revamped
A Bloody London Sunset
Summit at Sunset
Wicked Sunset
Sunset Rising
Sunset Burning **

** Additional Titles Forthcoming

* * *

The Logan Bringer Urban Fantasy Series
Bringer of Fire
Bringer Unleashed
Bringer's Law *

* Additional Titles Forthcoming

* * *

Gwen Reaper
(A Young Adult Paranormal Romance)
**Winner of the Paranormal Romance Guild's Reviewer's
Choice Award for Best Young Adult Novel of 2012!**

* * *

All titles published by Rutherford Literary Group

This is a work of fiction. Names, characters, places, and incidents either are the product of the author's imagination or are used fictitiously, and any resemblance to actual persons, living or dead, business establishments, events, or locales is entirely coincidental. The publisher does not have any control over and does not assume any responsibility for author or third-party websites or their content. Any trademarks mentioned herein are not authorized by the trademark owners and do not in any way mean the work is sponsored by or associated with the trademark owners. Any trademarks used are specifically in a descriptive capacity.

Published by:
Rutherford Literary Group
1205 S. Air Depot, PMB #135
Midwest City, OK 73110-4807

Cover art by Sharon Legg,
Sharon Legg Digital Art

Edited by Laura Matheson
Copy Edited by Vicki Rose Stewart

ISBN 098856906X
ISBN-13 978-0988569065

DEDICATION

This book is dedicated to devoted loved ones – my family, friends, and supporters – who've steadfastly encouraged me through challenging times while this novel was being written. Without you, I wouldn't be the person I am today.

CONTENTS

PART III – NEW REALITIES

ACKNOWLEDGMENTS

My heartfelt thanks to Tabby, the newest member of my family, who injects her youthful exuberance into both my life and my writing process, often with equal parts mirth and aggravation. My sincere thanks to my loved ones for supporting me through occasionally turbulent emotional events while this book was written. As always, a huge thank you to my dedicated publicist, Vicki Rose Stewart, for her continued support and encouragement.

Thank you to my editor, Laura Matheson, for her marvelous editing and mentoring skills. You were a joy to work with on this project. Special thanks to my covert artist, Sharon Legg, for sharing her talented artwork and permitting me to grace my novel covers with such beautiful imagery. As always, I give a hearty thank you to my graphics and font wizard, Brandon, for continued support and assistance.

Finally, a huge thank you and a big hug to my dedicated readers for your continued support, encouragement, and promotional assistance. Certainly, my unique collection of Sunset Vampire characters and storylines thrives under your energetic, grass-roots-level advocacy to others in the world. Thanks so much for all you do!

Part I

NEW HAVEN

CHAPTER 1

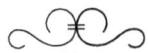

Caleb

Imagining killing people versus actually killing people are completely different experiences. The former questions your sense of innocence while the latter questions your humanity.

Contemplating either was abhorrent to me.

Yet, I'd recently partaken in each.

Grasping the repercussions of either was vast; certainly too much for me to process during the moments in which each had occurred.

In the fog that followed my recent experiences, I felt too overwhelmed to confront those realities.

As such, sleep was my preferred form of escapism.

In the space between restless dreams and consciousness is a timeless place of endless possibilities; a place I felt satisfied to dwell.

Unfortunately, my visit there felt far too short lived.

The moment my eyes opened, a host of unsettling thoughts and memories washed over me.

It took a few seconds to get my bearings as moonlight streamed in through the open blinds.

I lay alone in my bed, feeling slightly unnerved.

My last memory before falling asleep was of Kat curled around me.

I had felt safe then. And loved.

After a moment, my feelings of numbness, confusion, and bewilderment from Friday night resurfaced anew.

Accompanying them was a stark reminder that I'd killed two people.

While I felt anxious over that, strangely enough, I was devoid of either guilt or regret.

Despite the taint of death, I realized that it was nothing personal. It had been a matter of either living or dying; a simple choice, really.

It had been an exercise in survival, and I had prevailed. In the end, that was what mattered.

Memories from Friday night flashed through my mind in a series of disjointed images.

My walk home from the convenience store.

The two mysterious men who assaulted me; the ones who'd been stalking me around the city and campus, though I had no idea why.

I vividly recalled my surprise and feelings of panic at their strength and speed.

The memories of my desperate attempts to defend myself felt like permanent scars in my mind. My actions had culminated in two separate, and very awkward, acts with the combat knives that Kat had given to me.

In the end, there had been two deaths, and thankfully, neither of them was mine.

But that had been Friday night. I scarcely recalled anything from Saturday night. I'd only briefly talked to Kat and Alton and then slept again.

Though uncertain of the time or day, my visit with them must've been only a few hours ago because I still felt tired and sore. My entire body ached as I stretched my arms and then strained to read the display on my wristwatch.

Damn! Sunday evening! I slept through the entire day.

I groaned, rubbing at my eyelids with my rough fingertips. Even the joints in my fingers ached.

After pausing to listen for the sounds of voices

downstairs, but hearing only silence, I slowly sat up and rolled out of bed, ignoring the pain from my protesting muscles and joints.

I'd gotten the hell beat out of me Friday night.

It had all happened so fast, and I'd felt so ill-equipped to handle things.

Fortunately, I had handled things in the end...somehow.

Following a quick hot shower, I put on a pair of jeans and a t-shirt and quietly exited my bedroom.

As I stood at the top of the stairs, I heard the subdued conversation of familiar voices downstairs, but I couldn't understand what anyone was saying.

As I slowly descended to the first floor, the voices fell silent and multiple sets of eyes targeted me.

They were the four most important and beloved people in my life.

Actually, more accurately, they were vampires; not that I cared in the least. They were like family to me.

While I was relieved to see them, their intense expressions spoke volumes; concern that radiated toward me in veritable waves.

Still, who could blame them? Upon being attacked the other night, I didn't know if I'd ever see them again.

My beautiful mate, truly the love of my life, Katrina, stared at me from her seat on the couch. I could almost feel the pain reflected in her emerald eyes.

Alton Rutherford, my quasi-uncle for all intents and purposes nowadays, nodded back at me as he sat in one of the recliners, confidently poised like a king upon his throne.

Honestly, as one of the most powerful vampires in the world, perhaps the title truly suited him.

My surrogate vampire, Paige Turner, a sassy hellion who always had something snarky to say, was oddly silent at the moment. She leaned against the breakfast counter next to where her beau, Dr. Ethan Reynolds, sat on one of the barstools.

Ethan was one of the kindest and most sincere vampires

I'd ever met, and he had the best of bedside manners for any physician, either human or vampire.

"Hey," I said, nervously slipping my hands into the front pockets of my jeans. "Grim faces. You'd think somebody died."

Kat frowned at me.

"All right," Paige said. "You guys all harped on me to be on my best behavior. Just remember that funny boy here was the one who weighed in with the quips."

I made a half-hearted attempt at a grin, but I just wasn't feeling it.

I'm a bonafide killer now. Just like the vampires in my life.

There were no briefcase bombs this time, as had occurred at the Slovene conference; the latest violence and deaths had all been up close and personal.

My gaze shifted back to Kat.

She quietly rose from her seat and held her arms open to me, her expression full of strength and compassion.

I walked into her embrace, my arms encircling her hips. She hugged me against her warm body, conveying an immediate sense of comfort that permeated through me.

It felt amazing to hold her in my arms, much less be held by her in return.

She kissed the top of my head. "Feeling better, my love?"

"Yeah, I'm okay," I replied.

Okay would have to do; *better* was going to take time.

It was a nice start, merely standing there in her arms, safe and loved. I breathed in, reveling in her cherry blossom fragrance.

She pulled away from me slightly to look me in the eyes. "We're here for you. You're safe, and everything's going to be fine now."

An aura of reassurance washed over me; the tone of resolve in her voice sounded convincing.

I almost believed her.

"Sure," I said.

She held my face between her warm palms and kissed me on the lips. I pulled her body against mine.

During my confrontation Friday evening, I doubted such a simple act would've been possible for me again.

I'd expected the worst.

Thankfully, I'd been mistaken.

Kat stepped aside to let Paige and Alton greet me in turn with an embrace and kind words of encouragement.

Ethan shook my hand and warmly clasped me on the shoulder. "You're looking much better this evening."

If I was truly better, it was due in large part to their supportive presence, which was precisely what I needed at that moment.

Paige cleared her throat and I turned to look into her blue eyes.

She smiled and held up a can of Coca-Cola. "I bet my boy's thirsty."

I grinned and accepted the soda from her. "And maybe a little hungry."

"Yes, of course, you should eat," Alton said. "But let's have a little chat about Friday evening first, shall we? I'd like to listen to your recollections of the event."

Kat practically growled with displeasure. "It can wait."

"No," I said. "I'd rather talk things out now and be done with it."

As if I'll ever be able to put what happened Friday night out of my mind.

It felt as if it would haunt me forever.

Kat sighed, took me by the hand, and led me over to the couch to sit down. Alton returned to his spot on the recliner.

Ethan took a seat in the opposite recliner. Paige popped onto his lap and affectionately draped her arms around his neck.

"Cute. Are you his mannequin now?" Kat asked.

"Oh, can it, Warrior Princess," Paige said.

I almost laughed at that.

Kat arched one of her eyebrows at me, so I quickly took

a swig of Coke. As if I were suffering a penance, the cold fizzy liquid burned a path down my throat.

Alton stared at me. "Please, you may proceed when ready."

I took a deep breath while gathering my thoughts.

"I had just left the store," I said. "Roman needed cough drops."

Then I stopped.

Roman.

"Where's Roman?" I asked with a frown.

"Upstairs sleeping off the remainder of his illness," Ethan said. "He's fine. The vampire blood Paige injected in him on Friday should finish clearing the virus out of his system within the next twenty-four hours or so."

"Roman will be fine," Kat said. "Now, you were saying?"

I took another deep breath and nodded. "Yeah, I'd just left the store…"

It was much easier to recount what happened once I started. The story practically poured out of me like water through a floodgate.

Only it hadn't been a story, unlike some sensationalized thriller novel or movie; it had been real.

Throughout my ensuing narrative, the entire experience replayed in my mind like a bad movie. I rose from the couch and paced around the room, then sat down again.

Overall, it was easier to recount my experience than I had expected, though no less emotional in memory.

At least until I got to the combat portion of the event. At that point, I struggled to describe the disjointed images from my fight. I closed my eyes and rubbed my damp palms against my jeans as I wrestled with my memories.

I concentrated so hard, I practically forgot that anyone was there in the room with me.

I massaged my forehead with my fingertips.

"I'd thought I was prepared for a fight with someone. Maybe even two people," I said, turning to stare at the nearby television, which had been muted. "But nothing had prepared me for anybody like…them."

When nobody said anything, I blinked. I looked at Alton and focused my attention upon him.

"There was something wrong about the two of them," I said. "Something not quite normal. Something was off about them."

"Caleb, the mind can create illusions under stressful circumstances," Ethan said.

"No," I insisted, rising from my seat. "They weren't *normal* people."

I scanned the faces around me. Everyone was frowning.

"Look, I'm serious. I wasn't imagining it," I said.

"My love, nobody's implying that," Kat said.

"What do you mean by *not normal?*" Alton asked. "Describe what you mean by that in more detail."

I stood and quietly focused my thoughts while slowly pacing the room, carefully formulating words in my mind before saying anything further.

Then a sober realization struck me.

"They were like me when I was turning, just like back at the estate after you had injected the vampire blood near my brain," I said. "Only they were faster and stronger…as if they were more stable than I had been."

"Yeah, I thought their bodies looked somewhat feverish," Paige mumbled. "But the lightning flashes were distorting everything, and besides, I was in a hurry to handle things."

"Feverish?" Alton asked.

"Yeah, but it was really subtle," she said.

"It's a shame you didn't take any blood samples," Ethan said.

"Or finger prints," Alton said.

"Maybe even a photo or two," Kat said.

Paige sprang to her feet. "Oh, screw you guys and your damned CSI bullshit! I was trying to handle a dicey situation with no less than a shell-shocked kid and a sweaty guy who was the poster child for the plague."

7

"Kid?" I said. "Hey, I'm twenty-seven, if you haven't noticed."

"Enough," Alton said. "Paige, we're not blaming you for anything."

"Hindsight is always twenty-twenty," Kat said.

"And what's not to like about the sight of your hiney, Paige?" Ethan prompted.

Paige grinned. "Aw, now that's my man."

She returned to perch atop Ethan's lap.

Kat stood up, walked over to me, and wrapped me in her arms. "I'm so proud of you."

"I don't know what for," I said.

"You know, perhaps it's still not too late for the samples we need," Alton said. "Paige can lead us back to where she disposed of the bodies."

"Technically, we're still operating in a window where any blood samples taken will be highly viable for testing," Ethan said. "But I haven't practiced in Connecticut for a long time. I don't currently have lab privileges anywhere nearby."

"Fortunately, I have access to a lab where I can overnight the samples," Alton said.

"It sounds like a road trip is in order, shorty," Kat said, looking at Paige.

"Just great," Paige said. "I've barely finished burying them and now we gotta go dig 'em back up again."

Digging up dead bodies.

Bodies that I had killed.

I wasn't a squeamish person, but the prospect seemed somewhat grisly, no matter the necessity.

"I need to get my shoes," I said.

Kat tightened her embrace around me. "You're not going."

Part of me was more than happy to give in to her declaration, but a nobler part of me didn't want to be left behind.

Alone.

An involuntary shiver ran through my body.

Granted, Roman was upstairs, but somehow that was neither reassuring nor comforting at the moment.

"I don't want to stay behind," I said.

I felt Kat's chin settle on the top of my head, though she didn't press her full weight down on me.

"All right," she said.

"Good," Alton said. "It's decided then."

"But not until Caleb gets something to eat," Kat said.

"Hey, mothering me again," I warned, though my stomach betrayed me at that moment with a resounding growl.

The profile of her face appeared in my peripheral vision.

"Oh, hush," she whispered, her warm breath tickling my ear. Then she kissed me lightly on the cheek.

I couldn't help but smile.

* * *

Before we left the house, Paige actually took some hot soup and crackers up to Roman. Normally, I'd have teased her a little bit about that, but I was too proud of her to do that. It really was a nice gesture.

We stopped at one of the steak houses in New Haven so I could have some dinner. The five of us were seated in a large corner booth where I sat between Kat and Alton.

My hunger felt epic, so I ordered a complete rib eye dinner while the others ordered salads. By the fourth salad order, the waitress frowned and looked at me.

"You must one persuasive fellow to talk a group of vegetarians into coming to a steakhouse for dinner," she said.

"I won the coin toss tonight," I said.

"I guess you did," she said. "I'll bring you some fresh rolls. Don't worry, they're meatless."

"Well, snarkety, snark-snark," Paige said after our waitress walked away.

"Oh, no," I said. "She's snarking again."

"Yes, well, there will be no further snarking at the table,

thank you," Alton said.

"Snark-snob," Paige muttered, to which Alton gave her a wan look.

Small talk ensued, which lulled me into a comfortable state of mind. Being reunited with everyone raised my spirits.

I leaned back against the booth cushion and stretched my arm across Kat's shoulders.

As much as anything, it felt so good to do something semi-normal again. My life felt as if it had taken a sharp turn into the *Twilight Zone*.

Well, at least the sense of normality might last until we start digging up dead bodies.

I tried to put those thoughts out of my head, and was relatively successful throughout most of dinner. Instead, I focused on appreciating the company surrounding me.

Paige sullenly picked at her salad. "I don't see why we couldn't have just picked up a burger for junior here through a drive-thru and continued on our way."

"Yes, but this is nice, isn't it?" Ethan countered. "I mean, we don't get to do this together very often nowadays."

I nodded. "Don't I know it."

"The sooner we get out to you-know-where," Paige said, lowering her voice, "the sooner we can start to figure out why Caleb was attacked."

"You know, it's not so much about why they attacked him, but who attacked him," Kat said.

"Yes," Alton said. "After the Slovene conference, there's more than enough who's to pick from."

I fumbled with my fork, nearly dropping it.

"Look, can't it wait for just half an hour more?" I asked. "Let's just talk about something else."

Kat patted me on the thigh. "Fine. What would you like to talk about?"

"I don't know. Anything," I said. "The plural of moose."

"Easy," Paige said. "Mooses."

Everyone stared at her.

"What?" she said. "It's like fish and fishes, and goose

and gooses."

"The plural of fish is fish," Kat said.

"And the plural of goose is geese," Alton said.

Paige shook her head. "Fine, so it's meese then."

I laughed. "No, it's moose."

She frowned and looked at Ethan, who smiled and nodded.

"Whatever," she said, folding her arms before her. "Who the hell cares about moose anyway? Pick another damned topic."

"What color are you painting your toenails next"? I asked her.

"Oh, well, there's this new salmon-colored polish I bought just the other day," she said.

"Please spare me," Alton said.

Paige gave him a dirty look. "In fact, I bought two bottles since they were on sale."

"Salmon, huh?" I asked. "Hey, I bet you don't know what the plural of salmon is."

Kat chuckled while Ethan reached up to hide his grin with one hand.

Paige gave me an evil look and leaned across the table toward me. "I'm fixin' to bite you."

"So, dessert anyone?" Kat asked.

After our meal, while on our walk out to our vehicle, Alton tossed the car's keys to Paige. "As only you know our destination, you're the chauffeur. Please remember it's a rental."

She scowled and muttered something indistinguishable under her breath in response.

"I should point out, we'll need to make a couple of stops for some specialty items," Ethan said.

Following stops at both a twenty-four hour pharmacy and a Wal-Mart, we drove east out of New Haven city limits on the Governor John Davis Lodge Turnpike.

"Everyone turn your phones off. We won't want to risk our phones being used to track us any further," she said while powering down her smartphone.

As I powered mine off, I realized that such a thought hadn't even occurred to me. There seemed to be an awful lot of angles to consider when heading out to dig up bodies in remote locations.

Eventually, we passed a sign for Guilford and made our way south; it was territory far outside my scope of familiarity.

After traversing a series of gravel and dirt roads, we finally stopped near a rather remote, seemingly desolate area that hosted sporadic copses of trees.

In truth, the location had an eerie sort of feel about it.

I exited the vehicle with everyone else and visually scanned my surroundings. A cold wind sent a chill through me and I quickly zipped up my coat.

"It's only a short distance on foot from here," Paige said.

"I'll help carry some stuff," I said.

"Get back in the car, young man," Alton said.

"But—"

"I don't want to risk any of your stray DNA getting left behind. Unlike yours, ours would simply burn up during daytime," he said, pulling on a pair of leather gloves.

I started to protest again.

"And, mark my words, if I hear even one more attempt at argument over this, I'll put you over my knee," he said.

For some reason, that really irritated me.

"Hate to disappoint you, but I'm just not into that," I said.

Paige laughed aloud. "That's not what I heard."

I glared at her, but she stuck her tongue out at me.

"Paige, please retrieve the shovels from the trunk," Kat said.

Ethan appeared amused as he opened the driver's side door and reached into the vehicle.

The trunk popped open.

"Caleb, I realize the past couple of days have been troubling and stressful for you. However, you've responded in a commendable and highly respectable manner, and I'm very proud of you," Alton said. "That being said, you will obey me. You're staying here."

The king has spoken.

"Fine," I said, shrugging and folding my arms before me. "Whatever."

"Hey, that's my catch phrase," Paige said while leaning the shovels against her shoulder.

Kat offered me a sympathetic look as she held open the rear door and gestured with her hand toward the interior of the vehicle. I started to enter, but she gently caught my arm to halt me.

"Just so you know, I agree with Alton. His concern makes sense, my love," she said, lightly tapping me on the tip of my nose with her fingertip. "And I'm also very proud of you."

I offered her an appreciative look. "Thanks. That's something, I suppose."

As I scooted onto the back seat, Alton appeared in the door and handed me a small automatic pistol.

I looked at the pistol and then at him with a wide-eyed expression. "Seriously? Where the hell did you get that?"

"It's one of Roman's. The safety's in the trigger, so just point and shoot," he said. "I'm relatively confident that we weren't followed, but until we know who we're dealing with, I'd rather not take any chances."

I merely nodded, not sure what to say to that.

"We'll be back here immediately if something happens," Kat said. "Shoot first. Let us worry about the rest."

She frowned at me as she closed the door. I heard the locks engage and the car alarm's chirp as it activated.

I could easily tell from her expression that she wasn't pleased at all.

For one, Kat's never been in favor of me having a firearm. Granted, they didn't intimidate me, though I wasn't especially experienced with them. The fact that I was holding one at that moment only made me feel less at ease over my current situation.

There were a lot of unknowns at the moment.

Foremost, who's out there targeting me?

CHAPTER 2

Katrina

As I pulled on my pair of leather gloves, I took one last glance at Caleb sitting in the car. I was so very proud of how he'd conducted himself, and so grateful that his training had helped to save him.

But he was hardly adept at hand to hand combat.

Back at the house, while Caleb still slept, Alton and I'd had a brief discussion regarding how to proceed with his training from this point. At the very least, I felt confident that my mate was well on his way to being formidable for most any opponent.

Except actual vampires.

While I didn't like the idea of leaving him alone in the vehicle, Alton had made an excellent point about the potential for DNA contamination. Besides, given all that Caleb had recently experienced, I felt better not exposing him to corpses; particularly ones he'd helped to create.

As the group of us proceeded across the field, the moonlight cast the ideal illumination over our surroundings. These were conditions only a vampire could fully appreciate.

I breathed in the fresh scent of the ocean from the nearby bay, and I reveled in the soothing sounds of the wind and the telltale clunking of dry tree branches against one other.

Paige had selected an ideal location for disposing of the bodies. I doubted anyone would come across them for years, if ever.

Though, in truth, *if ever* rarely occurred. Given the rate that land continued to be developed in recent years, the most we could hope for was a few decades.

Despite the considerable burial depth, between Paige and Ethan it took only minutes to dig far enough to reach the bodies.

Paige had done well. She was so reliable regarding matters such as this.

Careless or short-sighted vampires didn't last long.

But then, wasn't that true of all killers? Only the most thorough and intelligent ones successfully eluded detection over the long term.

Paige easily leapt out of the impromptu grave, holding both shovels.

"Someone please hand me that pharmacy bag," Ethan said.

I handed the small bag of items to him and peered into the grave to watch.

As Ethan removed the plastic sheeting that covered the bodies, my breath caught in my throat, and not merely from the acrid scents of early decomposition.

Both of the men's faces appeared somewhat pale, much like a vampire's, though not quite as stark as was typical for my kind.

"They don't look normal at all for humans," I said.

"Yes, there's a strange pallor to their skin. Very odd," Ethan said. "But I'll know more once we run our tests."

"Caleb wasn't exaggerating after all," I said.

"Mm. So it would seem," Alton said.

As I stared at the bodies, my anger mounted.

I wished I could revive them just so that I could kill them all over again. After they dealt with me, they'd think Caleb had done them a favor.

Ethan used a bottle of water to rinse one of the men's forearms and withdrew a syringe from the sack.

"Two from each, please, as we discussed," Alton said.

I looked at him curiously.

He shrugged. "One for the lab, one for future reference, if needed."

I nodded. *Good idea.*

Evidence sometimes had a way of disappearing when it made its way into the wrong hands.

Minutes later, Ethan hopped out of the grave and landed across from me, sack in hand.

In turn, Alton jumped into the grave.

"Now what?" I asked.

"Their fingerprints will aid in our identification process," he said.

He withdrew a small device from his pocket and proceeded to press each of the men's fingertips against the screen.

"I'll go online to check them against the database after we've returned to the house," he said.

Once he had finished, he replaced the plastic sheet over the bodies.

With a single leap, Alton once more stood beside me.

Paige handed me a shovel and we proceeded to fill in the grave. It didn't take us long.

As we approached our vehicle, I noticed Caleb tentatively looking out through the opposite sides of the car windows, which were already fogged up.

That made me smile.

"Just look at that," Paige said. "Caleb couldn't see a car if it drove up beside him. Remind me not to take Mr. Heavy Breather on a stakeout."

In fact, Caleb jumped slightly as Paige used the remote to unlock the doors. I quickly opened the rear driver's side door to see a surprised expression on his face.

"Back already?" he asked. "That was fast."

"We're vampires," Paige said as she placed the shovels in

the trunk. "We're fast."

I slid onto the seat next to Caleb and stretched my arm across his shoulders. Alton opened the door opposite me and sat on the other side of him.

I held out my free hand before Caleb, my palm up and open.

"What?" he asked.

I arched one eyebrow at him.

His features fell. "Oh, all right."

He placed the pistol in my hand, which I quickly pocketed for safekeeping.

"You're not ready to carry one of those yet," I said.

"Then I need to start training very soon, don't I?" he asked.

Oh, clever man.

"Perhaps," I said. "We'll see."

"There's some other training I'd like for you to begin first, Caleb," Alton said.

"Really?" he asked. "What sort of training?"

"Oh, you'll find out beginning tomorrow," Alton said.

My mate flashed me a suspicious look.

"But I have class," he said.

"Don't worry," Alton said. "You can easily append this to your other training. Just set aside a little more time for it. It's important."

When Caleb flashed me a curious look, I merely nodded in knowing fashion.

"You'll see," I said.

* * *

Upon returning to the house, we unloaded the vehicle and gathered in the living room.

"I'm going upstairs to take a shower," Caleb said.

"I'll join you soon," I said.

I turned to Alton, who was staring down at his laptop which he had set up on the coffee table. He looked quite pleased with himself.

"Care to share in your good mood?" I asked.

"Success. We have positive results from the fingerprint scans on both of those men," he said.

Good. Because once we identify who sent them, they're going to forget all about Caleb.

They'll have my complete attention.

I'll make them regret their birth, and will welcome their return into oblivion.

Paige plopped onto the couch and picked up the television remote.

"Good, while you two sort that out, I'm going to catch the new season of *Cosplay Island*," she said. "It's an all-stars special and Steampunk Tranny Tim is returning."

Alton gave her a long look. "Steam-who?"

"Trust me. Don't ask," I said, absently waving my hand in the air. "It's just a reality program."

"Hey, it's not just a reality program," she protested. "It's *the best* reality program…as in, *ever.*"

I shook my head. The only reality I cared about was the one that certain parties were preparing to exit.

CHAPTER 3

Caleb

I woke abruptly to the sound of my alarm going off. I reached over to shut it off and lay there half asleep for a moment.

I hated Mondays.

The gray illumination peeking through the slats of the blinds suggested a cloudy and likely very cold day. I was half tempted to roll over and go back to sleep.

Two distinct things convinced me otherwise.

First, I wanted to see if there'd been any progress in identifying my attackers.

Second, I desperately craved normality; or at least, some semblance of it.

At the very least, I had to live a lie in convincing fashion, pretending to be just another mundane graduate student striving to complete his PhD.

It was a façade; a fabrication of reality. And yet, I was getting better and better at presenting it to the world around me.

In those moments when I was studying, or typing an essay, or just hanging out with friends at a local pub, I nearly believed it myself.

Almost, anyway.

However, I longed for an actual mundane reality; one with no rival vampire factions, assassins trying to kill me, or people I loved being in danger.

Maybe someday. Only someday couldn't come soon enough.

After a quick shower, I slipped on a pair of jeans and a turtleneck sweater and headed downstairs.

The living room was empty and I noticed that the door to the nearby study was closed. My human bodyguard, Roman, sat atop a barstool at the kitchen counter, nursing a glass of orange juice and looking more himself.

"You look almost human again," I said, walking over to pat him on the back.

"Yeah. Feelin' a lot better. Thanks," he said. "How about you?"

I shrugged. "Okay, or at least, on my way to it."

The study door opened and Kat walked through the living room to where I stood.

"Good morning, my love," she said, enfolding me in her arms. "Sleep well?"

I tightly embraced her, happy to hold her.

"Well enough," I said. "Actually, I barely remember my head hitting the pillow. The next thing I knew, my alarm's going off."

"It's no wonder. You're exhausted," she said. "Maybe you can go to bed early tonight."

She kissed me and separated from our hug to walk into the kitchen and over to a water kettle that was heating on the stove.

"That'll depend on what I find out in my classes today," I said. "I sense more lengthy essays in my future."

Graduate work was a full-time job all its own; including frequent overtime.

"Hey, where are Paige and Ethan?" I asked.

"They're sleeping in," Kat said with a wink.

I was happy for Paige. I knew how much she'd been missing Ethan, though no more than I'd missed Kat.

She poured hot water into three mugs with teabags and scooted two mugs toward me. "One of those is for Alton. He's in the study."

She placed the third mug in front of Roman, who gratefully nodded at her. "This should help to perk up your morning, Roman."

"Thank you, ma'am," he said.

I carefully transported my two mugs into the study without spilling either. Alton looked up at me as he sat behind the oak desk.

"Good morning, my boy," he said, accepting one of the mugs. "Mm. Earl Grey."

He gestured to the notebook computer screen before him. "Come around here. I'll show you what we've discovered."

He opened up a photo of one of my attackers. It may have been the light that night, but for some reason the photo didn't make him look as pale as I'd recalled.

"He's Angelo Potenza, age thirty-two," Alton said. "A third-generation American of Italian heritage."

"You mean, he was," I said.

"No, he still is," he said. "Merely more dead than he was last week."

What could I say to that?

I took a tentative sip of hot tea.

"Potenza has an arrest record going back to age eighteen. He's from Philadelphia; his last known address of residence, though arrest records within the past year place him in and around Newark, New Jersey and New York City. His adult record reflects mostly aggravated assault, petty larceny, and disorderly conduct charges," he said. "Though I wouldn't be surprised if his juvenile records are filled with similar references."

"Do you know who sent him after me?" I asked.

"Not as yet," he said. "But I will in time."

"Was he a vampire?" I asked. "Maybe turning?"

Somehow, I doubted I'd have been able to kill one

vampire, much less two. But if they'd been like me when I was in the process of turning, that might be another story.

He frowned. "Not as such. But we should know more when we get the blood test results back."

He brought up the photo of my other attacker; again with a more normal-looking complexion.

"Donnie Norwood, age twenty-nine," he said. "He's originally from Compton, California, but his recent address indicates New York City. His arrest records are similar to Potenza, except there are added charges referencing both stalking and witness intimidation."

"So these guys were just thugs?" I asked.

He took a sip of his tea. "This is a lovely blend."

He cleared the notebook screen and lightly patted my shoulder. "This is all preliminary information; just the beginning, so to speak. For now, you only need to concern yourself with college and your research. Incidentally, I'll expect a progress report on your dissertation subject very soon."

My mind buzzed with quandaries concerning Norwood and Potenza, but clearly Alton wanted me to focus on more pressing matters.

"Just go to class?" I asked. "It's going to be hard to focus on that after all that's happened."

"Perhaps," he said. "Still, that's your mission, remember? That's why you're here. Let Katrina and me worry about these other matters."

He draped his arm around my shoulders and guided me back toward the study door. "Now, why don't you get some breakfast and carry on with your day. Do stay close to Mr. Lee, won't you? We'll chat more this evening. Oh, and don't forget, you and I have some additional training activities to add to your regimen, as well."

Great, more things to occupy my already limited time.

"Have a productive day. We both have a full agenda, it seems," he said. "Oh, and thank you for the tea."

Before I could say anything further, he promptly closed

the study door on me.

"Um, you're welcome," I said.

I wandered back to the kitchen counter where Roman still sat, only to discover Kat was busy cooking breakfast.

The combined smell of eggs, bacon, and pancakes made my mouth water.

"I hope you don't mind turkey bacon, Roman," Kat said. "It's much leaner and healthier than pork."

She spared a warm smile as she glanced back over her shoulder at me. "Caleb has grown to like it."

I sat on a barstool next to Roman as she presented him and me with heaped platefuls of food.

"Thank you, ma'am," Roman said.

"Dig in," she said.

"Wow, this looks and smells amazing," he said. "Sure beats our usual bowl of oatmeal."

"You're in for a treat. Kat's a great cook," I said.

She sat a bottle of maple syrup on the counter between us.

As I expected, everything tasted absolutely wonderful. Among all the other things surrounding Kat's daily absence in my life, I missed her preparing meals for me.

"Oh, I'm in heaven," I said.

She reached out to caress the side of my face with her soft fingertips. A pleasurable shiver ran through my body.

"Nobody's going to believe me when I tell them the General made breakfast for me," Roman said.

He paused, as if catching himself, and warily looked up at Kat. "That is, unless you have an objection, General. I certainly don't openly discuss personal matters involving you, Mr. Taylor, or the household."

She appeared amused. "Meals are safely open for discussion, Roman. Besides, I enjoy shocking the troops from time to time."

And, just like that, my mate, the love of my life, went from being my lover back to being figurehead in charge of a combined vampire-human army.

I didn't think I'd ever get used to that.

It was yet another of my secret realities that must not be revealed to anyone.

After she prepared a second set of pancakes, she leaned back against the kitchen counter and watched me eat with a satisfied expression.

Roman finished eating first and went upstairs, so I helped clear the counter of dishes.

"Thanks for breakfast," I said.

She took me in her arms and imparted a lengthy kiss, which I returned in kind.

"Will you be here tonight, or is this your way of saying goodbye?" I asked.

I was half-afraid to ask that. I realized that she and Alton were both probably needed back in London, but I didn't want her to leave town yet.

"This is my way of saying have a good day today," she said. "I'll be here for a few more days."

"Until?" I asked.

She lightly tapped me on the tip of my nose with her fingertip. "Until I follow up on some leads, and I'm satisfied that you're safe."

"I'm glad you're here," I said.

She nodded. "Me, too."

After a quick kiss, she said, "Okay, go do something academic."

I winked at her. "Hey, my entire day is academic."

Then I paused. "Wait, that sounded all wrong."

She shook her head and giggled in an uncharacteristic fashion.

Frankly, it was a lovely sound coming from her.

* * *

Before I knew it, the day passed quickly. I silently commended myself on a practiced sense of subterfuge, playing at being just a normal student among my peers.

"How was your weekend?" asked Natalie, a fellow grad student.

"Pretty routine," I lied. "Studying and watching some TV. You?"

"Oh, I got you beat," she said. "I went to a frat party with one of my girlfriends Friday night. Then Saturday it was dancing out at clubs all night long."

Yeah, I got beat, all right. Friday night, I was almost beaten to death!

I listened as she proceeded to describe the club guys she had trouble choosing between.

Such was my day.

By early evening, I stopped by Yale's main library. One of my inter-library loans had arrived. It was a rare copy of a book published in 1908 by my dissertation subject, Dr. Oliver Simonson.

For some reason, Alton had insisted that I write my dissertation about Simonson. It was part of my bargain for being able to attend Yale with a full ride, courtesy of *Uncle Alton*.

Simonson was considered an early evolutionary biologist, even before the term had been properly coined and widely accepted. The book I checked out was a detailed study on diseases of the blood.

Upon skimming through it, I quickly anticipated hours of complete and utter boredom.

I received a text message from Roman: *You going to be much longer?*

I texted: *Why? Got a hot date on a Monday night?*

He texted: *Funny.*

I scanned the interior of the library and noticed him sitting in a corner with a book propped open before him. He frowned at me.

I texted: *Need a little more time here.*

His reply was: *Ok.*

Because I'd grown to become a cringing masochist in my research pursuits, I decided to browse the catalog system for any books on phlebotomy, just for some essential background information.

A few minutes later, a text from Kat interrupted me: *Coming home soon?*

I replied: *Still at the library. Need more time.*

She didn't reply, so I continued my search.

I used my iPad to look up the materials in the online catalog and made my way to a relatively deserted portion of the stacks to search for the books in question.

Too bad they don't have these available as eBooks.

As I picked a book from the shelf, I thought I heard a shuffling sound nearby.

"Roman?" I asked.

I turned to exit the aisle and found myself face to face with Paige. "Geez!"

She smirked at me. "Surprise. You're sure jumpy, kiddo. You nerds aren't very observant."

I shook my head with exasperation and turned to walk in the opposite direction, only to practically run into Katrina.

"Crap," I muttered with a start.

She steadied me by grasping me by the upper arms.

"You vamps are so damned stealthy," I said.

Kat arched one of her eyebrows at me. "Well, somebody's awfully grumpy."

I rolled my eyes and she released my arms.

That's when I noticed her outfit with satisfaction.

Oh, so very sexy.

Her fitted blue jeans, knee-high boots, and black leather jacket made her look like an edgy movie star.

She appeared both lethal and desirable.

"You're dressed to kill tonight," I said. "What are you two out doing?"

"I'm relieving Roman," Paige said. "He gets off at sunset, you know."

"Hard to believe it's already sundown," I said as I looked at my watch.

It was nearly seven o'clock.

"News flash; it gets darker earlier in the fall, nerdo," Paige said.

"Finally taking your science courses more seriously, I see," I said.

"Well, snarkety-snark-snark to you, too," she said. "Don't you watch the weather forecasts on the local news? They tell you these things, you know."

"Only old people watch the local news," I said. "Young people Google it."

She flicked me on the ear with her fingertip.

"Ouch!"

"Don't get lippy with me, twerp," she said.

I rubbed at my ear. "Well, I hope I didn't hold Roman up from anything."

"He said he didn't mind, really," she said.

I nodded.

"Slave driver," she added.

I gave her a withering look.

"So, watcha lookin' up there, smarty-pants?" she asked.

"It's a book on phlebotomy," I said.

Paige made a sour face. "Ew, like when they sever part of your brain in one of those sanitariums?"

"That's lobotomy," Kat said. "He's talking about the ancient art of bloodletting."

"Oh, yeah. Well, that's something I know a helluva' lot about," Paige said. "You could've just asked me."

"Yeah, but it's your impromptu demonstration that I might not survive," I said.

"All right you two, that's about enough," Kat said. "I need for my mate to focus on another topic."

She wrapped one arm around my waist and guided me back to the nearby table where I'd left my backpack.

I pulled out a chair for her and then sat in the one next to hers.

"You're rather carefree, leaving your backpack lying about," she said.

"Not an issue," I said. "Usually, there's a dependable

bodyguard somewhere nearby to watch over it."

"Mm," she said. "Point well made, I suppose."

"So, how's the investigation going?" I asked.

"Anymore leads on those two thugs?"

Paige snickered. "Thugs? What're you, Philip Marlowe now?"

Kat gave her a flat stare.

"I'm just askin'," she said.

"Not as many leads as I'd like," Kat said. "But I have a matching set of keys that Paige removed from their pockets. Most likely, they're for wherever they were either staying or operating out of. So, I'm trying to track down any locations they frequented here in town."

"Good idea," I said. "Except who could you ask about that? It's not like we know any of their local contacts, if they even had any."

"Admittedly, challenging," she said.

"Too bad you can't just trace their phone signal activity or something," I said. "I mean, the NSA does it all the time. Hell, they record everyone's phone conversations nowadays, so it's got to be stored somewhere that can be accessed."

"Good thinking," she said.

"Go ahead, pat him on the head," Paige said. "*Good, Caleb.*"

Kat glared at her.

Paige held up her hands. "What? I tease; it's one of my key roles in his life."

Kat shook her head. "Actually, Alton's working on the phone tracking angle. He's hacking their phone chipsets as we speak," she said. "But I have another idea in the meantime."

"Yeah?" I asked.

She handed me her smartphone. "Would you mind looking at these photos?"

"Sure. What am I looking for?"

"Paige said that, on the evening you purchased your new smartphone, you'd seen one of the men who'd been following you," she said.

"Oh yeah, that's right," I said. "He was leaving one of the shops."

"Think you could pick out which building he exited?" she asked.

"Why not check them all? They were just down the street from the AT&T shop," I said.

"Too obvious. It'd appear too suspicious walking up to random doors like that," she said. "However, if you act like you know where you're going, nobody pays you any attention."

"Unless someone's watching for strangers," I said.

"Oh, you're a clever boy," she said with a wicked expression.

She placed a forefinger beneath my chin, lightly pressing the tip of her sharp fingernail against my skin.

"Now, clever boy, your somewhat impatient mate wants to know if you can pick out the correct building," she said in a slow, sensual manner. "Can you?"

Whoa...

An involuntary shiver coursed through my body.

"I'll do my best," I said.

Paige placed her chin on her propped up palm. "Isn't it weird when she talks to you like that?"

I felt myself blush. "I don't mind so much, really."

Kat removed her fingertip with a sly expression and looked down meaningfully to the smartphone in my hands.

I cycled through the digital photos, mostly of a series of various storefronts and building facades.

The building pictures ended and I stopped at the photo of an adorable Labrador retriever puppy.

"Aw, what a cute puppy," I said. "Are we getting a dog?"

"What? No, never mind that one," she said. "I just couldn't resist snapping a photo when I saw him."

Given all the dark events that had intruded into our lives, it was nice to know she still embraced a softer side of her personality.

"The buildings, my love," she gently prompted. "I'm

waiting."

"Oh, you kids and your kinky roleplaying," Paige said. "So endearing."

Kat growled at her.

I couldn't help but grin as I scrolled back through the photos. Eventually, I selected one with a brick frontage and a small alley beside it.

"That's it," I said.

"Hm. A travel agency?" she asked.

"Well, that's where I recalled one of them exiting, anyway," I said.

She stood up and pocketed her phone. "Okay then. It's worth a try. I'll see you back at home in the next couple of hours."

"And, by any chance, would my sexy mate have time to go out to dinner with me tonight?" I asked.

"As a matter of fact, I think she might," Kat said. "After I check this out."

"Bring your credit card, kiddo. Remember, the submissive one always pays the tab," Paige said. "Or else, the sub *pays*. Am I right?"

Kat and I simultaneously looked at her.

She made the sound of a cat screeching and then a whip snapping sound.

"Are you quite finished?" Kat asked her.

She shook her head and sighed. "What? No sense of humor here? I'm using some of my best material."

I returned my attention to Kat. "Be careful."

"Always, my love."

She leaned down to give me a quick kiss.

As she walked away, I took a moment to appreciate the lovely view of her swaying behind.

"Oh, please put your tongue back in your mouth, pervy. You're getting the tabletop all wet," Paige said. "You can properly worship her ass when she gets home tonight."

"Hey, you'd feel differently if it was your butt I was admiring," I said.

"Trust me, tiger," she said in an alluring voice and patted her butt with the palm of her hand. "You're not ready for action this hot."

"Whatever," I said.

"I'm just sayin'," she said. "Now get with the program, brainiac. Ethan's only in town through tomorrow, you know. Once I drop you off at home, I've got a hot date with my own ass-worshipper."

CHAPTER 4

Katrina

As I exited the campus library following my chat with Caleb, I slipped on a pair of leather gloves. Given my intentions, I wanted to avoid leaving fingerprints.

Most people would have found it a foreboding evening for a walk, but the cold wind and moonless sky didn't bother me one bit. In fact, they were the perfect condition for dissuading onlookers. Most people were more interested in quickly making their way indoors or to their vehicles.

In addition, the travel agency had alongside it a small, dark alley ideal for a secluded approach.

The blinds covering the shop's glass door and windows were closed, but there was a dim illumination from within. As I expected, particularly given the time of evening, the door was locked.

One by one, I cycled through a set of keys that we had removed from the bodies of Caleb's attackers, only to find they either wouldn't fit in the lock or didn't turn the tumblers.

With an irony that only fate could bestow, the last key on the ring actually worked.

I quietly slipped inside and paused long enough to verify that nobody was present. Then I closed and locked the door behind me.

The sole light source was a relatively dim ceiling-mounted fluorescent light at the back of the small office, but I had no problem seeing clearly with my vampire vision.

One scan of the poorly furnished shop revealed that, while it had indeed been a travel agency, it hadn't been in operation for quite some time. The most recent brochures or paperwork were dated three years prior.

However, the place smelled as if it had just undergone a cleaning. There didn't appear to be a speck of dust on either the floor or any tabletops.

I searched the available desks, filing cabinets, and shelves for anything of interest, but everything appeared relatively benign.

I walked to the rear of the shop where there were three closed doors along the back wall.

Behind one door was a small bathroom

Another door led to an empty closet containing buckets, mops, and cleaning supplies. The fresh waft of cleaning products simply reinforced the fact that they'd been recently used.

I removed my glove and reached down to touch the mops.

They were still relatively damp, suggesting that someone had used them within the past twenty-four hours or so.

I put my glove back on and moved to open the third door, revealing a narrow set of carpeted steps leading upstairs.

I paused before them and listened for any telltale sounds.

Hearing nothing, I unsheathed a combat knife from inside my jacket and stealthily made my way up the stairs, which curved to the right as I ascended.

Boards from two separate steps squeaked as my weight pressed upon them.

I paused but still heard nothing.

At the top of a small landing, there was a solid wooden door with both a lock on the doorknob and a deadbolt lock.

I placed my ear against the door, but heard only silence beyond.

The door was secured, but fortunately two of the other

keys on one of the key rings fit the locks.

With one hand grasping the door knob and the other holding my knife at the ready, I slowly opened the door, which creaked as it swept open.

I was presented with a darkened, sparsely furnished apartment that also smelled of recently used cleansers.

Like the downstairs area, it was unoccupied.

I slipped my knife back into its sheath.

Aside from the single, open-flowing living room-dining room-kitchen, there were two Spartan bedrooms and a central bathroom; all of which had been scrubbed to the point of spotlessness.

Even the walls mildly smelled of bleach.

There were no clothes, belongings, or anything resembling personal effects left anywhere in the apartment.

The place had been professionally cleaned.

No, more than merely cleaned, it's been cleansed.

Someone intended to obscure any evidence and reveal no trace of who'd been staying there. That suggested we were faced with professionals.

That bothered me.

It also suggested that someone was already well aware that their two operatives had either been detained or were dead.

I made one final sweep of the apartment, to no avail, and decided to leave.

One thing for certain, this place is a dead end.

The question was, did the disappearance of Caleb's two attackers successfully dissuade whoever was in charge, or merely stir a hornet's nest?

No, I knew better than to contemplate the answer to that.

Caleb was still in serious danger.

Anger welled inside me like a dangerous, simmering volcano pending an eruption.

No. When I finally erupt, I'll do so at precisely the moment that satisfies my sense of retribution.

I locked everything back the way I'd found it and left the abandoned shop. A quick evaluation of the nearby trash dumpsters was less than helpful; each had already been emptied, likely earlier that day.

On my walk back to the house, I considered the situation and found too many loose ends for my satisfaction.

Maybe Alton's having better luck.

CHAPTER 5

Caleb

By the time Paige dropped me off at the house, I was feeling really hungry. I only hoped Kat showed up soon so that we could go get something to eat.

My thoughts gravitated to her investigation, and I wondered if she had found *someone* to eat.

Alton was holed up behind the closed door of the study. It sounded like he was talking on the phone.

At least, I hoped he was on the phone and not merely talking to himself.

Paige and Ethan had gone out for a night on the town together, and Roman was who knew where.

I sat on the couch channel-surfing as I waited for Kat. Fortunately, there was an interesting documentary covering the American Revolution on the History Channel.

After another half hour, I was feeling so hungry that I wandered into the kitchen for something to snack on.

I'd no sooner opened a box of rosemary and olive oil flavored crackers when Kat walked through the front door with a notably displeased expression on her face.

Something must have happened.

"What?" I asked.

"The keys fit, but everything had been completely wiped

clean inside and out," she said.

"Crap," I said.

In my distraction, the box of crackers slipped from my grip.

A rush of air swirled around me. Suddenly, Kat stood before me holding the box of crackers in her gloved hand.

She slyly smiled at me. "Drop these?"

"Show off," I said.

My super heroine. My vampire.

The sweet scent of cherry blossoms wafted between us as I glimpsed her soft lips.

Passion flared in me; I wanted her so very much at that moment.

I reached up to take the box of crackers from her while at the same time stepping forward and crushing my lips to hers in a lengthy, heated kiss.

She was an amazing kisser.

I wrapped my free arm around her waist to pull her body against mine as I kissed her again.

Both her arms went around me in a firm grip, and she nipped at my bottom lip.

She pressed me backward until the small of my back impacted the kitchen counter, my lips hungry for hers.

I felt her fangs extend, and they raked across my tongue.

Someone cleared their throat from across the room and Kat separated from our kissing; adopting a stern expression before slowly looking back over her shoulder.

"Your timing really stinks," she said.

Alton chuckled. "Terribly sorry. But I couldn't help but overhear your comments when you arrived. We're dealing with professionals, then?"

She reluctantly disengaged her arms from around me and turned to face Alton.

"Based upon what little I found, anyway," she said. "That's the telling part, in fact. The scent of cleansers was fresh and even the mops they used were still relatively damp, so they hadn't been gone for long when I arrived. They were exceptionally thorough."

"Mm," he said, nodding his head. "That does complicate matters somewhat. I received a report this evening from Sir Osborn; things in London are going to require our attention in the very near future."

"That's unfortunate," she said. "And inconvenient. However, I'm not leaving Caleb with matters up in the air, especially after what I discovered this evening."

Something in her tone bothered me.

What the hell kind of professionals are we dealing with, anyway?

"You and Gavyn are just going to have to handle things until I can return," she said.

I had met Sir Gavyn Osborn on my last visit to London. He was a vampire, and one of Alton's most trusted friends and allies, dating all the way back to the medieval period. He owned and operated a quaint pub called the Red Griffin that also served as a central gathering point for Alton's forces.

As I recalled, Osborn seemed very capable in his own right.

Alton sighed. "Yes, I'm afraid I must concur. Gavyn and I should be able to handle things well enough for the time being."

"What's next?" she asked.

My stomach growled and Alton looked at me with mild amusement.

"I believe that you should take your mate to dinner," he said. "We'll talk more later."

Kat arched one eyebrow as she looked at me. "You still haven't eaten dinner?"

I felt heat rise in my cheeks.

"Hey, enough with the mothering," I said. "I was waiting for you, and now it's getting kinda late and I'm hungry."

She walked over to the couch where my coat was draped over the back. With a quick motion, she tossed my coat to me.

"Bundle up, my love," she said.

Instead, given her exchange with Alton, I felt as if she was actually saying, *buckle up.*

Prepare for rough waters ahead.

* * *

In order to save time and remain closer to home, we went to one of my favorite New Haven hangouts.

Prime Time was a pub on Temple Street that my friends and I frequented. It had a cozy charm about it and the food was better than you'd expect from the average pub.

Seated beside one another at a small table tucked away at the back of the dining room, we browsed our menus.

Despite the dark mood that overshadowed the evening, it felt really good to spend some time alone with Kat.

I lowered my menu to gaze across the table at her.

She locked eyes with me. "And what have I done to earn such a reverential look tonight?"

"Just happy to be here with you," I said. "Happy to spend some quality time together. It reminds me of when we first started dating. Do you remember the place I took you to then?"

Her eyes narrowed slightly, as if in contemplation.

"Ah, Café Circa," she said. "It was your favorite restaurant. Downtown Atlanta."

I grinned. "With the long, finished oak bar."

"And the barstools at the tables," she said.

Such a fond memory. It felt almost like a lifetime ago; back before worldwide vampire politics and intrigue interrupted us.

I reached out to hold her hand.

"I love you," I said.

Her responding expression was both endearing and innocent-looking.

She squeezed my hand. "And I love you. You make my heart soar."

"See? I said I saw them come in here," said a familiar-sounding voice.

42

Chance Noble approached our table while tugging at the hand of a sheepish-looking Trey Baker.

I rose from my seat for a quick embrace with Chance and handshake with Trey.

"Kat, you remember Chance and Trey?" I asked.

"Of course," she coolly said. "From that night at the bar."

Kat rose from her seat like a huntress preparing to take down her prey, but Chance bravely moved toward her. An awkward moment occurred between them as Chance started to move closer to Kat, presumably to attempt a similar greeting.

But Chance was kept at bay as Kat reached out to shake her hand instead.

"Katrina," Chance said.

"Chance," Kat said.

"Edgy-looking outfit," she said. "I love your boots. I have a brown pair of Sesto Meucci's almost like them."

"Really? What are the odds?" Kat asked.

"It takes a real woman to pull off stiletto heels for any length of time," she said.

"I'm rather fond of stilettos," Kat said.

For some weird reason, I couldn't help thinking that she meant knives rather than footwear.

While it was hardly a Mexican standoff, I couldn't help feeling as if the two of them were sizing each other up.

"So, fancy meeting you two here," I said, just to break the ice.

"Yes, and at this time of night, no less," Kat said.

"Chance and I were on our way back from a movie when she said she noticed you two coming in here," Trey said in a nearly apologetic tone. "We didn't get another couple of miles up the street before she insisted we drive back here."

"I said I was hungry," she said. "You ate most of the popcorn at the movie, you know."

"Uh, yeah," he said. "So, here we are."

"Who goes out to see movies on a Monday night?" Kat asked.

I gave her a sharp look.

"It was a busy weekend," she replied. "And besides, I hate Mondays, so it's better to do something fun to take the edge off."

"Well, you two are welcome to join us, if you'd like," I said.

It seemed like the polite thing to offer, though Kat gave me a wan look.

"Oh, no, we'll leave you two-" Trey started to say.

"How nice," Chance interrupted. "We'd love to."

I glanced at Kat, whose tight-lipped smile didn't quite meet her eyes.

"Well, just marvelous then," she said in a less than convincing tone.

I nearly winced.

Oh, a disaster in the making.

Honestly, I just wanted to crawl beneath the table at that moment. And by the expression on Trey's face, he must've felt much the same.

Chance took my seat so she could face Kat from across the table. I moved to the seat beside Kat. Trey took the chair beside Chance, but hesitated as if wondering whether to sit or not.

"Well, isn't this is nice?" Chance asked. "We haven't had much of an opportunity to get to know each other, Katrina. You were only briefly in town when you were last here."

"Mm. So true," Kat said.

By the time the waitress took our drink orders, I was already tempted to ask for the check.

Chance neatly folded her hands on the place mat before her. "So, what's the latest on your exploits, Katrina? We hardly know anything about you."

I looked at Chance, wondering what her game was all about. I felt confused, to say the least.

Trey chuckled. "C'mon, Chance, you make her sound so mysterious."

She gave him a flat look. "Are you shushing me, Trey?"

He swallowed hard as his complexion flushed. "What? No, I-"

"You were saying, Katrina?" Chance asked, once again focusing her full attention on my mate.

Kat sat tall in her chair; nearly imposing looking. She regarded Chance as if closely assessing her.

That's not a good sign.

"Saying? I haven't said anything, yet," Kat said.

"It seems like Caleb's hardly said three words about you," Chance said. "So, it got me to wondering, are you some spy or secret agent or something?"

Kat arched one of her brows. "Something like that."

I nearly gaped at her and both Trey and Chance seemed momentarily taken aback.

Kat forced a chuckle. "Seriously, though, I'm just a businesswoman who travels quite a bit."

"Corporate consulting," I quickly added.

Chance looked at me. "Oh, yes, you said as much that night at Carlucci's. Strategic planning and restructuring or some other sort?"

Kat spare a momentary glance at me with an arched brow. "Carlucci's?"

I looked back at her sheepishly. "Oh, yeah. It's a restaurant over on Wooster Street. We should try it sometime."

"You mean that I should," she said. "You've obviously sampled the menu already."

I stared at her, wondering about potential innuendo in her statement.

Fortunately, her attention quickly returned to Chance, and I made a conscious effort to slowly exhale the breath I'd been holding.

Why the hell am I feeling so guilty? Nothing happened that night. Chance and I only talked. Besides, Paige had waited outside for us.

I absently rubbed my palms against my jeans.

"Getting back to your earlier question, Chance," Kat said. "I cover a span of projects and expertise, often multiple layers simultaneously."

Our drinks arrived, and for some reason, I relished the temporary lull in conversation.

I looked over at Trey and he looked back at me with a forced smile.

My throat felt so dry that I practically gulped at my tea.

"You're gone so much; it must be difficult maintaining a long-distance relationship with Caleb," Chance said.

I almost choked on my tea.

Everyone stared at me.

"Okay—just down my windpipe," I struggled to say. "Fine now."

"I think you'll find that my relationship with Caleb is rock-solid," Kat said.

"Mm-hm," Chance said while staring back at her.

Thankfully, the awkward moment was broken by Chance's smartphone ringing.

"Excuse me," she said, reaching into her jacket pocket and getting up from the table. "What's up?"

I watched as her expression darkened.

"What? I'm out—Trey and I are having dinner with Caleb and—" she said. "What, Dad? Caleb, he's—just a minute."

She appeared unnerved when she looked back at us, and proceeded across the dining room toward the exit.

"That was odd," Trey said with a perplexed look.

Kat frowned as she stared after Chance, seemingly lost in her own thoughts.

"Yeah, she told me once that she and her father have sort of a strained relationship," I said.

Trey shrugged. "I dunno. She hardly mentions him. But she and her mom seem really close."

I nodded. "Yeah, she said as much to me once, too."

Then, just as suddenly as she had walked away, Chance walked briskly back to the table.

"I'm sorry, but I have to go," she said. "Trey, can you take me back to my apartment?"

"Yeah, sure," he said.

"Everything okay?" I asked.

She appeared a little out of sorts, which seemed unusual for her.

"Oh, it's a family thing," she said. "My dad's just being an ass again. So much melodrama with him. I have to try and buy some train or plane tickets so that I can get home ASAP."

Trey got up from his chair and inclined his head toward me and Kat. "Well, it was—nice."

"Sorry you have to leave. I hope everything works out okay," Kat said cordially to Chance.

As Trey helped her with her coat, she froze and stared at Kat. "Thanks, but I'm sure you know how screwy families can get sometimes."

"More than you know," Kat said. "Safe travels."

Chance gave me a quick hug. "I'll message you."

"Okay," I said.

I sat back down as she and Trey walked across the dining room together.

"Well, that was unpleasant," I said. "You don't like Chance much, do you?"

I immediately realized that it was a stupid thing to ask.

Kat patiently looked at me. "No, Caleb, I don't like her, and I'm relatively sure the feeling's mutual. But of course, she has quite the crush you, I see."

"What?" I asked. "She and Trey—"

"Are friends, I suspect," she said. "Little more."

"She's barely turned twenty," I said.

"And you're a whole what? Twenty-seven as of July?" she asked.

Okay, that obviously wasn't the proper tack to take with her.

I rubbed my palm against my forehead as a weary feeling permeated my body.

"Well, I'm only interested in being friends. I've already told her as much," I said.

"That's good," she said, staring at me. "So, I suppose that I'll be reluctantly tolerant of your friendship."

Honestly, it had suddenly turned into a night from hell.

"Now, with that over, let's try to put it all behind us and recapture the moment," she said, reaching out to grasp my hand.

I offered my best reassuring smile despite the mild headache that had formed throughout my temples. In fact, I had nearly lost my appetite altogether.

* * *

By the time we returned to the house, I had a full stomach and my headache had largely subsided.

In the end, Kat and I had enjoyed a nice meal and visit together. And while we hadn't quite recaptured the emotional tone we'd experienced prior to Chance's unexpected arrival, we had enjoyed each other's company.

We had barely walked through the front door before Alton presented me with a four-foot length of cylindrical leather-wrapped wood. It was a couple of inches in diameter and rather weighty.

"Wow, I could really wallop someone with this," I said.

"That's not for walloping, it's for training," he said.

"Oh," I said. "How so?"

"Often, a blunt instrument is the most available item to use in defensive situations," he said. "I'm going to issue techniques for you to begin practicing with."

"Well, you can forget about him practicing tonight," Kat said. "I already have plans for him, thank you."

I grinned at the suggestive look in her eyes.

"Very well," he said. "We'll go over things in the morning then."

"Later in the morning," I suggested. "I'm thinking about sleeping in."

He arched one brow in a nearly imperious fashion. "Oh, really?"

"Or not," I said.

"Earlier is better," he said.

Before I could say more, Kat took me by the hand and led—rather, half-dragged—me upstairs to our bedroom.

Later that night, she lay in my arms as I dozed.

The effect of my day's stresses had finally abated and I was more than content to lay there next to her.

I wished it could last forever.

However, reality had its way of interrupting even the most blissful of moments and, before long, the day's events resurfaced in my mind.

"You don't need to feel jealous of Chance, you know," I said.

"What? Hardly," Kat said. "I feel no more threatened by her than a fly buzzing about my head. My challenge is not swatting it, that's all."

No, she really didn't like Chance at all, did she?

"My mistake then," I said.

She scraped a sharp fingernail across my bare chest in soothing fashion.

"If you want to remain friends with Chance, I'll accept that," she conceded, albeit in a glum tone of voice. "Though I can hardly imagine why you'd want to."

"Thanks for being flexible about the situation."

"Hm," she said. "I don't know how I let you talk me into it."

Then she made a purring sound. "Actually, your talented tongue just made a rather compelling argument, my love…without even saying a word."

Amidst the darkness, a smile formed on my face.

CHAPTER 6

Caleb

The next morning, well before breakfast, Alton wasted no time instructing Roman and me in how to incorporate the baton-like cylinders into my workout regimen.

"Where did you come up with these? You didn't bring these all the way from London, did you?" I asked.

"No, I constructed them for you," Alton replied.

They're rather heavy," I said. "My wrist feels strained already. Ever hear of carpal tunnel syndrome?"

His unsympathetic expression spoke volumes. "It may take some time to acclimate yourself to them. Use them slowly and methodically at first, and then increase speed once your muscles have strengthened."

That seemed reasonable enough.

"We'll need to wake a little earlier in the morning, too," Roman said. "We don't want to shave any quality time from your training."

Speak for yourself, Roman.

"Fine," I said.

It was a disparaging thought. I felt like I didn't get enough sleep as it was. Between course readings and class assignments, as well as researching my dissertation subject, much less actually attending classes, I already filled most weekdays.

Of course, my most recent lack of sleep was due to quality time spent with Kat the prior evening.

Face it, she wore me out.

Outside of Kat, my workouts and continued combat training—secret from any of my college friends and peers—took their toll on my early mornings, as well.

I caught a glimpse of Kat out of the corner of my eye, closely scrutinizing me.

I winked at her and the corners of her mouth upturned slightly.

Was it all part of a plan to keep me so busy that I didn't have time to get into further trouble?

Yeah, right. Trouble somehow always finds me in the end.

After exercising and combat training with Kat and Roman, I spent most of the remainder of the day in classes.

After lunch, I received a text from Yale's library informing me that one of the books I had reserved through interlibrary loan had arrived. It was one of the few I could find that had been written entirely by Dr. Simonson.

I hurried to the library with Roman in tow.

The book, *Field Studies on Diseases of the Blood*, was acquired through the Boston University School of Medicine and was published in 1908 by a defunct publisher, Firbst & Lachimann, Ltd.

As books went, it was a veritable tome, filled with arcane medical jargon and a litany of case studies. Upon cursory inspection, Dr. Simonson certainly seemed competent.

As if I'd have known otherwise.

I was no medical expert, but I tried to look on the bright side.

Well, at least it's in English.

I located a nearby comfortable chair and thumbed through the book. Within an hour, I determined it was likely going to take days just to make heads or tails out of anything in it.

"Where am I gonna find time for this?" I asked.

Following one of my mid-afternoon classes, I considered

heading back to the house. However, I felt rather pensive and thought that I'd feel too tempted by distractions.

Instead, I went to the student union to find a comfortable spot for some more reading from Simonson's book.

Fortunately, one of the lounge rooms was relatively deserted, so I camped out on an oversized recliner in the corner. Roman secured a small study table in an inconspicuous area across the room from me.

With a heavy sigh, I made my debut excursion into blood disorders case studies. Aside from the frequent use of my iPad to look up medical terminology, it was occasionally quite fascinating material. Written when the field was still in its infancy, Dr. Simonson's book seemed to have been on the leading edge of it.

I lost track of time, and before I knew it, evening had arrived.

At approximately six o'clock, I received a text message from Roman: *Late night?*

I sent: *Overtime averse? Long day?*

I looked across the room at him but he was slouched down in his chair ignoring me.

He responded: *Oh, funny man now? More bruises tomorrow morning for you. ;-)*

I chuckled and texted: *I'll wrap it up.*

I'd had more than my fair share of sore muscles and bruises from him since combat training began.

"Pain encourages proficiency," he had said to me on more than one occasion.

All teasing aside, I admired that the guy really knew his stuff and he was a good mentor. Alton and Kat had chosen well.

Then I received another text from him.

Belay that. Paige is en route.

I sent: *Thx.*

Another twenty minutes later, he texted: Clocking out. See you tomorrow.

I looked across the room to see him gathering up his

notebook computer into a backpack and he nonchalantly left the room.

Seconds later, Paige appeared in the entryway with her arms crossed before her. Ethan stood behind her with a grin on his face.

She rolled her eyes at me as they walked over to where I sat.

"Pack it up, nerdo," she said, nudging at my shoe with the tip of hers. "Ethan's leaving tonight and we're not spending his remaining hours hanging out in a study hall."

I gestured around the nearly empty room. "It's a lounge."

"No," she said. "*It's-a-lame.*"

"Fine," I said. "Home?"

"Nope," she said. "Club."

"Kat's gonna love that," I said.

"Red's not here to care," she said.

"What?"

"Yeah, she and Alton left after sundown to check on some leads," she said.

I wondered why Kat hadn't mentioned that to me. Hell, she had never even bothered to send me a text message.

"Oh, don't look all forlorn," she said. "She'll be back later tonight after she drops Alton off at the airport."

I'd nearly forgotten that he was returning to London already. For some reason, things felt like they were happening so fast around me since last Friday night.

She repeatedly snapped her fingers. "Hey, back to reality, kiddo. My last wager was 'club' as I recall."

"Restaurant," I countered.

"Bar," she said.

"Witches Brew?" I asked.

"Hm. Catchy name. Close by?"

"Walking distance," I said.

She gave me a suspicious look. "Okay. I'm sort of surprised I haven't been there already. I thought I'd already scoped out all the dives with potential."

"Well, we won't know for sure until we go there," Ethan

said.

"Follow me," I said.

I quickly packed away my book and iPad and led the way outside and across campus.

"You're gonna love this place, Ethan," I said, slipping one strap of my backpack over my shoulder.

"I'm intrigued," he said.

He draped his arm across Paige's shoulders as we briskly walked the couple of blocks over to Grove Street, not far from campus.

We rounded a corner and nearly ran into it.

Paige scanned the front of the building and groaned. "No fair! Aw, crap."

Ethan laughed.

Witches Brew was a popular coffee and tea cafe that served some of the freshest bagels and rolls in the city.

I held the glass doors open for them.

Paige glared at me as she entered.

I pointed over to the counter. "I distinctly recall you saying 'bar.' This has the best coffee and bagel bar in town."

"You're such a lame-butt," she said, plopping onto the seat of a nearby booth. "Just you wait. I'll have my revenge."

"Promises, promises," I said.

"Nice place," Ethan said.

"Oh, don't encourage him," she said, propping her chin on one upturned palm with a dejected expression.

"Drinks are on me," I said.

"Yep," she said. "Just as quickly as I can pour one over your head."

I purchased French vanilla cappuccinos for Paige and Ethan and Earl Grey tea and a chicken salad sandwich for me.

"That's all you're eating?" Paige asked.

"I'm not that hungry."

She stared at me. "You're normally a stomach with legs."

I ignored her.

"Sorry you have to leave tonight, Ethan," I said. "You'll

be missed."

Paige leaned against him as he wrapped his arm around her. "Ditto," she said.

"Paige is going to need a fresh supply of batteries after you leave," I said, trying to keep a straight face.

Paige stabbed the end of her forefinger in my face. "I'm gonna beat your ass."

"Yeah, I'm sorry I can't stay longer," Ethan said with a rueful look. "I'll try to make it back up here again soon...before any battery shortages."

I actually think that Paige was blushing.

It was easy to see how great a couple the two of them had become, and I felt very happy for them.

But I still felt guilty about my presence in New Haven causing Paige to be separated from him.

"When's your flight?" I asked.

"I've got a red-eye at one-thirty in the morning," he said. "I figured since it's only a short nighttime hop to Atlanta, I'd fly ordinary commercial."

That made sense. Sunset Air had excellent vampire-friendly service, but their prices were definitely the top end of premium, based upon the invoices I'd seen.

"How's your research coming?" he asked.

Paige groaned. "Oh, no. Snore-time. You had to ask, didn't you?"

Ethan chuckled. "Sorry about that."

She stood up. "No, no, you history buffs have your little nerd chat. I'm going to find something chocolaty."

He handed her some cash and she gave him a quick kiss on the cheek before heading toward the bakery counter.

I told Ethan about the book I had checked out, as well as some other information I had learned. He even asked to look at the book in question.

After a few minutes of rapid leafing and scanning, he laid the tome down before him.

"Interesting. It's an odd specialty for that time period," he said. "You'll want to investigate any of his European connections. That's where all the cutting-edge studies were taking place, anyway."

His insights were definitely helpful.

"Thanks. I will," I said. "Was that a former interest of yours, too?"

He smiled. "Me? No. I was too preoccupied with myself at the time. But I remember having occasional discussions with colleagues."

It occurred to me that I knew very little about Ethan's past.

"Where you human or vampire then?"

"Vampire," he said, lowering his voice. "Though only recently turned."

Wow, cool.

"Do tell," I said.

"You're really interested?" he asked.

"Oh, very," I said. "I'm a history sponge, remember?"

He leaned across the table toward me, so I met him halfway.

"Stop me if this gets boring."

I shook my head. "Yeah, right. Not likely."

"So, I was turned in—" he said.

I held up my hand. "Hey, no human backstory?"

"Even less noteworthy for that period, I'm afraid," he said.

"Try me," I said.

He paused for a moment, as if in silent reflection.

"I was born and raised in central Connecticut, just outside of Middleton. My father was a member of the Middleton council and my mother a midwife," he said. "Oh, how I loved it there. I knew from the time I was a boy that's where I wanted to live out the rest of my life. Of course, life had other plans."

"Siblings?" I asked.

"Two younger brothers," he said. "They took after my father, each becoming farmers in their own right when they were grown."

"But not you?" I asked.

He shook his head. "Me? Nope. I was fascinated by my mother's midwifery skills. I even helped with deliveries by the time I had turned eight, though social modesty precluded more active participation in the advanced activities.

"As such, I spent far more time helping my father and brothers in the fields than that," he said. "Still, I never developed an appreciation for farming."

"Was your father disappointed?"

"Maybe at first," he said. "But even back then physicians were highly regarded, and they earned a great deal of respect in their communities. When I expressed an interest in pursuing medicine, such as it was, my father encouraged me.

"My father used his contacts with regional clergy and managed to collect the attention of a competent physician in a neighboring county who was willing to take on an assistant," he said. "However, it was expected that I attend college. Fortunately, Doctor Sedgwick was a kind man. He not only tutored me on basic knowledge in physiology, but sponsored my entry into medical school. Between some of my father's savings and Doctor Sedgwick's influence, I was accepted to Harvard."

"Very cool," I said. "You're a Harvard man."

"Snob," Paige said as she sat down before what had to be the largest chocolate muffin I'd ever seen.

Both Ethan and I stared at it.

"Hey, stop sizing up my muffin," she said.

He and I simultaneously broke into laughter.

At first, she frowned. Then she scowled.

"Oh, very funny, you pervs," she said. "Get back to yammerin' before I fang you both."

Ethan stretched his arm across her shoulders and she snuggled beside him before delving into her snack.

"Anyway, by 1856, the year I turned twenty, I had graduated from Harvard and had fallen for a lovely young local woman named Deidre, who I'd met while attending college," he said.

"She was a fellow student?" I asked.

"No," Paige said. "They first saw each other on Sundays at the local church."

I stared at her.

"What?" she asked. "Spoiler. I've heard this already."

He looked at her with an endearing expression.

"Within a year, Deidre and I were married. We had a wonderful year together before she became pregnant," he said.

"Unfortunately, and as often was the case back then, she died giving birth to our son, who subsequently died within hours of delivery. Though the midwife was experienced, there'd been birthing complications, and neither Sedgwick nor I were able to stem her internal hemorrhaging."

He paused to take a drink of his cappuccino and I could see his eyes turn glassy. Paige reached over to hold his free hand.

"I'm so sorry, Ethan," I said.

What a tragic event.

I thought back to Katrina's own story of having lost her husband and children to disease within a short time of one another.

Throughout the ages, life seemed to be rife with senseless tragedy.

"I was devastated, and felt lost for months afterwards," Ethan said. "Nothing stemmed my intense feelings of loss and sadness. I think the only thing that propelled me onward was my work in medicine. In the years that followed, as I deprived Death of each potential victim, it seemed like a series of small victories, of sorts."

That was an interesting notion to me.

"Of course, you can't cheat Death forever," he said. "He always seems to get his due in the end."

I stared at him. "So, is that why you still practice medicine as a vampire today? To keep cheating Death?"

"Now? No," he said. "I do it because I thoroughly enjoy medicine and helping others. Although there may be a small component of penance for what I am now, as well."

I looked into his eyes, wondering why he felt that way.

"Penance?" I asked.

The edges of his mouth upturned slightly, though in a bitter fashion.

"By the time the Civil War started in 1861, I had been actively practicing medicine itinerantly from town to town. Naturally, the Union Army aggressively recruited doctors, and I volunteered my services," he said. "I was commissioned a Captain, and spent most of my time in field hospitals."

"Wow," I said. "I can only imagine what you saw during the Civil War."

"You're a historian, so you've read about how brutal it was," he said. "Still, to experience it was something else entirely."

"Hey, I'm eating here," Paige said.

I gave her a wan look. "Oh, please. You eat, sleep, and dream blood."

"Yeah, true."

Ethan shook his head.

"The field hospitals were horrible places, and I still remember the stench and foulness that accompanied sounds of pure human misery. For all of the carnage on the battlefields, the carnage in the field hospitals was much worse," he said. "For every person I managed to save, three or more died. I felt the loss of Deidre all over again with each human soul that passed, but took some solace in the few that I managed to help."

One of the baristas stopped by our booth.

"Can I get anybody anything?" she asked.

"Maybe another Earl Grey?" I asked.

"You got it," she said.

Ethan paused for a moment before continuing his story.

"In May of 1864, I was assigned to a smaller brigade during the Wilderness Campaign in Virginia. In truth, it was really just a series of uncoordinated skirmishes, rather than a formalized campaign, but no less bloody than any of the other major battles that I had seen," he said. "By then, everyone was so tired of the war. It all seemed so pointless...seemingly endless, really."

"Hey, wasn't that was the first time U.S. Grant engaged Lee's own Confederate forces?" I asked.

Paige held up one hand. "Down boy. Sit now. Sit."

I gave her my best deadpan expression.

Ethan remained silent until the barista delivered my fresh cup of tea. Then he scanned the dining room.

"Getting sort of busy in here all of a sudden," he said. "I'll talk more on our walk back home."

I could barely wait for us to exit the place.

Fortunately, it was a cold night and there were scarcely any pedestrians to share the sidewalk with.

Not long after we began walking, Ethan continued his story.

"One night, two soldiers conveyed a severely injured man to the surgeon's tent, which at the time struck me as odd because most engagements ended by sundown," he said. "The man's body had been so riddled with musket balls I was amazed he was still alive. Apparently, he was the sole survivor from some bloodbath of a skirmish that had occurred a couple of miles outside of camp.

"I feverishly worked to remove the musket rounds from the man's body, and was amazed that he had held on as long as he had. By the time I had finished, it was nearly midnight, and I dismissed the two orderlies who had been helping me," he said. "Given the man's ragged breathing, I figured he had only hours to live. Not wanting him to die alone, I pulled up a chair and dozed as I sat vigil at his bedside."

"He was the vampire," Paige said.

I gave her a dirty look. "Spoilers, remember?"

She winked at me. "Oops, sorry."

"Okay, so the man woke within an hour or so, and seemed remarkably recuperated despite his overly pale skin color. He told me that his name was Noah, and that he was grateful to me for saving him. Though in reality, it wasn't anything that I hadn't already heard from others whose lives I'd saved," Ethan said.

"Noah?" I asked. "Hey, he wasn't—"

"The legendary flood guy with the animals? Nah, different Noah," Ethan interrupted.

"Oh," I said. "Go on then."

"He rested in one of the recovery tents for another day, and then reappeared in my tent the following night. I was amazed that he could even stand," he said. "It was when he told me that he'd lived for over two hundred years that I doubted his sanity, much less his constitution. As if that wasn't enough, he offered me immortality as a parting gift."

"Man, that's surreal," I said. "What'd you do then?"

"I laughed at him, thinking his mind had been sadly affected either from battle trauma he had experienced or his injuries," Ethan said. "However, he swore he could prove his claims and asked me to accompany him into the woods, where he displayed some amazing feats of strength and speed."

"I still can't believe you went with him," Paige said. "Seriously? Some crazy-sounding guy asks me into the woods, and I'm dropping him with the nearest heavy piece of wood."

Ethan chuckled. "I'm not ashamed to admit I was curious, though I still wore my service revolver."

"A lot of good that would've done you," she said.

"Well, of course, I didn't know that at the time."

"Okay, okay, what happened next?" I asked.

"As you can imagine, I was stunned, as well as scared, but he reassured me that he meant me no harm."

Ethan paused to look sidelong at me. "Much like you, he had an innocent face."

That made me smile.

"Then the man explained the power of his saliva and blood, and it immediately occurred to me how much easier it would be to help people with such abilities," he said. "I really hadn't given much thought to the idea of eternity at the time, but was definitely still affected by how fresh Deidre's loss in my life had been. Besides, I had grown so weary of the war, and the death, and the sickness. It was overwhelming in its scope."

Paige reached out to hold Ethan's hand as we continued our walk.

"A tempting offer," I said.

"Yeah, so much so that I agreed to his offer. We left my unit behind in the middle of the night, and journeyed to an old cabin in the middle of nowhere, far away from any battlefields. I lost track of time, but during nearly a week of painful blood exchanges using a really odd method of transference Noah had acquired from an old Indian ritual, I was turned," he said.

"Do you remember much about it?" I asked.

He shook his head. "Towards the end of the process, I lost my faculties as if in some prolonged fever. By the time that I awoke, all I knew was that my life had been changed forever. The world looked, sounded, and felt completely different then."

"I remember something of that," I whispered.

Unlike Ethan, my body had been too weak for the turning process. I had nearly died before stemming the process by saturating my body with raw sunlight and its strong ultraviolet radiation.

"Now, I'm once again merely human," I said.

He reached out and clasped me on the shoulder. "It wasn't your time yet."

"Sometimes, *yet* feels like never."

"A word of advice," he said. "Enjoy the time that you spend, no matter in what form. It's about your journey, not your destination."

I considered that for a moment.

"So, what happened next?" I asked. "After your turning."

"After a few days showing me how to feed on animals, just in case people weren't available, and then important lessons on the dangers of sunlight, I told him I felt the need to return to my unit. More than a week was a long time to be gone and unaccounted for, you see," he said. "But I felt honor bound to return to resign my commission and not be labeled a deserter. However, Noah urged me not to try returning to my unit, particularly given that my body had been strongly craving blood."

"That was idiotic," Paige said.

"Hey, it was a matter of honor," Ethan said.

"So, did you go back to your unit?" I asked.

"After a couple of days, I got up the urge to venture back just after sundown," he said.

Then something occurred to me. "Ah, I bet the camp had moved on by the time you returned."

Ethan's expression darkened. "Not so much."

We walked around the corner onto our street.

"I smelled the stench of burning flesh miles before I got close enough to see what had happened for myself," he said. "My old encampment had been attacked, maybe only a day or so prior. It looked like a slaughter had occurred."

"That had to be shocking," I said.

"In truth, while gruesome, it was prophetic. I mean, it was pretty obvious that my army days were behind me by that point," he said. "It made resigning my commission unnecessary. It was relatively common for people to be lost and unaccounted for during or following battles. I simply returned to Noah, and he helped me learn the ways of my new life."

"And yet, you remained a doctor, didn't you?" I asked as we reached our front porch.

"I couldn't deny what I had become, but it didn't change how I felt about helping people," he replied. "I just had to be a hell of a lot more careful about it. And it helped me to learn to curb my appetite for human blood. To this day, it's the one thing that I hate most about what I am now. My profession is my penance; plying my trade in return for partaking in human blood."

Paige looked up at him with a sad expression. "You don't

need to pay penance, Ethan. You don't owe anyone anything."

He bent down to warmly kiss her and she reached up to hug his neck.

They were a lovely sight.

"I love you for who you are," she said.

"Love?" he asked.

She smiled. "Yeah...love."

I grinned as I opened the front door for us.

Paige and Ethan made their way upstairs hand in hand as I walked over to the couch to pick up the television remote.

At that moment, I longed to hold Kat in my arms.

CHAPTER 7

Katrina

After sundown, Alton and I made the hour-long drive on Interstate 95 through waves of cold drizzle to New London to meet with the vampire who lay territorial claim to much of the state of Connecticut. We hoped to learn more about other vampires who might be operating in and around New Haven.

I was determined to locate those responsible for attacking Caleb.

"Newton's a bit of a traditionalist," Alton said. "We only visited briefly at the Slovene conference, but he seemed like a sensible, though quiet, sort of fellow."

"Benjamin Newton," I said. "I wonder. As in, Sir Isaac Newton?"

"You sounded like Caleb just then," he replied.

A faint smile crossed my lips.

"Not Isaac himself, per say, though Benjamin claims to be distant relative," he said. "Mind you, I've never explored his claim on that."

"Don't you trust anyone?"

"Very few, and rarely at face value," he replied. "I trust you."

Benjamin Newton's estate was rather large compared to

the properties surrounding it, though most homes in the area were relatively grand by contemporary standards.

Upon pulling around the sweeping circle driveway, we were quickly approached by two vampire guards wearing rain coats. Alton immediately rolled down his window as one guard approached our vehicle.

"I'm Alton Rutherford," he said. "And this is my associate, Katrina Rawlings."

"You're expected. Pull your vehicle over there," prompted the guard, pointing to a nearby paved easement.

The estate's interior appeared orderly, but decorated in a manner reminiscent of an early colonial museum interspersed with modern conveniences.

We were conveyed to a large den where a tall vampire stood from his seat in a reading chair strategically placed before a lit fireplace.

It all appeared remarkably rustic; a vision of the perfect country gentleman's estate.

"Mr. Rutherford," he greeted, extending his hand toward Alton. "So good to see you again."

"Miss Rawlings, welcome to my estate," he greeted me in turn, taking my hand in his.

Following further pleasantries, Alton and I sat together on a settee before Newton, who returned to his high-backed reading chair.

"My territory extends through most of Connecticut and then continues into Rhode Island to the east and a brief portion of the southeastern tip of New York to the west," he explained. "My western territory borders with Rudolph Pitt's area."

"I'm unfamiliar with that name," I said.

"He claims much of southern New York, but particularly New York City proper," Newton replied. "The entire city area is his; something he's very possessive of."

"Yes, I've heard of Pitt," Alton said. "He wasn't at the conference, as I recall."

"Ah, well, he keeps to himself for the most part,"

Newton said. "However, we get along well enough, and there have never been any disputes between us."

"Would there be any reason that Pitt might be interested in New Haven?" I asked. "Or any other vampires who you're aware of, for that matter."

Newton frowned. "To my knowledge, Ms. Rawlings, you're the only vampires who have recently taken up residence in my territory, though Mr. Rutherford arranged that with me well in advance beforehand. Has there been some trouble that I should be aware of?"

I briefly described what had taken place with my mate.

"Oh, dear," he said. "I'm terribly sorry to hear about that. I do hope that your mate is well."

"He's improving, thank you," I said. "But I'm very interested in locating those responsible for attacking him."

Newton adopted a grave expression. "That's certainly understandable. However, I think it important to note that I'm remaining solidly neutral in the recent rise of vampire factions around the globe."

"Why is that?" Alton pressed.

"You might say that I'm a traditionalist," he said. "I like the way that things have been maintained over the centuries. It's worked quite well, overall. Maintaining individual territories around the globe is quite a manageable arrangement."

"So long as you're one of the vampires in control of a territory," I added.

He nodded in deference. "Naturally. How very egalitarian of you to point that out."

"Yes, well," Alton quickly added. "We're not here to challenge the merits of the past, though I'm mindful that flexibility is often helpful in the face of evolving conditions."

In addition to our conversation, another scan of the dated room décor suggested to me that Newton was likely not only a traditionalist, but also an antiquarian.

"I must agree with Alton," I said. "Times are changing, and we must be prepared to change with them."

"You sound a lot like that fellow, Bob Dylan," he said. "However, traditions are important; they're stabilizing, which is something people are quickly forgetting."

"I'm afraid that even Bob Dylan has been passé for some time, Mr. Newton," I said, glancing sidelong at Alton. "Incidentally, do you have Amish roots?"

Hasn't Newton listened to contemporary music in over forty years?

Alton gave me a sharp look. "What Katrina means is that, traditions aside, modernity in moderation has its merits."

I repressed a sigh. That wasn't what I meant at all.

Newton comes off as an old fuddy-duddy.

Wait, fuddy-duddy? Now I sound dated, too.

"...respect your personal choice in being progressive, Rutherford," Newton said. "I merely ask that my own traditions be respected, particularly in my own territory."

"Certainly," Alton said. "We mean no disrespect, and we appreciate the courtesy you've given us in permitted our temporary residence in New Haven on Katrina's mate's behalf."

Newton appeared more settled. "Very good. In the meantime, if I hear anything further regarding other vampire activities, I'll see that the information is forwarded to you."

We exchanged farewells and were escorted back to our vehicle.

"Well, that was less than helpful," I said as our vehicle pulled back onto the main road.

"Mm," Alton murmured. "Back to square one, I'm afraid."

"What now?" I asked.

He remained silent for a time, appearing to be in deep thought.

We traveled westward on Interstate 95 when both of our mobile phones received text messages. Alton pulled off to one side of the highway to check his message as I retrieved my phone.

My message was from Gavyn Osborn, one of Alton's most trusted vampires; a knight from his own period.

"A new group of vampires has appeared in London," I said. "The latest patrol has located their operational center and requests orders."

"It appears we received the same message," Alton said. "We should return to London immediately. Matters like this require both of us, so we can't continue to be derailed by dead ends here."

"I see. So, Caleb takes a back burner to vampire politics then?"

"Please. Need I remind you of what happened the last time we had a sleeper cell operating in London?" he countered.

"You mean the one that Caleb stumbled upon?" I asked meaningfully.

"Yes, well," Alton said. "Such as it was."

"Mm-hm."

He gave me a sober look. "In the meantime, I'll send my best investigators here to take up where we're leaving off. We'll bide our time until the culprits are identified. Then we act decisively."

Admittedly, he made a good point about sleeper cells; they had to be rooted out as quickly as they were located. But the idea of leaving Caleb with our investigations unresolved made me grit my teeth.

"What if our nameless entities return to New Haven?" I asked. "Or, worse yet, make another attempt against Caleb?"

"Caleb is in secure hands. For the time being, we need to keep him occupied, as well as under tighter scrutiny," he replied. "He'll be just fine."

I looked sidelong at him.

"Trust me," he said. "I know what I'm doing."

Famous last words.

CHAPTER 8

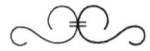

Caleb

Despite feeling very tired, I had trouble falling asleep while Kat was out on her adventure with Alton.

It wasn't as if I was overly worried for her safety, just merely concerned. To say that she was capable in her own right was an understatement.

Kat was like a red-haired Wonder Woman; my own personal super heroine. In fact, if anyone deserved their own comic book, it would be her.

I was still parked on the couch, watching a cartoon marathon on television when the front door opened.

I looked over the back of the couch to see Paige, returning just past midnight from dropping Ethan off at the airport.

"Oh, I thought you were Kat and Alton," I said.

"Well, you don't have to look so disappointed," she said.

I let that go unanswered.

She plopped down onto the nearby recliner, one leg casually draped over one armrest. To her credit, she waited quietly for nearly fifteen minutes before harassing me.

"What the hell sort of crap are you filling your brain with now?" she asked.

"*McCluck*," I said.

"What the cluck?" she asked.

I gave her a wan look. "Oh, fun—ny. That's my favorite cartoon you're talking about there."

"Somebody, please shoot me," she said, pressing the back of her head further into the recliner cushion.

"Just watch it for a while before passing judgment," I said. "It grows on you."

"Whatever," she said, folding her arms before her.

To her credit, she watched TV for a time before saying anything further.

"Okay, so who's the chicken wearing the trench coat?"

"He's the hero, Bantam McCluck, police detective," I replied.

"Right. And who's he beating up?" she asked.

"Robbie the rooster," I said. "He's one of the town's biggest mobsters."

"What town?"

"Barnville," I said.

She groaned and pressed her fingertips to her temples. "I should've known."

I pointedly ignored her.

"Okay," she said. "I need popcorn and lots of beers for this."

Around 2 a.m., Kat walked through the front door, fully engaged in a mobile phone conversation. Most notably, Alton wasn't accompanying her.

"No, just give me the short version," she said, casting off her black leather coat and flinging it onto a chair as she proceeded upstairs. "Yeah, give me the scoop on what happened in the Baltics, too."

She never even paused to say hello.

More and more, I felt like even when Kat was around she was mentally somewhere else.

Alton's scale of endeavors seemed to be growing exponentially. I couldn't help feeling that it was becoming less a venture and more of an epic as time passed.

And I felt less hopeful that things might come to a

conclusion anytime soon.

Maybe that's why I was having trouble sleeping, though there seemed to be no shortage of reasons for that.

I would have scarcely noticed the passage of time had it not been for the *McCluck* episodes ending each half hour.

Finally, Kat came downstairs dressed in a pair of sweatpants and T-shirt. She sat on the couch beside me, curling her bare feet beneath her.

She wrapped her arms around my neck and leaned in to kiss me.

"I'm back," she said.

"Really? I scarcely noticed you'd left," I said.

"Why, Caleb, such sarcasm," she said. "It was just a quick errand, that's all."

"A mysterious errand," I said. "The nature of which is on a need to know only basis."

"Caleb—"

"And where the hell's Alton?" I asked, growing more agitated by the moment.

"He has some last-minute details to handle before returning to London to attend to urgent matters," she replied.

I shook my head over having to draw information out of her like that.

"Somebody's angry with me," she whispered into my ear before kissing it.

I remained silent, watching the television, but not really paying attention to what was happening.

"It was just a fact-finding endeavor that we undertook," Kat said. "I'd tell you if I was leaving for an extended period."

"Better pinky swears to that," Paige said.

Kat gave her a dirty look and then adopted a maddeningly patient expression as her gaze shifted back to me.

"Alton and I went to check into a lead," Kat said. "We're trying to find out who hired your two assailants."

"And?" I asked.

"We didn't find the answers we were seeking," she said. "The search continues for now."

"The search continues," Paige said. "Way to go, Agatha Christie."

"Oh, dry up," Kat said.

"With two beers in me already and a third on the way, not likely," Paige said. "At least, not anytime soon, thank you."

Kat ignored her response, instead looking at me while stroking her fingernails lightly across my cheek and down my neck.

It felt pretty amazing, actually.

"Alton said to remind you about your new training regimen," she said. "He said he'll want an error-free demonstration the next time he sees you."

"Don't worry," I said. "I'll be able to bludgeon someone with a heavy stick like the best of them by then."

"I know you will," she said. "Still, it's a rather ungainly looking routine, if you ask me. I'd have preferred advancing your knife fighting techniques instead."

"Alton's ancient," Paige said. "He probably learned it in Ye Olde Branch Beating School. Hey, maybe next month, he'll teach you how to string a lute."

I chuckled aloud at that.

Kat ran her fingers through my hair as she snuggled beside me. "You're up especially late."

"Can't sleep," I said.

"Consequently, he's torturing me with cartoons," Paige said before crunching on another handful of popcorn.

"What are we watching?" Kat asked.

"*McCluck*," Paige said. "It's really pretty good."

I smiled at Paige and she winked back at me.

One of the program's characters made a screeching sound.

"*McCluck?*" Kat asked. "Hey, isn't that woman a chicken?"

"Her name's Polly Poultry," Paige said.

I grinned. She was catching on fast.

"An investigative reporter, as well as Bantam McCluck's girlfriend," I said. "She's a French Hen."

"Odd, but strangely endearing," Kat said, leaning her head against my shoulder.

At least she was trying. However, I was still annoyed by how she had abruptly left town with Alton without even a word to me.

Still, it was times like this, just quietly curled on the couch together watching television, that were among the most enjoyable moments.

I want a lifetime filled of moments with Kat just like this one.

That would make me truly happy.

After the episode finished, Kat said, "It's getting pretty late. Shouldn't we get upstairs to bed?"

"Mothering me again," I chastised.

She playfully nipped at my earlobe with her teeth.

"There's nothing motherly going through my head right now," she whispered.

"Hey, just take your tawdry sex-capades upstairs, you randy wench," Paige said. "I'm trying to watch *McCluck* here."

Kat stuck her tongue out at her, then reached out to take me by the hand and lead me upstairs.

"And try to keep the headboard banging to a minimum up there!" Paige yelled after us. "I've got vampire hearing, you know!"

* * *

It was only after sex that Kat shared with me that she would be joining Alton on his impromptu departure for London.

"You could have mentioned this earlier," I said.

She gave me a sly look. "Yes, but then I probably would've missed out on sex."

She removed her suitcase from the closet and began packing.

"So, instead you used me and you're just going to fly away?"

"My mate gets snippy when he's tired," she said.

"Don't change the subject," I said.

"Caleb, a sleeper cell in London is something we have to react to with a sense of immediacy," she said. "Surely you remember how dangerous that group beneath the city became during our spring break visit?"

"True, I suppose."

Subways seemed like creepy, ominous places following that nearly lethal experience.

She folded some articles of clothing that had been hanging in the closet and neatly placed them into her suitcase.

"Besides, you're very busy here and I don't want to be a distraction to your progress," she said.

"I'm more distracted when you're not here," I said.

She gave me a sympathetic look and walked over to enfold me in her arms. She kissed me on the top of my head.

"I so love you, my dear," she said. "I wish that I could stay, but we both have our obligations and objectives to confront."

I tightly hugged her body against mine and tilted my head upward. Her warm lips met mine.

"Both of them keep mounting, too," I said. "I'm starting to resent words beginning with 'O' as time passes."

She smiled into her next kiss.

"I miss the life that you and I had after Chimalma was eliminated," I said.

"I know," she said. "Me, too."

"Do you think we'll ever get back to that again?"

"I certainly hope so," she replied.

That wasn't exactly the reassuring response I had hoped for.

"You could have lied a little bit," I said.

"True," she said. "But then it would feel even worse when the truth finally raised its ugly head, wouldn't it?"

I held her close as her response echoed in my thoughts.

"When do you have to leave?"

"Just before dawn," she replied. "Alton chartered a Sunset Air flight for us already. He has a way with arranging things on spur of the moment."

Damn Alton's efficiency.

CHAPTER 9

Caleb

I didn't sleep much at all before Kat and Alton left. However, sleep or not, my training continued with all of the promptness that Roman could muster.

Training was followed by rigorous coursework at the campus, though my attention span was scarcely focused. My mind kept wandering to thoughts of Kat, worldwide vampire factions, and hopes to return to a simpler life; the kind we'd lived not so very long ago.

I longed for my old life, boring and routine though it might have seemed to others.

There's one key difference between watching an exciting, adventurous life presented in the movies and living one in real life; a movie will eventually end, leaving you with the vicarious thrill sans all of the lingering wounds and emotional baggage.

During the next couple of weeks, my patience wore especially thin as my conversations with Kat were few, as were my periods of relaxation from a grueling schedule.

Still, while my disposition grew darker, my weapons training techniques improved considerably. Perhaps that was due to needing a physical outlet for my frustrations.

At one point, Roman barely deflected a baton strike

toward his shoulder.

"Hey, you're not actually trying to maim me, are you?" he asked.

I stepped back. "Sorry."

"Let's take five," he suggested. "Do some more stretching, and maybe throw in some pushups while you're at it."

"Punishment, coach?"

"Let's call it constructive venting," he said.

"How about a vacation instead?"

"How about if I kick your butt for you?"

"Exercise Nazi," I muttered.

Later that day, I texted Chance Noble.

Let's do lunch.

She replied: Can't.

Why not?

Trouble at home.

After reconsidering further texting, I called her instead. When it went to her voicemail, I called her again.

She picked up after the first ring.

"Caleb, it's not a good time," she whispered.

I heard men's raised voices in the background. One man, in particular, had a particularly New York-sounding accent.

"…gonna want me to do about that now?" the man demanded. "That wasn't part of the deal."

"What's wrong? Chance, are you okay?" I asked.

"My dad's really upset right now," she whispered. "In fact, he's arguing with some other—"

"Chance? Are you on that goddamned phone again?" snapped someone with a gruff-sounding voice.

"I gotta go, Caleb," she insisted.

"Call me when you can," I said just before the line went dead.

Just when I thought my own life was pretty crappy...

I remembered her telling me that her relationship with her father hadn't been an easy one.

I made a mental note to try calling her again in a few

hours if I hadn't heard from her. Then the day's events swept me up again, and it was during my early evening walk home from the college before I thought of her again.

Oddly enough, that's when my phone rang.

"How about a little privacy for this, Roman?" I asked.

"Sure thing," he said.

He slowed down until he was a short distance behind me.

"Chance? Are you okay?"

"Hi, Caleb," she said. "Everything's better now."

"What was that all about? I mean, I heard arguing in the background."

"Yeah, that was my dad and one of his business associates," she said. "Listen, I know this is going to sound crazy, but I think my father's had people stalking me in New Haven."

"What? Are you kidding?" I asked. "Hey, where are you now? Are you safe?"

"I'm fine, really," she said. "I couldn't wait to get away from there. In fact, I just arrived back to my apartment here in New Haven."

Well, it was a relief that she was safe.

"Listen, what's going on with you and your dad?" I asked.

"I hate talking about this over the phone," she said. "Can you meet me for dinner?"

"Yeah, sure," I said. Then I realized I'd need to clear that with either Roman or Paige. "Uh, I might need a short time to reschedule something, but I should be able to meet you. What time and where?"

"Something? Caleb, you're always so charmingly mysterious," she teased. "Okay. How about Prime Time, say an hour from now?"

"Sure thing," I said. "You know all my favorite places."

"Hey, what are friends for?" she asked.

"Burying a body?" I countered.

"Ew, that's a really bad reference after the day I've had,"

she said.

"Sorry. I'll see you there in about an hour."

By the time I cleared my evening plans with Paige, including convincing her to follow me from a discreet distance, it was getting late. But I made it to Prime Time on Temple Street only about ten minutes behind schedule.

Chance had already secured a booth for us. As soon as she saw me walk in, she rose to give me a warm hug. She looked like her usual self—the stylish young Hollywood look—complete with designer jeans and leather jacket.

After we ordered our drinks, I couldn't help but delve into the topic at hand.

"Chance, what happened today?" I asked. "And you said that you think your dad is stalking you?"

She took a deep breath and let it out slowly.

"Yeah, pretty screwed up, isn't it?" she replied. "Sometimes I think I just want to get into my car and drive somewhere—anywhere—and start a new life."

"Admittedly, very tempting," I said. "I get it."

"You do?" she asked, her eyes wide with surprise.

"Uh, yeah...I mean I can see the appeal."

"Mister Perfect wants to escape his life of luxury?" she asked. "Somebody get the smelling salts for me."

I scowled at her. "All right, Sally Sarcasm, let's just get back to your crazy father issues, shall we?"

She gave me a peculiar look. "Fine, but we're returning to your situation again very soon."

I shook my head at her.

"So, Dad calls me last night and practically threatens me to come home immediately. I texted Mom and she seemed to think it was important, so I went home," she began.

"Your dad threatened you?"

"Yeah, he's just being a dickhead," she said. "I've told you that I don't get along with him very well. Sometimes I can't stand him."

"Sorry," I said, motioning with my hand for her to continue.

"I no sooner get home and Dad is all in a huff about what I've been doing and who I've been seeing here in New Haven," she said. "Honestly, it was like he was an FBI agent grilling me over a crime or something."

"That was this morning?" I asked.

"No, that was last night, barely ten seconds after I walked through the front door," she said. "This morning, some guy—hell, maybe some private eye that he hired or something—shows up at the house and they start arguing. Then Dad calls me into the den and this guy, who I don't even know, starts asking me a hundred questions. Half the crap he asked was the same stuff my dad and I went over the night before."

"What sort of stuff?"

She shook her head. "Like, who do I hang out with on campus? Then he asked if I was dating anyone, or how many men? Then he asks if I'm dating women, too! Like it's any of their damned business—"

Nearby patrons looked over at us, so she fell silent.

"Really? So, are you?"

"What? No," she snapped. "I'm all about the guys, thank you. I mean, carpet-munching is cool if you like that sort of thing."

I tried not to laugh aloud and she started to blush.

"Ah, but *you're* a carpet-diving sort of guy, aren't you?" she said with a sly grin.

I felt the heat rising to my cheeks. "Yeah-yeah, whatever. Back to your father and the stranger."

"Good for you. Anyway, so I'm answering these questions and Dad finally smartens up and digs into the guy for asking personal questions like that," she said. "That's when you texted and called. By then, I was ready to just walk out on both of them."

"Sounds intense. So, did you?"

Chance waited until the waitress delivered our drinks and then left before she continued.

"Oh, how I should have. Instead, it was another series of

more stupid and prying questions," she said. "I'm not submitting myself to that again. My dad can go screw himself."

"Does your mother know that you hate him so much?"

"She knows," she replied. "But hey, who am I to interfere. Mom seems fairly happy with their arrangement, though I can't say that I applaud her taste in men. It seems as if it's just so damned hard to find somebody that's worth having nowadays."

I glanced across the room at a couple who were holding hands across the table and staring lovingly into each other's eyes. It made me think of Kat, and how I wished that we could get back to that stage again.

But with all of the clandestine vampire crap happening around the globe, and with Alton nestled right in the middle of it all, I doubted that I'd have Kat back to myself anytime soon.

I loved Kat, but was it enough to get us through all that was happening? Hell, I hardly even ever saw her nowadays; unless, of course, I was at death's door.

I wondered how much longer I could endure our current arrangements. While I realized that it wasn't Kat's fault, I couldn't imagine enduring successive years of this.

"Hey, are you listening to me?" Chance asked, snapping her fingers once to get my attention.

"What? Yeah," I said.

"Well, you sure looked pissed off all of the sudden," she said.

"Huh? Sorry," I said.

"Listen, if this is a bad time for you, I can—"

"Nah, it's fine," I said. "I'm sorry. I've just been a little preoccupied with some things, that's all."

"Yeah? Well, I haven't seen much of you lately, either," she said. "Enough about my dickhead dad. Whatcha been up to?"

I shook my head. "Aw, just crap."

"C'mon, you just endured my drama queen dissertation.

It's time to put the crown on your head for a while," she said.

I chuckled. "Is that what I am now, a drama queen?"

"Sure, we all are sometimes," she said. "The crown gets passed around a lot. It's all about the human experience; especially in college."

I looked into her eyes.

The human experience...

"What?"

"Ah, yeah, you're probably right," I said.

"So, girlfriend problems?" she pressed.

I paused to collect my thoughts.

"Yeah, some," I admitted. "It's like we never see each other much anymore. Not that with all these damned research obligations and classes that I have any time. Then all my spare time is filled with—"

Her eyebrows rose. "Yes? I've wondered what it is that you do in your spare time. It's not like you're hanging out with me or your other friends that much. Although I see you hanging out with that slice of handsome who's rooming in that big house with you. What's his story, anyway?"

"Hey, have you been stalking *me* or something?" I asked, trying to keep my tone mild.

She gave a half-shrug. "I jog around the campus a lot, and I've seen you two hanging out. I noticed that he follows you back to your house a lot, so I just figured. That is, unless you're playing for both teams..."

My eyes widened. "What? No, it's nothing like that. He's just a friend of a friend who needed a place to share expenses. And what with Kat being gone so much and everything, and it just being Paige and me."

"Oh, yeah, your *sister* Paige," she said. "I'm still perplexed with your family tree."

Warning bells went off my head for some reason.

"Yeah, what about it?" I asked. "We don't get to pick our family, you know. I know a lot of people with odd family circumstances."

She held up her hands. "Hey, true," she conceded. "And

hell, I'm hardly one to talk, am I?"

I decided to steer the conversation back toward safer waters. "Speaking of which, where does that leave you with your father? He sounds sort of controlling."

"Yeah, control is his thing," she said. "Though it comes off more like anal retention, really. He's a plus-sized A-plus personality."

I had to laugh at that. "I know the type."

"Oh, who's your A-plus pain in the butt?"

"Not pain in the butt per say," I said. "I dunno. It's complicated."

"How complicated can it be? What sort of complicated?" she pressed.

"It's really not that easy for me to explain."

"It's Katrina, isn't it?" she asked. "Distance is supposed to make the heart grow fonder, but I think that's only true for occasional trips versus a lifestyle. What is it about Katrina's job that's keeping her away so much? Do you think it's another guy?"

My heart ached over that possibility. "No, at least, I'm fairly sure that's not the case."

"For your sake, I hope not," she said. "Been there, done that. But still, how can you know for sure if you're always apart?"

I really didn't suspect that Kat might be seeing other people. If there was one thing that Kat was all about it was fidelity.

"Nah, it's gotta be her job," I said. "It's demanding right now; maybe more than ever, actually."

"What is it she does again? Corporate raiding or something?"

If she only knew how close to true that moniker might be...

"Just a lot of travel and long hours spent on various projects," I said.

"Listen, Caleb, you need to do what's healthy for you," she said. "I know I seem like one to talk about that, given what's happening, but I mean it. You've got to sort it out in your head and decide if this is what you really want in life."

"I'm too busy to sort out anything outside of my daily schedule," I said.

"Take a weekend out of town," she suggested. "Hell, take a week. That's what I'd do. In fact, I've done that a couple of times in the past and it really helped. Get away from all of the crap and distractions and just find some place quiet to *contemplate*. Imagine what your life might be...make different plans, or just think about your life and dream about something more. It's the whole Ebenezer Scrooge thing; what might your life be if you made big changes in it? You'd be amazed how quickly things come into perspective after that."

I had to admit that her idea was very tempting and sounded remarkably therapeutic.

"I like the idea, but I don't even know where I'd go," I said.

"Pick someplace you've been before. Like, try somewhere that makes you feel like you wanted to stay there forever," she said wistfully.

I frowned at first, but then actually considered the possibilities.

It sounded rather tempting.

"Kat and I went camping a few times," I said. "It was amazing...the whole world just melted away while we were there."

She shook her head. "My idea of camping out for a grand escape is a five-star hotel, sunny days around a pool, and endless room service. Oh, and great shopping nearby, too. Maybe a spa."

I smiled. "You are such a diva."

She adopted a haughty expression. "Dah-ling, I put the divine in diva. Luxury is becoming on me."

Our food arrived and further conversation subsided as we ate, though my mind was racing with what she had suggested. Could I really just pack a bag and take off for a few days?

Kat would never permit it; especially not by myself. I'd definitely have to haul both Roman and Paige across country with me.

All prospects of blissful solitude quickly evaporated over that realization.

"I feel sort of like a prisoner in my own world sometimes," I said.

She stared into my eyes with a serious expression. "Yeah? Well, if that's true, then *escape* from it. As your self-appointed warden, I'm officially giving you a deferred sentence."

I gave her an appreciative look. "Thanks, I appreciate the sentiment, at least."

"Sentiment, my ass," she said. "Since when does your own personal sanity have to take a back seat to everything—hell, everyone—else?"

Her words echoed in the back of my mind throughout the remainder of our meal.

After we finished eating dinner, we exchanged a lot of small talk about classes, movies, and a host of quickly forgotten topics. However, my mind kept wandering back to contemplations of a brief escape from my daily grind.

Did I really want my life to keep going on like it had been? It might be months...or even years...before things changed.

Then again, what if things never did change?

That prospect sent a chill down my spine.

No...I didn't want that for myself.

Or did I?

"Hey, dessert or not?" Chance asked. "Or is your silence implying that I'm already getting too fat?"

"Huh? Nah, not for me," I said, snapping back to the present. "You go ahead."

"On second thought, the calories won't be as appreciated while stapled to my butt," she said.

"What's with the sudden worry over your body? You look great. You're an attractive woman."

She appeared amused. "Thank you. I didn't think you noticed."

"Sure, I noticed," I said. "Hell, you should see all the heads you turn on campus."

There was little doubt that Chance was an attractive woman. Never mind that both Anthony and Trey from our hangout group had both openly commented on that fact, as well.

She adopted a shy expression. "Well, I *was* asked out twice on the same day last week, now that you mention it."

"Cool. See?"

"Yeah, you're right," she said. "Bring on that raspberry cheesecake. Wave down our waiter before I lose my nerve."

I said goodbye to her in the parking lot and walked in the direction of my neighborhood while turning up the collar of my leather jacket against the chill air.

It didn't take long for Paige to catch up to me.

"So, how was dinner with Miss Cheesecake?"

"Stalker," I said. "And shut up; you love cheesecake like nobody else I know."

"Hey, I'm supposed to keep an eye on you, remember?" she asked. "I'm supposed to be stalkery."

"That's not a word."

"Give it a rest, Mister Webster."

What I wouldn't give to have just one weekend that didn't involve people watching over everything I did or everywhere I went.

Chance's getaway suggestion quickly returned to the forefront of my mind.

"What's with bein' all broody, kiddo?" Paige asked. "Don't tell me Miss Fashion Statement actually said something that caused you to light a brain cell."

"What is it with you and Chance?" I asked. "She's never done or said anything wrong to you that I can recall."

"Call it intuition. Never liked her; never will," she said.

"Yeah, well, she's still my friend, so at least try to be civil."

"Fine, no more taunting the rich girl from Easy Street," she said.

It struck me as both weird and slightly sad over how we all walk through life with so many misperceptions about the people around us.

As we continued our walk home, I contemplated that and a host of other things. Although one topic in particular, the prospect of a reflective weekend getaway, loomed heavily in my thoughts.

* * *

One week passed as my research into the history of those who studied blood diseases in early twentieth century Europe continued. I secured three promising obscure texts through interlibrary loan.

All that I needed was the spare time to read through them.

Roman persisted with our daily regimens of combat training, as well as the additional things that Alton wanted me to practice. Fortunately, my classes entered a lull of sorts, or as much of a lull as graduate courses could offer.

The fall season was in full swing, and I reveled in the cooler temperatures and colorful foliage. That more than anything made me pine away for a camping retreat.

But perhaps more than that, I craved time alone. I wanted to contemplate my future with Kat and all the prospects that went with it.

The urge to board the nearest bus bound for anywhere gnawed at me like a powerful obsession.

I steeled my resolve and resisted the temptation, though only barely assuaged by the looming Thanksgiving break that I highly anticipated.

"My Thanksgiving break is coming up in a couple of weeks. Are we going to be able to have everyone over at our home in Georgia?" I asked Kat during one of our rare phone visits.

It felt as if I hadn't been at our home in Pine Valley, just outside Atlanta, in years as opposed to merely months.

"I'm not sure that's going to be possible, Caleb," she replied.

"Well, where then? Here?"

Her lengthy pause wasn't encouraging.

"It may need to be here in London," she said. "I'm not sure that we can venture far from things at this time."

"They don't celebrate Thanksgiving in the UK," I said. "Can't we at least have it here in New Haven."

"I wouldn't oppose you spending Thanksgiving in New Haven," she said. "Although Alton and I may not be able to attend."

I felt stunned. She knew how important the holidays were for me. It was our special time together.

"I don't understand this," I said. "Why must our entire lives revolve around vampire politics?"

"Caleb, there's much more at stake than politics."

"You two aren't the only ones in London, you know," I said. "You're supposed to be surrounded by competent people. Or at least that's what you've tried to convince me of in the past. Were you just saying that so I wouldn't worry?"

"My love, you don't understand—"

"How am I supposed to understand when you won't actually tell me anything about what's really going on there? I mean, seriously, how am I—"

"*Caleb.*"

I curtailed a further tirade upon hearing the steely tone in her voice.

"What?"

"We can have Thanksgiving here," she said. "The entire menu can be traditional American cuisine, and I'll ask Ethan to fly over with you and Paige. You can even invite Roman if you like."

I took a deep breath and let it out slowly. At least we weren't cancelling the holiday altogether.

"Sure, I suppose that works," I said.

In truth, it wasn't what I would have preferred, but my life had devolved into an endless series of distasteful compromises over recent months.

"There, it's settled," she said, her tone lighter. "We'll chat more soon about the details, though we only have a few days remaining before we need to solidify plans. That will give you time to organize the guest list. Now I have to join Alton for a meeting with some prospective business associates."

We said our goodbyes pleasantly enough, but I still felt both unsettled and annoyed by the time I hung up the phone.

For a supposed compromise, my prospective Thanksgiving plans still felt like a crappy deal.

It was in that moment that I determined it was time for me to make some decisions about the rest of my life, including the future of my relationship with Kat.

A queasy feeling formed in the pit of my stomach over where those deliberations might lead, and I nearly changed my mind. But my future was worthy of more than just taking the easy route; the path of least resistance was no longer good enough for me.

It occurred to me that there had been a time in the not terribly distant past when that wasn't necessarily true. Whether due to low self-esteem or the strong desire to be with Kat, it wasn't that long ago that I would have caved in to nearly any demand.

But circumstances had evolved.

Or, just perhaps, I had evolved.

No matter the reason, the undeniable fact remained that life was too short for me as a human to settle for less.

CHAPTER 10

Caleb

The next morning, I abruptly awoke in a cold sweat in the middle of a particularly bad dream, convincing me more than ever that my life was too overwhelming for my own good.

There was no way that I could endure yet another day working on my doctoral thesis, or facing endless reading and assessment assignments, much less what felt like a perpetual regimen of extreme sports training combined with mixed martial arts.

Today was a day for self-preservation.

Normally, this would be the point where Kat would divine that something was wrong and she'd take me aside so that we could quietly discuss the matter.

But she wasn't there.

Worse, I was rarely able to speak to her.

Hell, I was lucky to work in occasional text messages, or the even rarer phone call. Even when we did chat, we felt so removed from each other; she remained steadfastly tight-lipped about what she had been doing.

Her daily life was practically a mystery to me.

It scared me to admit that sometimes it felt as if she and I were growing more distant with each passing week.

I wasn't so dim to realize that she was probably avoiding such topics because everything she was up to was dangerous. I felt certain she didn't want me to worry about her, or permit myself to become distracted from my own endeavors.

However, the truth was that, if this was what our lives were relegated to, it seemed like no quality of life at all for either of us.

Hell, all I really wanted was to be with her. But each day that possibility seemed more and more remote, becoming like some sort of daydream.

Sometimes it felt like our relationship was evaporating before us.

A rapid series of heavy knocks on my bedroom door made me jolt upright in bed.

"C'mon lazybones," Roman demanded. "Outta that rack and down in fifteen minutes or you'll do laps this evening."

"Right," I groaned.

"Hurry it up!"

"Oh, stick it," I muttered under my breath, throwing the sheet off of me.

The cool air assaulting my sweaty skin sent a shiver through my body.

Although I had formed a strong respect for Roman, in recent months he'd practically morphed from an instructive bodyguard into an insufferable drill sergeant.

I squinted my eyelids shut and grit my teeth.

"This shit really sucks."

As I leaned over the bathroom sink and splashed warm water on my face, I momentarily struggled to remember what day of the week it was. Lately, they all felt the same.

Downstairs, Paige was finishing putting on a set of black motorcycle leathers and gloves.

"Where are you headed to?" I asked as she picked up her helmet and a small book bag.

"Some stupid English test," she said. "My instructor won't let us take exams online. Something about student identity verification issues or some such crap."

"Yeah, some instructors don't like giving online exams," I said. "There's a big uproar in the teaching community about the inability to verify a student's identity online. They want to make sure that the actual student is taking an exam and not somebody standing in for them."

"Whatever, McLawyer," she said. "Most of my other teachers don't seem in an uproar over it."

"It's typically at the instructor's discretion," I said.

She stared at me with a flat look. "Again, whatever."

"Caleb, we'd better get started," Roman prompted.

Paige gave me a knowing look. "Looks like somebody's late for their workout time."

I gave her a dirty look as she slipped her helmet on.

Following training and exercises was an all-too-quick breakfast. Then I walked alongside Roman on our trek to the campus.

Our walk was relatively brief, but it was more than enough time to contemplate my circumstances.

As the office building relegated to the history department loomed before us, a crossroads loomed in my mind.

Did I really want to live this daily drudgery for the next few years? Could Kat and I survive our growing distance from each other?

The thought of living like I was for two or three more years turned my stomach. I felt as if I wanted to throw up into the nearest bushes.

"Hey, you okay?" Roman asked.

"What? Yeah, it's nothing," I said. "Just tired."

"Up too late playing video games last night?" he teased.

"If, by video games, you mean writing an essay on the economic conditions in nineteenth century Europe and their influence on scientific advancements, then yeah, maybe I was up too late," I snapped.

"Research and writing is why you're here, right?"

It annoyed me that my response didn't even faze him. That lack of recognition only further aggravated me and heightened the sense of unfairness about my situation.

We entered the building and I headed straight for the elevator.

"Hey, let's take the stairs. We'll get some extra leg work that way."

"Always looking out for me, aren't you?"

"*That's* what I'm here for."

He followed me upstairs to just outside Professor Gowan's office to discreetly ensure that everything appeared safe and then he reversed course to head back downstairs.

"Meet me in the lobby when you're done," he said.

Before I entered the professor's office, I hesitated.

My life felt like some macabre connect-the-dots game, and the doorknob before me was the next dot in my day, followed by a host of other linear dots afterward, all leading to...

Monotony.

I felt an immediate urge to turn and run.

To escape.

But then, escape to where?

With a heavy sigh of resignation, I turned the knob and entered.

* * *

Upon the conclusion of my meeting with Dr. Gowan, I was left with a list of further research reading and a lengthy essay assignment.

While I had mostly enjoyed the graduate work for my master's program, the process of pursuing my PhD seemed like a master's program on steroids. I contemplated my busy schedule designated for the remainder of the week as I descended the stairs toward where Roman waited for me.

I wanted to chuck it all by the time I reached the first floor landing.

As I reached for the door handle that would take me into the lobby, I once again hesitated, wishing I could do anything but continue my grueling timetable.

Instead, I longingly eyed the door to my right that led directly outside the building.

Fed up with everything, including my seemingly endless routine and obligations, I exited to outside.

As the sunshine hit my face, I felt as if I'd just walked into another world. A veritable wave of infinite possibilities washed over me.

I quickly proceeded toward the parking lot, away from the front of the building and the windows that might give my position away to Roman.

I knew it was the wrong thing to do, but my desire to avoid my grueling fate won out over my sense of obligation or duty.

What duty? I was an overwrought graduate student who also trained as if he was heading either to the Olympics or into the army.

I just needed a break, that's all. Maybe all I would need was just an hour or so off to myself.

As I walked toward the student union building, a forbidden notion taunted my imagination.

I didn't just need an hour away; I needed a few days off.

Of course, I knew that probably wouldn't fly with either Roman or Paige.

I took out my smartphone and texted Kat.

How about an impromptu visit? Maybe a couple of days together?

As I sipped at a hot cup of coffee from one of the café vendors, it took nearly half an hour before Kat replied.

So sorry, Caleb. Important activities to address. Maybe in a few weeks?

I closed my eyes and cursed under my breath.

Sure, I texted.

Sorry to disappoint you. Love you.

I texted, *Love you, too.*

It appeared that there would be no respite for me—for us—after all.

To be honest, it made me angry.

Once again, I wondered if I wanted to keep this up for weeks or months on end.

Despite the obvious luxuries of my accommodations—including no worries for expenses such as room and board or tuition, coupled with the opportunity that going to Yale afforded me—it certainly didn't feel like I was living a lifestyle of enviable quality.

Or at least the expected sacrifices felt like too much of a price to pay.

Somehow, being poorer but happier sounded better to me. I'd lived a modest lifestyle for most of my life, and yet it had been some of the most satisfying occasions in my life. Before Kat, I had lived a relatively fulfilling life devoid of vampire politics, hectic schedules, or people trying to kill me.

Granted, it had also been a life without Kat in it.

Although she didn't exactly feel like part of my life, either recently or at that moment.

What if this was as good as things would be between us for a while? Was it enough for me?

I took a sip of what had turned into very tepid coffee.

Despite my circumstances, the fact remained that I needed a break.

I need to contemplate things…my life…my future.

That's when a decision settled in my mind, and I rose from my seat with a renewed sense of purpose.

I practically jogged back to the house, entering through the front door and hearing complete silence.

It was a soothing sound.

As I closed the front door behind me and looked toward the nearby staircase, much to my surprise, my sense of determination hadn't waned.

I took the stairs two at a time, almost giddy with a mix of apprehension and excitement. As I entered my bedroom, I dropped my backpack onto the bed and unloaded most everything from it.

I had a plan.

However, how I proceeded during the ensuing minutes

would determine my hasty plan's success or failure.

I realized that I couldn't use my credit cards or other electronic payment methods; they'd track me down in no time. Instead, I retrieved a stash of cash that I had stored in my chest of drawers and hastily crammed three pairs of jeans, some trendy t-shirts, a spare pair of sneakers, and a few days' worth of underclothes into my backpack.

Scanning my belongings, I realized I'd have to leave my electronic devices behind or they'd track their usage. It was already bad enough I had a locator chip implanted in my shoulder. I felt a little bit like a tagged animal.

But I only had to exceed range of the detection equipment to drop off that particular radar.

The problem was staying ahead of it.

Granted, they'd probably still locate me in a matter of days, but that's all I needed; just a few precious days to clear my head and gather my thoughts.

I glanced forlornly at my iPad on the table.

I'd miss it.

Nevertheless, I grabbed my Kindle and two iPods that were loaded with movies and music. As long as I kept their wireless functionality turned off, they couldn't be tracked. Like my smartphone, my iPad had built-in cellular functionality, presenting the risk of being tracked.

There was little doubt that I was addicted to consumer electronics and their contributions to daily escapism in my life.

Hell, the entire human race was addicted.

It dawned on me that technology served as both the ultimate babysitter and an emotional pacifier.

I hurried into the bathroom to toss additional necessities into my backpack. I glanced up into the mirror at my reflection, noting the haunted look in my eyes.

The renewed urge to leave welled up inside me; though a wave of guilt washed over me over how upset the people who loved and cared about me were going to feel.

Then I almost lost my nerve.

But I knew deep down inside that getting away was exactly what I needed at that moment.

Just a few days of contemplation and solitude.

God, Kat's going kill me for this.

Hopefully not literally.

I swallowed hard and steeled my resolve.

It's not like it was forever.

Was it?

While I felt unnerved, I also felt liberated.

I've gotta clear my head. I'm no good to anyone like this.

Zipping my backpack shut, I hurried downstairs.

I left a hastily written note on the countertop:

Paige and Roman,

    I'm taking a few days to clear my head and gain perspective on my life. I hope you'll forgive me for leaving so abruptly, but I doubt you would approve what I need to do. Even though I can't expect you to understand what I'm going through, I hope you'll respect my decision.

    I'll message you periodically so that you won't worry about me.

Caleb

I figured that it was a pretty lame note, but it was the best I felt I could do on short notice.

Before I lost nerve, I exited through the front door, locking the door behind me.

Despite my reservations about continuing, I had scarcely reached the curb before an aura of satisfaction took root within me.

I smiled, feeling a pervasive sense of freedom and the hunger for possibilities like none I had ever felt before.

Part II

THE OPEN ROAD

CHAPTER 11

Caleb

Unfortunately, I couldn't contemplate anything with any hope of peace of mind until I left New Haven, well before Paige had an opportunity to track me down via the microchip nestled beneath the skin of my shoulder.

I hastily purchased a bus ticket for the earliest, farthest away destination, which was the twenty-something-mile trek to Bridgeport.

At the bus station, I grabbed a printed map and another bus schedule for the surrounding region.

I already missed my mobile devices.

During the shuttle to Bridgeport, I devised a series of routes to follow that might throw Paige and Roman off while economically conserving my limited financial resources.

I went from Bridgeport to White Plains, and then on to Yonkers before ending up in Jersey City.

By then I felt tired and my butt was sore from sitting.

Honestly, I was surprised that I'd made it this far without being intercepted. I was convinced that by now they were already diligently searching for me.

I momentarily imagined Paige discovering me missing and then saying, "Aw, screw him. He's more trouble than he's worth…"

It made me smile, but also made me feel a little bit sad.

Did it make me feel better to think they were going out of their minds trying to find me?

Once I had mulled that over, it made me feel guilty. However, I was also appreciating the freedom of the open road.

Having had enough of buses for the time being, I made my way to the nearest train station, though it was a bit of a walk.

As I boarded the train destined for Newark, my mind wandered further and I began to contemplate where I actually wanted to go. Traversing endless bus and train routes didn't entice me in the least.

It was evening by the time the train arrived at Newark, so I looked for a place to spend the night that was within walking distance to the station. I ended up in a cheap hotel that was so run down in such a cliché style that it reminded me of something out of a bad Hollywood film. Suffice to say, I checked beneath the sheets and mattress for pests before attempting to go to sleep.

The next morning began with a breakfast burrito and coffee from the nearest fast food restaurant. I boarded a train for a quick ride to Elizabeth, New Jersey. Once I exited the train, I located an Internet café to send a quick email Kat, Alton, and Paige to let them know that I was in no danger.

Then I was back on a train to Newark, where I changed direction and took a train northwest to Scranton, Pennsylvania.

At Scranton, I boarded a bus for Syracuse, New York and passed the time perusing state maps from the region to contemplate my future destination. Along the way, my mind wandered until my thoughts gravitated to Katrina.

The memory of her was almost painful to me.

She was the last person I wanted to think about at that moment. I couldn't bear to focus on her or our relationship.

But she was the reason I was there.

If not then, when exactly did I intend to contemplate the

central reason for my abrupt cross-country excursion?

I wasn't ready yet. That much I knew.

So I returned to alternating between perusing maps and passively staring out at the passing traffic and surroundings.

It's startling how quickly time passes when you're avoiding confronting strong emotions.

Before I realized it, we were nearly at the outskirts of Syracuse, and I stared dumbfounded at my watch to realize that nearly three hours had passed.

Where the hell did the time go?

I ate a quick lunch and decided to go on to Rochester and then to Buffalo. During the layover in Rochester and some heavy traffic, I was able to sit and mull things over for nearly four additional hours.

By the time we reached Buffalo, it was almost early evening, so I stayed in yet another cheap hotel. Despite room conditions that were somewhat improved from my previous experiences, I nevertheless closely examined the bed before going to sleep.

One thing was certain about life with Katrina and all its trappings: I tended to stay in upscale, well-maintained accommodations. The Spartan reality of my life before Kat was quickly reasserting itself, like a half-forgotten memory of days gone by.

In reality, it had only been more than a year since I met Katrina. And yet, in some ways it felt like a lifetime. Perhaps that was because my life had changed so drastically over that short duration.

I had experienced unimaginable passion and adrenaline-rushing excitement, as well as confronted moments of heart-stopping terror. It felt as if I had already lived an entire range of lifetime events.

But it was the lighter moments with Kat that I cherished the most. I reflected upon those and it lulled me into a state of relaxation.

Sometime during my musings, I fell asleep.

I abruptly awoke to the sounds of someone banging on

my hotel room door.

"Hey, open up," came a gruff voice.

The room was dark as my mind struggled to grasp where I was amidst renewed knocking.

I instinctually grabbed my combat knives from beneath my pillow before slipping into my jeans.

I tip-toed to the door and carefully glanced out through the security peephole to see a tall, heavily bearded fellow facing forward.

"C'mon, open up, asshole," he said. "I haven't got time for this shit."

He obviously had the wrong room and it sort of pissed me off that he'd woken me out of a relatively peaceful slumber.

I took a deep breath while slipping one knife into my back waistband, then unsheathed the other and held it at the ready.

I quickly unlocked the door and jerked it open, startling the guy. I snatched him by the collar of his leather jacket and jerked forward, catching him off balance.

"What the—"

I swung him downward onto the floor while placing the tip of my knife to his throat.

"Wrong damned room, *asshole*," I said.

"H-hey, what gives, dickhead? You called me," he stammered.

"I don't even know who you are, idiot," I said, increasing the pressure of the blade against his neck.

"Whoa, whoa, Peterson, back off," he said, holding his hands up with palms open.

"Peterson? Who the hell is Peterson?"

"Wha—You're not Blacktop Peterson?"

I stared down at him. "Do I look like Blacktop Peterson?"

Whoever the hell that was...

"Uh, how should I know? This is the drop, room 27 for Peterson," he said. "Are you a cop? You've gotta tell me if you are."

"Well, I'm definitely not Peterson," I said between gritted teeth.

"Oh…shit," he said. "I thought he said 27."

Despite my heart racing, I was really pissed off for some reason.

"I oughta—" I said.

"Hey, whoa-whoa," he said. "Let's just calm the hell down before someone gets jacked—"

"That's you," I said, pinning the guy beneath my knee while patting him down for weapons with my free hand.

I heard a door open across the hallway, but didn't want to take my eyes off the guy before me.

"Hey, man, are you selling to him instead?" asked a tentative voice from the doorway behind me.

I held the knife at the prone man's throat and reached behind me to withdraw my other knife. I turned to my newest unwanted guest.

"Do you want a piece of this, too?" I asked.

The man's eyes went wide and he took off at a dead run.

"H-hey, this don't have to end bad, you know," the guy on the floor said. "I don't want no trouble."

I gave him my best hard glare.

"Did you hear that other guy running down the hall?" I asked.

"Y-yeah."

I removed the knife from beneath his throat and rose to stand.

"You better beat him outta here."

The fellow slowly rose to his feet with his hands held above his shoulders and gradually moved toward the open door.

"Go!" I said.

He ran down the length of the hallway. I heard rapidly retreating, heavy footfalls and a door fling open at the end of the hallway. I carefully peered around the corner in time to see the metal stairwell door shut with a thud.

Despite the late hour, I wasted no time hastily packing my things and heading downstairs to check out. There was no way I was waiting around to see if the guy came back and with renewed courage and perhaps a gun.

The desk associate was wary to check me out, but I told him about my unwanted guest, for which he apologized profusely.

"Absolutely, sir," he said. "I'll make sure my manager is notified. Should I call the police?"

"No, they're both gone now," I said. "But I'd keep the phone handy, if I were you."

To his credit, the guy appeared sympathetic.

"I only charged you for half the normal rate. The manager left me his override card," he said. "But would you mind giving me a good rating on a customer survey?"

Seriously?

"Yeah, for you, sure," I said. "Not so much on my room experience."

He gave me a sheepish look. "Yeah, I don't blame you there, really."

The associate gave me directions to the nearest decent hotel, so I cautiously made my way out into the night.

What a weird night.

Suddenly, I doubted the wisdom of my road trip escape from New Haven.

Once I had checked into a hotel just down the street, I went to the bathroom and splashed warm water on my face. I looked into the mirror at my tired expression.

Lying in bed, I replayed the events from my recent hotel experience. I was annoyed over how awkward everything had felt, and I silently critiqued my actions and technique.

I need more practice on takedowns, I mused.

I almost made a mental note to ask Roman about it during our next workout. It was odd how easily my mind fell into routines, no matter how undesirable.

Over the course of various training regimens and events ranging from enlightening to nearly lethal, I had morphed into a decidedly different version of me over the past year. I could scarcely envision the person I had been before meeting Katrina.

I could have pondered if that was a good thing or not, but I already knew that would have been silly, as well as pointless.

I respected the person I had become; I was better equipped to live in the world around me, as well as survive its challenges.

The remainder of my night was restless despite my fatigue, and I slept very little.

The next morning, I undertook a bus trip to East Aurora, the historic township where Millard Fillmore and his wife had lived in the 1920s prior to his ascendency to the presidency.

Only a history nerd like me would appreciate that veritably forgettable moniker.

The journey permitted me more time to contemplate my life with, and lately without, Kat.

East Aurora was quaint and I availed myself of a cozy café with public Wi-Fi to send a message to Kat, Paige, and Alton to tell them that I was safe and would be in touch again soon. I kept my notes brief while trying not to dwell on the emotional, bordering on furious, emails from each of them. There was even a message from Roman in which he threatened to beat my ass when he saw me next.

It was nice to know he cared.

I lingered long enough to take in some brief sights and eat lunch before returning to Buffalo. From there, I took a train to Silver Creek, right off the shores of Lake Erie. Afterward, I went all the way to Cleveland, Ohio where I killed some time and awaited another train departure.

My life came full circle as I contemplated an emotional selection for my next destination.

Columbus, Ohio.

I was born and raised there.

When I was only a boy, my abusive alcoholic father died

there at Katrina's hands; a memory only recently returned to me thanks to the hypnotic ministrations of a London-based vampire psychiatrist named Dr. Roehl Guilhelm.

Perhaps the worst memory was that my mother died of cancer in Columbus while I was still in college.

I had many demons to exorcize there.

Night had fallen once my train pulled into Columbus. However, I remained in town and avoided a taxi ride out to my old childhood home on the outskirts of the city.

There might be demons, but I wasn't in the mood to be a demon hunter quite yet.

Instead, that night, following a quick meal, I decided to pick someplace restful for further contemplations.

I selected Ohio's Tar Hollow State Park, located just south of Laurelville on state highway 56. There were over sixteen thousand acres of forest woodlands to lose myself in. It was a scenic location that I'd briefly visited while growing up

It seemed absolutely ideal.

I was pleased to find that Laurelville actually supported an infrequent bus route, which I quickly secured passage on.

The road trip was restful and there weren't many people on my bus, so it was relatively quiet. Every time I tried to think about Kat and the issues that inspired me to run away, my mind rebelled. Instead, I morosely stared out the window at the passing landscape.

What was I going to do?

I couldn't just keep running away. My available timeline wasn't limitless.

Was it?

CHAPTER 12

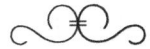

Caleb

When the bus pulled onto Main Street in Laurelville, I thought we'd landed in the midst of a cliché.

I had the distinct impression that the town might fit into the back of two semi-tractor trailers. Heck, for all I knew, the townspeople might all fit into the Greyhound bus that had brought me there.

I was the only person exiting the bus, and as I watched the bus pull away, I felt a wave of uncertainty wash over me. I spared a few moments to scan my surroundings.

It looked bleak and remote. The nearest homes that I could see looked as if they'd been built decades before I was born. The place seemed wholly removed from modern times; an anomaly stuck in a time pocket.

Had I just stepped into the *Twilight Zone?*

"God, I'm so screwed."

I hoisted my backpack over one shoulder and walked just up the street to a small diner called Cooper's Cafe, conveniently placed directly across the street from Laurelville Feed and Seed.

As I crossed the café's threshold, the half dozen customers turned to look at me.

"Just sit where you'd like and I'll be right with ya," said a waitress standing behind an old-fashioned counter.

"Sure thing," I said, making my way toward an empty booth situated before one of the front picture windows.

The other patrons quickly dismissed me and returned to their meals.

As I sat and perused the crumpled single-sheet laminated menu, the waitress arrived at my table.

"Hi, I'm Bel. Can I get you something to drink while you look at the menu?" she asked.

What an unusual nickname. Or is that her actual name?

"Um, iced tea, I suppose."

"I'll be right back," she said. "Oh, and our special today is fried catfish."

Minutes later, after looking over the menu and sipping some tea, I took out the brochure about the Tar Hollow State Park cabins.

"Tar Hollow, eh? Sort of missed the season, didn't you?"

I started slightly as I registered Bel's proximity.

"Probably, I really just need to find somewhere quiet," I said. "Seems nice and quiet here. I can probably still catch a few fish, too."

"Well, it's pretty dead in the off season," she said. "But if it's quiet you want, this is the place. This time of year, you'll have your pick of cabins at Tar Hollow. And yeah, any fisherman worth his salt can land some bass and crappie."

"Thanks for the info. So, how's the chicken fried steak?" I asked.

"Award-winning, just like the menu says."

I noted the wry expression on her face.

"What award did it win, exactly?"

"Blue ribbon at the Hocking County Fair."

Then she smiled. "Back in 1959."

Somehow the year 1959 seemed fitting in more ways than one for anything I had already seen in Laurelville.

"Do they use the same recipe today?"

"Oh, sure. But then, I think it's prepared by the son of the recipe's cook, too."

I chuckled. "I'll take it, mashed potatoes and all. Oh, and ranch dressing, if you have it."

As our eyes met, I thought that her hazel eyes practically twinkled.

"I'll fix you right up," she said. "I'll bring your salad out in a few minutes."

"Order up, Bel!" yelled the cook from the back kitchen area.

"Coming, Jim!" she yelled back. "Old fart."

I stared out the window at the town beyond and watched only a couple of vehicles pass by before my meal arrived. Fortunately, my food tasted much better than I expected.

Bel placed a check at the edge of my table. "Can I get you anything else?"

"Yeah, about how far away is the main office to rent a cabin at Tar Hollow?"

"Well, it's a few miles south of here, but you can't miss it if you follow highway 56."

"A few miles?" I asked.

"Just a few minutes by car," she said. "The guy you'll want to speak to is Garth. I forget his last name, but he's the only Garth in this area that I've ever heard of."

It sounded pretty straight forward. Then it occurred to me that walking there was going to be quite a hike.

"You have a vehicle, right?" she asked.

"Uh, not exactly," I said. "It sounds strange to say, but I just got off the bus. Any taxi service around here?"

She stifled a laugh. "Boy, did you land in the wrong town. I haven't seen a taxi come through here in months."

"Car rental?"

She shook her head. "Not so much."

Despite my practice of cautious budgeting, I quickly calculated a generous tip for her and laid out the cash onto the table.

"Thanks for everything," I said. "The food was pretty good...took me right back to 1959."

"I'll bet. As if either of us could legitimately claim to

know 1959," she said.

"Yeah, well, that's the history teacher in me talking," I said, picking up my pack and making my way out of the restaurant. "Thanks again."

As I stepped out onto the sidewalk, I sensed the major flaw in my impromptu plan.

No transportation in a one-horse town.

Then my eye caught sight of a dark blue moped with a for sale sign on it out in front of the Feed and Seed across the street.

"Well, beggars can't be choosers," I said.

An hour later, and with a serious dent in my cash reserves, I donned a small skullcap helmet and awkwardly rode down the street on my decidedly used moped.

Paige would give me so much hell over this right now.

* * *

Before venturing south, I made a quick trip to the town's only discount department store for what few toiletries and supplies I could squeeze into my nearly full backpack.

By the time I had secured a cabin from Garth at the main office and settled in, it was late afternoon. Realizing that I only had some light snacks for food, I puttered back to town where I purchased another backpack before heading to the local grocery store. At the camping supplies store next door, I procured a relatively inexpensive fishing kit.

Afterward, I began my drive back to the cabin and felt very appreciative for the moped.

Approaching the café, I saw Bel getting into a Jeep. We waved at each other as I passed by.

It was a cool but pleasant early evening by the time I returned to the cabin. I gathered some firewood from a neatly stacked supply on the back outer wall. Only as I carried the wood inside did I realize that I actually felt more relaxed than I had in days.

Maybe I've finally found where I need to be to think things through.

* * *

The next morning, I rose early for a quick breakfast and then walked to the nearby lake to do some fishing. I only had a couple of bites and tossed back the few small bass and a crappie that were too little to be worth cleaning.

As I appreciated the beauty and peacefulness around me, I mulled over my situation and all that had brought me there.

I couldn't deny that my existence was likely enviable to most people; that is, if you discounted the occasional attempts on my life or the violence that went along with renegade vampires showing up from time to time. In truth, some of it was sort of exciting. However, it was the life-threatening aspect that got old fast.

Then there was my situation with Kat.

I loved her. I really loved her.

But she was essentially an absent mate, perpetually on missions and building and organizing a veritable army for Alton. Even though she told me that she was doing it for us as much as for Alton, it nevertheless kept me away from being with her.

Then there was my doctoral program at Yale.

Yale.

I'd have never expected the opportunity for that; not in a million years.

Kat and Alton were spending thousands of dollars toward my education and living expenses, not to mention Paige upheaving her life with Ethan just to help protect me. Of course, Roman was doing his part, as well. He had even turned out to be a pretty competent trainer.

Granted, he was a bit of a drill sergeant a lot of the time. I could do without some of that, actually.

So many sacrifices were being made and opportunities being issued on my behalf.

And, while I realized the importance of each of those, I

still couldn't help feeling dissatisfied at times.

In the end, I was fully cognizant of everything that Alton and others were doing for me, which only made me feel guilty over feeling the way I did. But it really didn't alter my view—my visceral emotions—over the situation at hand, either.

I didn't care about vampire politics, or building coalitions, or even stemming the tide of mounting aggression against two opposing factions. I didn't even feel like a failure if I didn't complete my doctoral program. I only wanted to be with Kat, to have her in my life on a daily basis.

If we were together, I felt as though there was nothing I couldn't overcome or endure. My love for her would carry me through.

And yet, I wasn't enduring her prolonged absence in my life very well at all. What did that say about my true sense of commitment?

Or did it really mean anything in the end?

My fishing line tangled as I cast forward in frustration. "Dammit!"

I threw the small rod and reel to the ground, annoyed that I couldn't even enjoy a simple fishing excursion without things going to hell.

I took a deep breath and hitched my hands atop my hips. Then I slowly stretched my neck and back muscles to relieve some tension.

The sun was already on its trek toward the west as I glanced down at my watch. Half the afternoon had already passed.

Worse yet, I was hungry and I had no fish to show for it.

I picked up my rod and tackle and walked back to the cabin. I immediately went to the refrigerator to grab something to eat.

As I started to retrieve the items to make a cold sandwich, my stomach craved the menu at Cooper's Café.

I mulled over my finances, which could still endure a few meals before I had to be overly conservative.

I put everything back into the refrigerator and headed

out to my scooter.

When I walked through the café main doors Bel was delivering some food to a table.

"Hey," she said. "Back already?"

"What can I say? Best food in town."

Granted, it qualified as the only legitimate restaurant in town.

"Pick a place and I'll be right with you," she said.

I selected the same booth that I had on my first visit. It had an excellent view of both the entrance and the street outside; a good tactical location.

Roman would be proud of me.

"Already tired of eating all those fish you've been catching?" Bel asked.

I gave her a wan look.

"I warned you it was the off season," she said. "Besides, the fish are in their fall pattern, usually deep instead of the shallows."

"You fish?" I asked.

"No, but I've cleaned quite a few for my ex," she said. "And I pick up dozens of good tips each week working here."

I glanced at her left hand and noted a telltale faded circular area at the base of her ring finger.

"Well, I should hope you get good tips," I quipped. "You're a really good waitress."

She shook her head at me, though she smiled. "Thank you, kind sir. What can I get you today? The fried catfish is pretty good, if you're suffering fisherman's remorse."

Suddenly, the thought of fish didn't entice me very much. "Nah, how about the fried chicken instead."

"It's even better. Iced tea?" she asked.

"Yes, thanks."

"Coming right up."

As I sat there, I realized how much I appreciated running into someone like Bel. Somehow, her friendly personality made my situation here in town feel more comfortable.

As I ate a small salad that she brought to me, my thoughts returned to Kat and our future together. I barely noticed when my entrée was being delivered to my table.

"Deep in thought?" she asked.

"Yeah," I replied. "Thanks. This really looks good."

"There's some good things here," she said.

"You know, this whole town seems like something out of a nostalgic old movie," I said. "It's almost like an escape from the real world. All that's missing is James Stewart."

"You'd think so as a visitor," she said. "But people in small towns like ours one have just as many issues as people living in the city. The main difference is that here everyone else knows about everyone else's problems."

I nodded. "Makes sense."

"There's a lot to be said for the anonymity of big cities, if you want my opinion," she said. "Let me know if you need anything."

Halfway through my meal, Bel stopped by my table. "I'm getting off-shift in a few minutes, but Candace will take care of you from here. Normally, I'd stay late to finish your table, but I have to pick up my kids on time tonight. My parents have an event to attend."

"Oh, that's just fine," I said. "But thanks for letting me know."

She smiled at me and I watched her as she took off her apron. A nearly teenage-looking young lady wearing a waitress uniform handed a coat and purse to Bel.

"Thanks, Candace," she said. "Take good care of table four over there. He's a first-class customer."

"Sure thing, Bel," the young woman replied.

Bel winked at me while shrugging into her coat and then left through the front doors.

I liked her.

Her parting words echoed in my thoughts as I finished my meal.

There's a lot to be said for the anonymity of big cities, if you want my opinion...

I could appreciate how Bel might feel the way she did about small towns. Still, sometimes it felt like a person could practically drown in their anonymity in a big city. Certainly, New Haven and the Yale campus made me feel practically invisible at times.

When I thought about it further, so did Atlanta.

I'm sure that's something vampires find very appealing.

It struck me that those were two key words for me, vampires and found.

Now that I had stopped moving around the country, how much longer might it be before I was found...by a vampire?

More to the point, what was I going to do then?

CHAPTER 13

Caleb

After stopping by a convenience store to purchase some beer, which I slipped into an empty back pack I had brought with me, I rode the distance back to the cabin.

During the ride, I replayed the list of routes I had taken to get to Tar Hollow. I was confident that my circuitous journey permitted me many more days of solitude before Kat, or anyone else for that matter, might come close to locating me.

That's when the guilt washed over me; guilt for leaving New Haven so abruptly, as well as for going off the grid once I had.

Granted, I had taken the time to send multiple messages to reassure everyone that I was fine. But I knew Kat better than most and she was going to be really pissed with me.

I imagined a dark, oncoming storm in my mind's eye.

A shiver ran down my spine and I knew it wasn't from the gradually cooling evening air that impacted my face.

I sat quietly before the cabin's fireplace that evening and drank three beers before finally going to bed.

I slept restlessly.

The next day began with a cool morning breeze and a mostly clear sky. I rose early for a light breakfast and then sat outside with a mug of hot tea to appreciate the sunrise. Additionally, I busied myself unraveling the snarl of fishing line on my reel that I had acquired the previous day.

Later that morning, I set out for a relaxing walk through the woods. I'd always enjoyed the outdoors, and it was particularly beautiful here as the waning fall gave way to the precursors of winter.

It occurred to me that Thanksgiving was just a couple of weeks away. My thoughts gravitated to last year and my first Thanksgiving with Kat. It was hard to believe that we had been together for more than a year.

In fact, it had almost been that long since our life or death fight with the renegade vampire, Chimalma.

Kat and I had been through so much together in the short time we'd been together.

Had all of that been too taxing for us? Was our relationship threatened by too much drama?

There were no easy answers, and I considered those questions at length.

After a time, I arrived at an honest answer. No, to both.

I wished that Kat were there to share the beautiful, relaxing surroundings with me. Maybe between the two of us we'd be able to set everything right again.

But then the problem wasn't that I didn't want to spend my life with Kat. On the contrary, it was that I didn't think I could go on as we were, essentially without her regular presence in my life.

How did previous generations do it during times of wars and conflict abroad, when lovers were apart for years at a time?

I made my way back to the cabin by midday and decided that I once again craved a meal from Cooper's Café versus a cold sandwich.

Within the hour I was seated at my usual booth as Bel waited on me.

"Don't you ever get a day off?" I asked.

"I wish," she replied. "But when you have an ex who only

pays alimony and child support when the mood strikes him, you work more than you play."

"Can't you take him to court?"

"Sure, if I had the money to pay an attorney," she said. "And until he stops paying entirely, a judge really isn't going to take much notice."

While that might have been true, it certainly didn't seem fair.

"I'm sorry to hear that," I said, not really sure what I should say to that.

"Hey, we all have our burdens, right?" she said.

She said a real mouthful there.

"So, let's review for a moment. You've had the chicken-fried steak and then the fried chicken," she said. "What will it be today, I wonder?"

"Guess," I said.

"I'm guessing something fried," she said.

"Ha! Too easy," I said.

Her eyes narrowed as she thoughtfully tapped the end of her chin with her ink pen. "Meatloaf with mashed potatoes and gravy?"

I shook my head. "Cheeseburger, well done, and fries."

"You got me there. Still, the fries are deep fried, so I was close," she said. "Iced tea?"

"Coke," I replied.

"Well, you're just full of surprises today, aren't you?"

I shrugged. "I can be."

"I bet," she said. "I'll get this started for you."

I didn't have to wait long for my meal, which was good because my stomach was already growling.

After checking on a handful of other customers, Bel returned to my table.

"How is it?"

"Great," I replied.

"Are you enjoying your stay at the cabin?"

I considered how to answer that.

"What? Are the fish being really mean to you?" she asked

with a feisty expression.

"Yeah, but it's really relaxing, too," I replied. "I'd like to come back again during the spring or summer sometime."

"I know it's not really my place, but I have to ask about something. Candace, Jim, and I have been trying to guess what brought you to Tar Hollow," she said.

"Oh? Is there an office pool for it?" I asked.

"No," she replied. "Jim says he's not much on gambling. Although I say that's strange because he loves bingo night at the Baptist church in town."

"Ah," I said, nodding my head. "So, what's been guessed so far?"

Bel sat on the end of the booth seat across from me and leaned across the table. "Well, Jim thinks you're on the run from the law, but then he watches too many legal dramas on television, which is where he gets most of his ideas."

I chuckled at that.

"As for Candace, she thinks you're an introverted author who's traveling the country seeking inspiration as you work on your next big novel," she said.

"That's actually an enticing thought," I said. "What about you?"

She smiled. "I think it's a little bit of both."

"Oh, really?" I asked with a penetrating look. "Do tell."

"I don't know why, but I get the impression that you didn't plan to come here," she said.

"Why would you say that?"

"Well, you expected to rent a cabin," she said. "But you didn't seem all that knowledgeable of the area, and you didn't arrive with any luggage to speak of, much less any means of transportation. If you had been planning this for some time then you're either highly disorganized or a really bad planner."

"What if I simply enjoy living life spontaneously?"

"Maybe," she conceded. "But I'm not convinced."

"Bel, order up!" called Jim from the kitchen area.

"Great timing, as always," she muttered. "Hold that

thought."

She quickly made her way to the small window behind the counter that separated the kitchen from the front part of the diner.

I realized that I had better come up with a plausible answer before she returned to the topic. It would seem overly suspicious if I tried to remain elusive about my reasons for being in Tar Hollow. Sometimes simple truths are the most believable.

In retrospect, I liked Candace's idea of being an author seeking writing inspiration. Unfortunately, it couldn't be further from the truth, and the truth was far too strange, and potentially dangerous, for the average person to discover, much less understand.

Bel brought me a fresh glass of cola and looked like she intended to continue our previous conversation.

"Hey, Bel," Jim called from the kitchen. "Company."

We both looked up to see a twenty-something bearded man wearing a faded denim jacket walk in through the entrance.

"Hey, Bel," he said. "Got a minute?"

She appeared none too pleased to see him.

"What? I told you not to bother me at work, Kevin," she said.

"Aww, get off me," he said. "Can we talk outside?"

"Only if you're bringing the check that's two weeks late," she said, folding her arms before her.

He scanned the dining room before looking at her. "Look, let's take this outside."

I watched as the two of them went out through the front entrance and moved away from the doors. From my vantage point, I could see them talking at the far front corner of the building.

After a few minutes of what appeared to be arguing, she pointed her finger in his face in accusatory fashion.

He slapped her hand away from him and shoved her shoulder, causing her to lose her balance and fall backward.

He walked away toward an older model Ford pickup parked nearby.

A flood of bad childhood memories washed through me as I watched.

Before I fully registered it, I had risen from my seat and purposefully walked outside, flinging the front door open as I went.

"Who the—" the man started to say.

I didn't cease my momentum toward him and caught his forearm as he opened the driver's side door to his truck. I swung him around into an arm bar while propelling him face first against the side of the vehicle with a heavy thud.

"Asshole, what is your—"

"Shut up!" I said. "So, you like to push women around, do ya?"

"Mind your own damned business!"

"Wrong answer," I said, rotating his arm into a more painful position.

"Hey, ow, OW!"

"I don't *ever* want to see or hear that you've laid a hand on Bel, you got me?" I demanded.

"All right, all right already!"

I used my free hand to slip his wallet from the back pocket of his jeans and flipped it open.

"Well, Kevin Truitt, now I know where you live," I said. "And I don't want to hear about you giving Bel any trouble, period. Got it?"

"Yeah, yeah, got it," he said.

I released him from the arm bar and shoved him away as I stepped backward.

"Oh, and one more thing," I said, making sure that my hand gravitated toward my nearest concealed combat knife, just in case he did something stupid.

He looked at me wide-eyed as he turned around, gingerly rotating one of his shoulders.

"What's that?" he asked.

"Pay your damned alimony and child support on time," I

said flatly.

"Yeah, I'll do that."

"When?"

"Tomorrow," he said. "I can get the money to her by tomorrow."

"Good," I said. "Because I'll be checking to make sure you do."

"Wha— Who the hell are you?" he asked. "You a cop?"

"No, I'm much worse," I said, anger welling inside me.

I'm someone who remembers someone like you growing up; someone who knows what men like you can become. And I'm not about to endure people like you anymore.

He must have read my features because he jumped inside the cab of this truck and had scarcely started the engine before he slipped his truck into reverse and backed out, momentarily burning rubber against the pavement.

I watched him pull out onto the street and then turned to see Bel staring wide-eyed at me.

"Are you okay?" I asked.

She nodded. "Yeah, thanks. Who *are* you?"

"I told you already," I said. "My name's Caleb."

"Oh, well yeah, but I meant—"

"I'm just a guy who's trying to escape his own problems on the open road," I said. "Just trying to find a little peace, really."

She considered me for a moment. "A little peace."

"That was the idea, anyway," I said.

A gusty wind blew in from the north and I looked up at the darkening sky. It looked like a storm was moving in.

When I looked back at her, she was staring at me.

"It doesn't matter much where you go, everyone has problems of some sort," she said. "The difference isn't whether you have problems; it's how you choose to confront them."

I was struck by the stark logic in what she said.

"You know, you're pretty wise for someone living out in the middle of nowhere."

"Nah, that's just something my dad has said since I was a little girl," she said, rubbing her arms against the chill in the air. "I suppose it stuck over the years. That and I've learned over time that it's actually true."

I considered what she had said as I politely guided her toward the diner's entrance and held the door open for her.

Everyone looked up at us as we entered, and even the cook, Jim, had stepped out into the dining room to see what had taken place.

"You okay, Bel?" he asked.

"Fine, thanks," she said. "Kevin's not usually so…physical…when we argue. Is it any wonder he's my ex?"

"Who could blame you?" I asked.

"There's a heavy storm moving in from the northwest," Jim said. "Hey, you're the guy with the moped, right?"

"Jim, you *know* that he is," Bel said. "And his name is Caleb."

Jim appeared slightly uncomfortable. "Well, just didn't want to seem too familiar. Anyway, you better get going soon so you don't get caught out in the really bad stuff before you get back to your cabin."

"Thanks, I'll do that," I said, pulling out a large bill from my wallet and handing it to Bel. "Here, this should cover it."

"I'll get your change," she said.

I walked past her to exit. "Nope, the rest is your tip. Take care, okay?"

"Sure thing," she said. "Thanks again, Caleb."

As I exited the building and walked toward my scooter the wind felt even colder and I heard thunder in the distance.

"Caleb," Bel said from behind me.

I turned to see her leaning out through the front door.

"Thank you," she said. "That was very brave and kind of you."

"My pleasure," I said.

I pulled my skull cap helmet on, feeling a little awkward as I mounted what had to be the least masculine machine in the county.

I waved to her as I pulled out onto the street.

* * *

I made it back to the cabin just as the lightning and thunder exploded in the darkened skies.

After securing my scooter on the front porch, I went inside and laid my damp jacket over a nearby dining room chair.

Then I went to the fireplace to arrange some chunks of wood for a fire, if only to cut the slight chill that I felt. As I squatted down to light the kindling, I reflected upon all that had transpired at the café.

Then Bel's voice replayed in my head.

It doesn't matter much where you go, everyone has problems of some sort...

Had traveling across the country, eventually ending up in Tar Hollow, actually helped to solve any of the problems that I left behind in New Haven?

Not really.

The difference isn't whether you have problems; it's how you choose to confront them.

Who would have thought that I would receive such sage advice in such a remote, one-horse town?

I plugged my small set of external speakers into my iPod and turned it on.

As evening set in, the flash of lightning momentarily lit the cabin's windows and thunder sounded outside.

I looked out the nearest window to see the rain beginning to fall, heavy droplets striking against the glass. Then another flash of lightning illuminated outdoors, revealing a semicircle of six individuals just inside the treeline outside the cabin.

"Oh, shit," I muttered.

CHAPTER 14

Caleb

My first thought was that Bel's ex, Kevin, had secured some muscle to work me over following our encounter at the diner. At least, he struck me as the sort of guy who might do something like that.

Though their appearance outside startled me, I remained calm and carefully waited for another flash of lightning to permit further inspection. However, they had disappeared from view by that time.

The sound of my heartbeat thrummed in my ears as I contemplated any number of other unsavory possibilities. Unfortunately, the prospect of one or more of them being vampires came to mind.

Suddenly I wished that it might merely be Kevin and some thug acquaintances.

I retrieved my jacket and extracted a combat knife and one of the flashlights with infrared bulbs from an inside pocket.

Regardless of whether they were vampires or humans, the odds dictated one against six, and that certainly wasn't a ratio that favored me.

A knock at the door caused me to start.

They're knocking?

I waited, half-surprised the door wasn't already flying off

its hinges and inward at me.

Another knock sounded.

I took a deep breath and, in that singular moment, I decided that I wasn't going to make things easy on whoever was waiting outside for me. I'd make them work for it.

I used the fingers on my flashlight-wielding hand to twist the knob as I steadied my knife for action. The door's hinges creaked as a slight gap opened.

My breath caught in my throat as I lightly thumbed the switch on my flashlight.

My eyes narrowed as a flash of lightning lit up the porch area.

"Hello, Caleb," greeted a familiar voice.

Katrina stood before me, her long leather trench coat swaying slightly in the wind as rain blew onto the porch. Her emerald eyes practically glowed.

"Still alive, I see," she said.

How ironic was it that Skylar Grey's "Back from the Dead" played over my iPod speakers?

"So it would seem," I said. "For now, anyway."

"May I come in?" she asked. She looked at my bike parked on the porch to her right. "Or are you planning on running us down on your Moped?"

I curtailed a sour expression, though inwardly I was admittedly relieved that it was her and not Kevin or other enemy vampires. Never mind that she was likely angry with me.

"Did you come here just to insult me?" I asked.

She gave me a dark look. "Don't even go there."

There were times when I knew better than to push topics with her. This was clearly one of those times.

I opened the door and stood aside.

As she slipped past me, I looked out at the group of five vampires standing in the rain, staring back at me with curious expressions.

"What about them?" I asked. "Sort of a small army you have there."

"It took a small army to find you," she said. "But they're fine where they are for now."

She leaned past me and issued a rapid series of hand motions.

The vampires stepped back into the treeline and practically melted into the night.

I shut the door and turned to face her.

She glanced down at my hands. "Are you planning on stabbing me, or merely giving me a dose of UV?"

"What? Oh, sorry," I said, practically dropping the knife and flashlight as I placed them on the nearby dining room table.

She removed her wet leather coat and tossed it over the back of one of the wooden dining room chairs. Her boot heels made heavy thumps on the wood planking as she walked over to my iPod and switched it off.

The ensuing silence felt palpable.

I stood there, wondering what I should say first. There were suddenly so many thoughts and feelings running through my mind that it seemed impossible to sort them all at once.

With more heavy thumps from her boots, she made her way back over to stand before me, towering above me, a look of disapproval evident on her face.

"I'm very cross with you at the moment," she said. "But at least you're safe."

She reached out and tilted my head upward. Then she slowly bent down to briefly kiss my lips in a firm, almost possessive fashion.

"I was worried sick about you," she said.

As she pulled away from me slightly, the flat of her palm slapped the side of my face, shocking me.

The impact stung like hell.

"Wha—"

"That was for all the worry and fear I felt while desperately trying to find you," she said.

I was almost willing to admit that maybe I deserved that.

Almost.

"I left a note telling you not to worry about me," I said. "And I sent periodic emails that I was safe."

She gave me a wan look as she drew her smartphone out of her vest pocket to make a call. I took the opportunity to rub at my still stinging skin.

"I found him," she said. "He's safe…for the moment."

I narrowed my eyes at her, but she pointed her index finger at me in a warning fashion.

"Don't start with me," she said, placing her phone in speaker mode and setting it upon the dining table.

"You're on speaker now," she said.

"Young man, it goes without saying that I'm extremely disappointed in you right now," Alton began. "You gave us all quite a bit of a scare and caused no small amount of disruption both in the UK and the States. What the hell were you thinking?"

He sounded reminiscent of a father scolding his teenager.

"I wasn't trying to scare or worry anyone," I emphasized with a meaningful look at Kat. "I repeatedly checked in, in fact, just to make sure you understood that."

"Yes, well, despite all that I'd still probably strangle you right now if I was there," he said.

Kat's free hand moved in a blur and her palm once more impacted the side of my face.

Thankfully, it was the opposite side, though my jaw nevertheless ached from the impact.

"Hey!" I snapped. "Enough with the slapping already!"

"That was for Alton," she said.

"Fine, he's pissed. You're pissed. I get it," I said. "But I've had more than enough of feeling everyone else's pain for the moment."

Nobody said anything to that.

In fact, the awkward silence built to an uncomfortable level.

"Yes, well, I'll let the two of you sort things out from here," Alton said. "Caleb, you and I are going to have a long chat the next time we see each other. Understood?"

"Yeah. Got it," I said.

"Goodbye for now," Alton said.

Kat pocketed her smartphone and stared at me.

"Yes?" I asked, waiting for what I believed to be the beginnings of an argument.

"You should've thought about the possible cause and effect before you just up and ran away," she said. "I've tried to convey to you in the past that your actions have consequences."

"I didn't run away," I said. "I just had to clear my head; regain some perspective. I needed to think."

"About what?" she demanded. "What did you have to think about that you ran halfway across the country to consider? And why alone? Why from me?"

How could I explain?

"You probably wouldn't understand right at the moment," I said. "And besides, I didn't exactly run from you. *You* were already halfway across the planet."

"How can I even begin to understand you when you won't even talk to me about it?" she asked. "You shocked me when you just up and left. You didn't even try to discuss things. You just abandoned us."

I looked into her eyes and saw both pain and anger directed at me.

"*Abandoned?*" I asked.

"Yes, abandoned," she said. "You, running off like that. What you did hurt me."

Despite the aggravation I still felt, a pang of guilt surged through me.

Admittedly, I probably could've handled things better, I supposed.

"Well, I wasn't trying to hurt you," I said.

She stared at me.

I stood my ground, though just barely, and looked her in the eyes.

"Or make you angry with me," I added.

She stepped closer to me, towering above me.

"Did you honestly believe for one moment that striking out like that wouldn't make me feel either angry or abandoned?" she demanded.

At that moment, I didn't know what to say.

"Well?" she asked.

"I—"

"I've given you practically everything you could need or want, including my love," she said. "Never mind what Alton's done for you."

"I'm grateful for—"

"And yet you abandoned it all at the drop of a hat," she said.

Roiling emotions inside me boiled over.

"No, you don't understand at all," I insisted. "Sure, you and Alton have provided so much for me...a home, tuition, bodyguards, and what not. But you've also taken something very precious from me."

The words, however raw, tumbled from my mouth before I even realized I'd said them.

A look of shock appeared on her face.

She arched a single brow at me. "What have we taken from you, then?"

"*You*," I said. "I don't care about big houses, or tuition, or new cars, or any of it. I only want you."

Her eyes narrowed. "I've already given myself to you, fully and wholly. I have given you my full commitment. I am your *mate*."

I shook my head. "But nowadays only in absentia."

"That's not fair," she said. "You know why I've been away, and it's certainly not by choice."

"Still, it's not what I want," I said. "I want to be with you, not thinking longingly about you while you're somewhere halfway across the world. Half the time I don't even know if you're alive or dead until the next text message appears.

"Hell, after everything I've recently experienced, I know for certain that all I really need is to have you in my life," I continued. "And on a regular basis."

She placed her index finger below my chin, the sharp tip of her fingernail pressing dangerously into my skin, and she pressed upward.

I tilted my head upward in compliance as she drew even closer to me until I felt her warm breath against my face.

"Don't you toy with me," she said. "If this is a ploy to defray blame over how you've behaved—"

"I'm not toying with you," I said. "You'd know if I was lying."

I saw the hard look of assessment in her eyes.

"Fine. You've acted out and made your dramatic, so-very-emotional point," she said. "What's next, then? I'm supposed to just ignore what you've done?"

"Maybe not ignore," I said. "But you could try to forgive."

"How can I forgive what I don't even understand yet?"

"Because you say that you love me," I said. "Because, even if you're pissed at me—"

"Oh, I'm very pissed," she said.

"Yeah, well, you hopefully still care."

She paused, as if considering that for a moment.

"Because, deep inside where few can see, you're kind," I added.

Her features hardened. "Listen to me. I'm not at all a kind woman, Caleb," she said. "Especially where either my heart, or my trust, is concerned."

I swallowed hard, suddenly feeling as if I was playing with a coiled serpent that was ready to strike at any moment.

"You're wrong," I said. "Maybe not with other people, but you've always been kind to me."

Her firm resolve appeared to momentarily waver.

"And as for your trust, I've never betrayed it," I said. "Not once."

Her facial muscles relaxed slightly. Slowly, she withdrew her index finger from beneath my chin.

Though relieved, I resisted the temptation to reach up and see if her fingernail had drawn blood.

"Still, what you did was wrong," she said. "I'm not going to just overlook that. It was a serious lapse of judgment of your part. And it was recklessly dangerous."

"How can I say I'm sorry so that you'll believe me?" I asked.

The corners of her mouth upturned. "You could begin on your knees."

I started to smile, but her gaze turned cold.

Apparently, she wasn't kidding.

I dropped to my knees before her, staring into her abdomen, her clothes still damp from the rain.

I breathed in her scent and felt a familiar carnal desire rise within me. The mere prospect of holding her body in my arms again was irresistible.

It had been too long.

She snapped her fingers above my head and I looked up.

While her expression was almost menacing, her body was also painfully ravishing, which only heightened my attraction toward her at that moment.

Maybe we're due some makeup sex?

"I know that look," she said. "But you can forget it. You should be so lucky right now."

Oh, I should, indeed.

"Don't forget why you're actually down there," she added coolly.

I swallowed. "Kat, I'm so very sorry if my actions were reckless," I said. "And I wasn't trying to hurt you. But you need to understand, my perspective on life has matured quite a bit since I left."

She folded her arms before her and stared down at me.

Something told me that she wasn't convinced of my sincerity.

"We should talk about this," I said. "I can help you to understand what I've been feeling."

"Perhaps," she said.

"Look, I feel really silly down here," I said. "Maybe we could chat over on the couch instead of like this?"

"Why? Are your knees getting uncomfortable?" she asked.

"A bit," I conceded.

"Good."

If that was a sign of things to come, I was probably in big trouble.

"Kat, at this point, I don't know what our future holds," I said. "But I do know that this isn't helping either of us."

After silent moments passed while I stared up into her eyes, my neck felt strained at such an angle and my muscles started to ache.

"I suppose," she conceded.

Well, that hardly seemed like a shining endorsement.

I stared back into her abdomen and reached out to encircle her waist in my arms.

Then I firmly pressed my lips to just above her belt line and kissed her.

"Don't toy with me, Caleb," she warned.

"I'm not," I insisted. "Unless you've forgotten, you're my mate, remember? I'm supposed to be allowed to kiss you, dammit!"

The muscles in her stomach went taught, almost like stone. "Of course, I remember you're my mate," she shot back. "Why the hell else would I even be here?"

The intensity in her eyes alone was intimidating.

"I wouldn't know."

She remained silent and her gaze reverted to staring ahead, as if looking at something far away in the distance.

"I wouldn't have expected that from you. How can you even say that? What's gotten into you?" asked Kat.

I paused to gather my thoughts.

"I feel like we're drifting apart," I said. "Like I'm losing you to something with greater pull than I can muster enough strength to counter."

She looked down at me with surprise.

"Why?" she asked. "What's changed between us for you to say that?"

Despite the many centuries of experience that I knew she

had, veritable lifetimes more existence than that of my own, her expression reflected sheer confusion toward me.

"Our distance, both physical and emotional," I replied. "It's like a barrier that's formed around you over time…first like a fog, subtle and amorphous. Now, it's like a thick cloud that's nearly impenetrable."

I looked down at the wood floor and a tired sense of resignation flowed through my body. I felt both weary and helpless.

She squatted before me, placed her fingertip before my chin, and tilted my head upward until I gazed into her piercing eyes.

"Your reckless actions concerned me," she said. "Now, your words worry me. What's happening with you?"

"Me?" I asked. "It's us! Don't you see that?"

"What about us?"

"There isn't any *us* anymore, that's what!"

She appeared taken aback by my response.

"That's ridiculous," she retorted.

"Oh, really? I never even see you anymore."

"Caleb, I can't exactly fly back every weekend as if I'm working some nine to five office job," she said. "You know what's at stake, as well as how unpredictable what I'm doing is."

"I can't even call you anymore," I continued. "Hell, our contact is a series of stupid text messages."

"Now you sound like some spoiled teenager," she said, standing up.

"Teenager? Maybe I just sound like that because you're like – what? – almost twenty times older than me. Which means you should understand far better than me what I'm trying to tell you."

"Oh, you're really driving me crazy right now," she said. "At times like this I can't see how this relationship even works between us."

"Well, it's *not*, in case you hadn't noticed. So maybe you need someone much older than me…maybe another vampire then?" I countered. "Somebody who's so much wiser and capable at handling this insane life we're having to live."

"It's becoming apparent to me that you're obsessing over everything. Perhaps you simply have too much free time on your hands," she said.

Something inside my brain snapped as weeks of emotional strain, stress, and fatigue flooded back through my memory.

I jumped up to stand before her.

"Free time?" I demanded. "Look, my life has turned into an endless slog. I can't handle this pace anymore! My life is nothing but an endless damned stream of combat training and physical workout sessions and classes and stupid papers and then perpetual research for a thesis topic that I didn't even choose. Hell, Alton has me looking down some dark rabbit hole with no bottom. Now I don't even have a life anymore! I hate this! In fact, I can't stand it anymore...I want to be anywhere else, doing anything else."

Her eyes widened.

"I hate this life! I don't have you or freedom or downtime," I raged. "I can't keep this pace up anymore. Dammit, I'm not some friggin' vampire; I'm only *HUMAN!*"

I suddenly realized that my fists were clenched at my sides as I glared into her eyes. I felt as if standing on the edge of a precipice and very nearly ready to fall over the edge.

She frowned, studying me at length as if divining her future from a cup of tea leaves.

"Well? Aren't you even going to say anything?" I demanded.

"Your haunted-looking eyes," she said softly, placing her warm palm against my cheek. "I haven't seen that look in such a long time.

"It's a visage that I prayed might have been banished forever, and now I'm staring back at it once again. It breaks my heart to see you this way," she said.

I felt too stunned to utter a single word.

CHAPTER 15

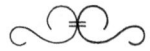

Caleb

The saddest expression commanded Kat's features.

How could I have realized that she hadn't been divining our future in her expression, but rather reflecting on the past?

My past.

I felt spent all of the sudden. My entire body felt ragged and emptied of strength and energy.

I reached out to place my hand around hers, grateful even for that limited contact, yet realizing that it was much more than I'd had in weeks, with her away in Europe.

In an instant, I was wrapped in her arms, my face pressed against her shoulder. My own arms embraced her tightly.

It felt as if had been forever since I had held her.

"Come," she said, guiding me toward the couch.

She sat alongside me, cradling one arm around my shoulders.

"Take a moment," she said. "Then tell me everything."

I took a deep breath, suddenly feeling unprepared to unload what was the culmination of months of building tension, self-doubt, and angst.

"My life," I began. "It feels like its spiraling forward out of control, full-tilt and mixed with both routine and menace, but neither in a manner or direction that I care for it to go. And worst of all, I feel like you're less and less a part of it..."

I told her about the conflicted emotions I had experienced; including my feelings of guilt for all that's been done for me, and yet, having found myself wanting for more, or at least different circumstances.

She listened as I recounted my fears about what felt like our waning relationship and her obligations that I felt powerless to balance in our relationship.

Of course, I confessed my feelings of regret over holding Alton responsible for her obligations, given how he'd saved my life more than once. Not to mention how he'd generously offered himself as a quasi-avuncular figure in my life.

Of all my conflicted feelings and emotions, guilt appeared to figure prominently among them.

The thunderstorm outside raged for a time in a manner that seemed to mirror my own tumultuous inner feelings.

I don't know how long I spoke, but it felt like an endless stream of thoughts, feelings, and even confessions, poured forth like a flood. I left nothing out, recounting events and inner feelings that spanned fear, shame, anger, and anxiousness.

Most of all, no matter the consequences of my revelations, I felt unbridled relief at getting everything out in the open.

By the time I finished talking, I felt nearly exhausted. That's when I noticed that, while it was still dark outside, the thunderstorm had ceased, save for droplets of rain occasionally pelting against the glass window panes.

Kat pulled me close against her again, holding me in place and gently nuzzling the top of my head with her chin. I had almost fallen off asleep when she finally spoke.

"My dear, sweet, Caleb," she said. "You maddening, precious, silly man. You drive me almost insane at times.

"Why did you wait this long to tell me these things? Why endure this on your own at such length?" she asked.

"I don't know, really. At first, I just tried to brave my

way through it, or ignore it completely," I replied. "Then it felt too imposing to confront, wearing on me day after day."

"Why didn't you tell me?"

I reveled in her embrace. "I sort of tried, in my own way. But I always ended up feeling as if I was imposing, or standing in the way of your duty to Alton. Eventually, it felt as if we didn't even have time for a phone call. But—"

"But what?"

I took a deep breath. "It wasn't easy trying to press my concerns with you. You can be a very insistent woman, but lately it's as if you've grown evasive with me much of the time."

I felt her body tense and she remained silent.

After a few moments, her body relaxed again.

"Yes," she conceded. "Yes, I suppose that can be true sometimes, particularly lately."

I let out the breath that I hadn't realized I'd been holding. It was a considerable concession on her part.

She kissed me on the cheek, which felt very reassuring.

"But I'm still really put out with you for just up and leaving so abruptly."

Yeah, I sort of figured that might be the case.

She retracted her arm from around my shoulders and started to rise from the couch.

"Where are you going?" I asked.

She stared down at me, then walked over to the small dining room table and gathered her leather coat that was draped over the back of one chair.

"You stay here. I'm returning to the hotel to coordinate some details and retrieve my things," she said. "In addition, the vampires outside will need to switch shifts with the humans soon."

"What? There's more people with you?"

"You thought otherwise?" she countered. "This was a twenty-four hour operation comprised of two teams; humans during the day and vampires at night."

"Look, just send them home," I said. "You can see I'm

147

perfectly safe here, especially now that you've found me."

"*Caleb*," she warned.

"Okay, okay. Do whatever you feel's best."

"Much better. You have no idea what's been going on lately," she said.

I started to argue but she held up her hand. "Yes, I realize that I haven't exactly been keeping you fully informed about matters, either."

I settled back down, contented that she had at least conceded that.

"Don't go anywhere until I get back."

"It's not as if I have any place else to be."

She walked back over to me, her boot heels thumping against the wood floor. She stared down at me until I met her gaze. "No more running from things, either figuratively or literally."

I nodded.

She bent down to give me an all-too-brief kiss.

"You're going to be the death of me someday," she said.

My eyes widened. "I hope not."

The edges of her mouth upturned ever so slightly before she turned and exited the cabin, firmly pulling the door closed behind her.

I listened as a vehicle drove away from outside the cabin. The strange thing was I hadn't even heard one pull up out front since she arrived last night.

For the first time in forever, it had felt as if she and I were the only two people in the world.

I wanted to try more of that again very soon.

"Well, all in all, I suppose that went better than it could have," I said aloud, standing up to stretch and then massage my neck.

I felt completely exhausted, both physically and emotionally.

Then, as if on cue, the sound of heavy rain pelting against the cabin's roof generated a din of noise that drowned out the silence.

I plopped back down onto the couch, uncertain as to what to do next.

Multiple thoughts collided in my brain all at once.

Despite telling her everything, Kat was still put out with me. Not to mention Alton was annoyed and disappointed in me.

My recent cathartic days of contemplation seemed far less satisfying in retrospect.

Then my mind went numb and I just stared at nothing, the sound of the rain almost hypnotic and soothing.

Eventually, despite the combination of periodic thunder and steady rainfall, the growl of a motorcycle engine grew louder until it sounded like it was right outside the cabin.

I got up and opened the front door just in time to see Paige removing her helmet.

Her blue eyes looked cold and flat, and she stared at me as she walked up onto the porch to stand before me.

Her denim jeans and black leather jacket appeared soaked through from the rain.

"Paige?" I asked. "Long time, no see."

She said nothing, staring back at me with a cold expression.

"Listen, I'm sorry about what's happened. I mean, I've missed you really badly," I said. "And frankly, I could use a friend right now. Maybe you could come in and dry off and then we could talk?"

The look in her eyes turned nearly feral.

"You're a fuckin' idiot!" she yelled.

Before I could say anything, her fist impacted the side of my face, knocking me off balance.

I stumbled backward against the door jamb.

As I rubbed at my jaw in shock, she turned and stalked away while replacing her helmet over her head.

I lurched forward to the edge of the porch as she mounted the cycle and revved the engine.

"Paige, wait!" I shouted as cold rain pelted against my aching face.

Ignoring me, she gunned the engine and her spinning back tire pivoted the cycle around in a semi-circle as mud spewed out from behind.

My eyes widened as I half-stumbled backward on the wet porch, struggling to retreat back inside the cabin as a continuous arc of wet mud sprayed against the front wall and one window, splashing toward me.

I barely managed to slam the front door shut in time before hearing the muted sound of water and mud striking the opposite side of the door.

Damn, she's really pissed!

I absently rubbed at my throbbing jaw as her cycle's engine roared and quickly grew distant.

I opened the front door ajar to see her taillights disappear into the night as she sped away.

Apparently, I had screwed up royally with her, too.

Crap.

I'd never seen her that angry before; at least, not toward me.

I grabbed my jacket, flung open the door, and ran outside into the rain. Dodging muddy puddles while shrugging into my jacket, I ran across the small field outside the cabin and into the treeline.

Fortunately, the trees had been culled enough that I was able to dodge between them as I ran forward toward a place where the winding road that Paige was on might intersect.

I hurried to cut her off. I had to talk to her. Maybe I could reason with her as I had Kat; help her to understand what I'd been going through.

Two figures appeared before me, surprising me. I lost my balance and fell backward, though someone caught me from behind before I impacted the ground.

Their glowing eyes, pulsing with either emotion or hunger, told me they were vampires; doubtless, some of the ones who had accompanied Katrina to the cabin.

"You can't leave," the female vampire before me stated.

The fellow who caught me from behind waited until I

righted myself before letting go of me.

I pointed toward the distant sound of Paige's motorcycle engine.

"I'm trying to catch Paige," I said. "Maybe now I can't, but one of you can."

"That's not within the parameters of our orders," said the tall, broad-shouldered vampire standing beside the female vampire. "The General was very specific."

I shook my head. "Well, thanks for nothing then."

"We would help if we could," the female vampire said, glancing up toward the waning night sky. "But you should return to the cabin now. The thunderstorm is surging again."

I turned and walked back to the cabin, not caring about the penetrating cold rain. I heard the vampires following not far behind me.

A vampire stood on the porch of the cabin just outside the front door.

"I cleared the cabin already," he said. "It is safe inside."

"Thanks, though I was just here a few minutes ago," I said, stopping just inside the doorway. "Do any of you want to come inside from the rain?"

"Thank you, but that's outside the parameters of the General's orders," said the vampire standing by the door.

It surprised me how formal they were, almost like soldiers. Of course, given the way they kept referring to Kat, I had no doubt that Alton and she had likely formed a literal army by now.

"It's a nice night, rain or not," said the vampire who had caught me in the forest. "This beats the city anytime. I'm tired of cities."

"Country bumpkin," teased the female vampire.

"To each their own," he countered.

I shut the front door, leaned back against it, and wondered how much had transpired in the UK and Europe that Kat hadn't ever mentioned to me.

That was yet another issue with our communication challenges.

My thoughts quickly returned to Paige's reaction on the porch.

Between Kat and Paige, I felt completely on the outs with both of them; though I held out hope that, after our earlier chat, Kat might come around.

I retrieved a cold beer from the fridge and held it against my jaw. I sat down at the small dining table to ponder things further.

I felt tired and numb. Of course, I'd already been up for most of the night.

After consuming half of my beer, it occurred to me that it was more early morning than night.

I pushed the can away from me. "God, please don't let me turn into my father."

With him, anytime was a good time for alcohol.

No, I'd never be a monster like him.

I'd shoot myself in the head first.

I went to the sink to fill a glass with water and tried to contemplate matters further, but I was still too dumbfounded to come to terms with Paige's reaction.

I drank a full glass of water and then refilled it.

Once again, my life felt as if it was in flux.

What had started out as my grand journey for self-actualization had turned into a veritable nightmare for my closest relationships.

It felt as if I had effectively managed to turn my life even further upside down.

I heard some vehicles pull up out front and I glanced at my watch, surprised that only a little more than an hour had passed since Kat had left.

She walked inside toting a small leather satchel, a backpack with two sword handles sticking out of the top, and a small suitcase, which she placed on the floor just inside the doorway.

She stared at me with a curious expression. "What happened outside?"

"Don't ask," I said.

"On top of that, what happened to the side of your face?" she asked. "What happened while I was gone?"

"Paige happened while you were gone, that's what," I said, absently rubbing the side of my face with my palm.

The edges of her mouth upturned slightly.

"You're charming everyone's hearts tonight, I see," she said.

"Yeah, I've already figured that out," I said.

"You brought it on yourself, you know."

I steeled myself from wincing and ground my teeth together.

Tell me something I don't know already.

"Live by the sword," she said as she carried her suitcase past me and into the nearby bedroom.

I tried to reflect positively on her decision to locate in the bedroom, but then wondered if I might yet end up being tossed out onto the couch instead.

"Yeah," I said. "I get it."

I finished my second glass of water as she set up a portable computer on the dining room table.

"Are we past the point, too?" I asked.

The point of no return?

That thought chilled me to the bone. If there was one thing I had solidified in my mind during my absence, it was that I loved her—needed her—more than I had previously realized.

She was the one woman in the world who filled the empty void in my life.

And my heart.

She stopped what she was doing and looked up at me with an arched brow. "Past the point?" she asked. "Are you asking if I still love you?"

For some reason, I was almost afraid to even acknowledge the framing of her question.

"Yes, of course, I still love you," she said. "Or I wouldn't be here right now. Exactly what's been going through your head since I left?"

I exhaled a breath I hadn't realized I'd been holding.

Well, that's something.

I definitely didn't know what I would've done if she had said otherwise.

"I love you, too, you know," I said. "That never changed. That was never the issue."

She sat down in the empty chair beside mine. "Caleb, I'm very upset with you about what you did," she said. "It was irresponsible, as well as selfish. And particularly risky."

I nodded, but said nothing.

"Nobody I've loved as much as you has ever just up and left me like that," she said. "I was shocked. And it hurt."

I gazed into her eyes and could practically see the pain reflected in them.

"It wasn't you I was leaving," I said. "It was my situation. You were already well on the other side of the globe."

"You keep saying that, but that's where you're wrong," she said. "Wherever I place you, wherever I provide for you, is where I am; even if it's by proxy through those I entrust to watch over you."

I pondered that. It was an unusual, somewhat foreign, concept to me.

But then I supposed it also made a little sense.

"I'm sorry."

What the hell more could I say, after all?

"Before my team and I showed up tonight, were you actually planning on coming back?" she asked.

"Yes, I was," I said. "In fact, I'd intended to call you in the next day or so."

A sardonic thought crossed my mind. "That is, if you hadn't found me by then," I added.

"You gave us a run for our money, you evasive little rabbit," she said with the first twinkle in her eye I had seen since she found me. "Granted, you still had that small tracking device implanted beneath the skin near your shoulder. However, at first, we were limited to being within close enough proximity to you before we could find you with the beacon tracker."

"What do you mean by 'at first'?"

She smiled, but she looked like a cat that had just cornered the rabbit.

"Within a couple of days, Alton secured the use of a surveillance satellite orbiting somewhere over the United States," she said.

"What the—?"

"Tracking you was relatively easy then," she continued.

"How the hell did Alton manage to use an orbiting satellite?"

Her expression turned wry. "He's remarkably resourceful, you know," she said. "In fact, he still surprises me, from time to time."

I shook my head.

She reached out and squeezed my hand to get my attention. Her expression had turned serious again.

"Don't ever do something like this to me again, Caleb," she said in a hard tone. "If you want to leave me, you better tell me up front first."

"But I wasn't actually leaving you," I said.

She squeezed my hand firmly, using her tight grip for emphasis, though not enough to cause me overt pain.

"Never. Do. It. Again," she insisted. "Understood?"

I didn't say anything, but merely nodded.

"Say it," she said.

"Never again."

She moved her face to within an inch of my own. "Good," she said. "And don't ever forget."

Maybe it was the way that she stared into my eyes, or maybe it was the tone of her voice. Either way, for some reason, I had the feeling that was to be my only warning.

I swallowed hard, but remained silent.

"So, we're good now?" I asked.

She released my hand and reached up to firmly grasp my chin instead.

"Not even close," she said. "You still have fences to mend."

"With you?"

"With me," she said. "With everybody, it seems. I can't begin to tell you how pissed Paige and Roman were."

"All right," I said. "Maybe I'll start with you."

"Smart man," she said sardonically, releasing my chin and tapping me on the end of the nose with her fingertip.

I reached out to take her hand in mine and softly caressed the top of it with my thumb.

I missed her affection toward me. It felt like a painful absence, in fact.

She gazed into my eyes with a curious expression. "Yes?"

"Please forgive me," I asked.

"I'll consider it," she said.

I gave her my best confident look, despite how tired I felt. "I'm going to make this up to you. Actually, we need to make this up to each other."

Her eyes narrowed. "Perhaps," she said. "But we're both going to have to work at it."

"Makes sense," I said.

She let go of my hand and motioned toward the bathroom.

"Go take a shower," she said. "You're not going to bed smelling like you are right now."

"Maybe a shower, but it's sort of late for bed now," I said, glancing outside. "It'll be dawn soon."

"Shower," she ordered.

I knew better than to argue.

Afterward, as Kat took her shower, I lay atop the bed amidst the sporadic flashes of lightning through the window.

My mind felt so tired and numb that I blankly stared at the ceiling with scarcely a thought firing in my brain.

I awoke with a start, lying on my side and not sure how long since I had dozed off.

I felt surprised that the room was relatively dark, though some subtle glow of light emanated around the edges of the nearby window.

As I rolled over onto my back, I stared up at Katrina's sedate-looking features. She was propped up on one elbow, watching me.

"Good morning," I said. "At least, I think it's morning."

That's when I realized that someone had secured a dark covering over the room's windows, which made sense given the vampire beside me.

"It's around ten o'clock," she said. "So, yes it's morning."

She gave me a quick kiss on the lips.

"I'm sort of—"

"Surprised that I'm in bed with you?" she interjected.

"Well, no," I replied.

Then I reconsidered my response. "Well, actually, maybe a little. But I'm pretty happy about it."

She tapped the tip of my nose with her fingertip. "You drive me absolutely crazy sometimes, Caleb."

"You said that earlier," I said. "You know, they say it's the ones you love the most who stimulate the strongest emotions in you."

"I love you, and yet, I still want to strangle you," she said.

"See? True love," I said.

"You're fortunate that you're so charming," she said, caressing my face with her fingertips.

I closed my eyes, appreciating her soothing attention.

Her caressing moved to my neck, and then down to my chest and across my abdomen.

Then her fingers moved much lower and she kissed me; softly at first, and then much more passionately.

Then time stood still.

CHAPTER 16

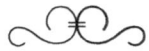

Caleb

I was dozing again as one of Kat's legs lazily lay across mine. Her free arm was draped across my chest and I felt her warm breath against my ear.

"This is nice," I said. It was the first time we'd made love in many weeks.

"Mmm," she murmured.

My stomach growled.

"Hungry?" she asked.

"Yeah, but there's not much in the fridge," I replied.

"You were getting low on cash," she said.

I frowned. "Did you go through my wallet?"

She patted my chest with her hand. "Of course, I did. I rifled through most everything, in fact."

"So much for boundaries," I said.

"Under the circumstances, you expected less from me?" she asked. "But then, none of my efforts actually told me what I really wanted to know."

She reached up and lightly tapped my forehead with her index finger. "There's where all the really interesting information is located. And I can't rummage through there like I can your pockets."

"What do you want to know?"

"Everything," she said. "No more secrets. Not anymore, my love."

There was a hint of concern in the tone of her voice; caring versus sounding intrusive or demanding. And yet she had sorted through my belongings while I slept.

That aspect of it annoyed me.

"I'll try," I said.

"And I'll try harder to listen," she said. "I did a lot of thinking while you slept earlier this morning."

"I wasn't asleep for that long."

"I'm a fast thinker."

"What were you thinking about?" I asked.

"You."

I gave her a wry look. "Let me guess…you've thought about my recent behavior and now you think that I'm broken and unreliable."

Her expression turned serious. "Not broken so much as wounded. Though not beyond saving, I hope."

"You mean not beyond redemption."

"No, I mean not beyond healing," she clarified. "You are, as you said, human. It's possible that both Alton and I have laid more upon you than was realistic for you. Each person has a different tolerance level."

I didn't know exactly how to respond to her concession, but I felt a lump harden in my throat, and I was happy in that moment that I didn't have to. It felt as if a great hurdle had been overcome; one that I'd formerly felt was unassailable.

She finally understood a little of what I'd been going through.

"You don't have to hold everything inside of you until you break," she said. "You don't have to do this alone anymore. If you're willing to try again, we'll work on some adjustments—as well as concessions—for you."

"What about Alton?" I asked.

"I'll handle Alton," she said. "But you'll still need to talk with him about this. He deserves to hear everything from you."

I dreaded that.

"He's not going to think less of me, is he?"

"I won't lie to you; he's very disappointed right now," she said. "But I think we can help him to understand some of what you've been going through."

"Oh," I said. "I see."

"He will come around, Caleb," she reassured me. "He cares about you; very much, in fact. That's another reason he's so disappointed with you at the moment."

I sighed. *Fair enough.*

"Then there's Paige," I ventured.

Paige had been so angry when she punched me in the jaw. I felt lucky that my head stayed attached to my body, in fact.

"She practically took my head off," I said.

"Hardly," she said. "Unlike you, I've actually seen her take someone's head off before."

My eyes widened and a chill went through me over her matter-of-fact tone.

"Don't dwell on Paige for the time being," she said. "She's an altogether different creature, and she has her own system for handling emotional situations."

That sounded far less reassuring to me.

Kat's smartphone buzzed and the bed lurched as she whipped around to snatch it from the nightstand.

"A dark-haired woman in a Jeep?" she asked.

I quickly rolled over. "She's okay. Don't hurt her."

Kat gave me a flat stare. "No, let her continue."

She calmly laid her phone down and gave me an inquisitive look.

I shrugged. "Her name's Bel. She's a waitress at Cooper's Café. She's been very welcoming to me since I arrived here."

Her brow arched.

"It's not what you're thinking—"

"And precisely what am I thinking?"

I gave her my best wan look. "You know what...we're not doing anything."

"I should hope not, particularly for your sake," she said. "That being said, why is she coming here?"

"Hey, I didn't invite her or anything."

"Well, she's on her way here now so you better get up and put some clothes on."

I rolled out of bed and half-stumbled into my only remaining fresh pair of jeans and T-shirt from my backpack while Kat watched me with a dubious expression.

"We're just friendly acquaintances," I said.

She flung the sheets from over her and stood, her nude body looking ravishing to me.

"You're, uh, going to put some clothes on, too, right?" I asked.

She gave me a hard look and pointed out toward the living room. "Go."

I closed the bedroom door and hurried toward the front door as I heard the sound of an engine outside.

I opened the door just as Bel stepped onto the porch holding what looked like a foil-covered dish.

"Hi, Caleb," she said. "I wasn't sure if to stop or not when I saw the SUV parked out front."

"Hi, Bel," I said, opening the front door. "Really, I'm glad you stopped by. Please come in."

She stepped inside. "I'm not interrupting or anything am I?"

"Not at all," I said. "My partner decided to join me here."

"Partner? Well, you left the café last night in a hurry and forgot the dessert that came with your meal. So, then I thought about how kind you were to step in with—Anyway, I decided to bake this for you," she said, handing me the pie. "It's just a small way to say thank you for your help with Kevin."

I peeked beneath the foil to see, and smell, a fresh apple pie.

"I love apple pie," I said. "Thanks so much. Won't you come in?"

I shut the front door in time to turn around and see Kat entering the room.

"Um, hello. I'm Bel."

Kat crossed the distance between them to extend her hand. "Katrina. I'm Caleb's significant other; his partner, as he just mentioned."

The term mate had become so ingrained to me that it sounded awkward for Kat to be classified in any other way. However, no human that I'd ever heard of had used the term mate, either.

"Pleased to meet you," Bel said. "I hope that I haven't intruded."

"You mentioned Caleb's help with something, I believe?" Kat prompted. "Kevin?"

"Well, yes," she said. "My ex, Kevin, was being an ass, as usual, and Caleb kindly intervened at the café last night."

"Ah. Well, Caleb is an easy touch, and he's all about knights in shining armor," Kat replied with a pointed look toward me.

I tried not to wince.

"I'd better get going," Bel said, once again looking at me. "I just wanted to drop off this pie for you."

"Thank you," I said. "That was very kind."

She smiled at me. "You're welcome. Perhaps I'll see you at the café again soon."

I glanced at Kat, whose brow arched inquisitively.

"Perhaps," I said. "Though I'm not exactly sure when we're leaving."

"Likely sooner than later," Kat interjected.

"Oh," said Bel. "Well, if I don't see you again, Caleb, it was very nice meeting you."

I shook her hand. "The pleasure was all mine."

I held open the front door for her.

"By the way," she said, lowering her voice as she stepped beside me. "Kevin brought over a check for the most current child support payment. He promised to get together what he's overdue on very soon, too. I can't thank you enough."

I waved goodbye to her before closing the door.

"Aren't you a regular Prince Charming," Kat said. "She's very pretty."

"There's no need for jealously," I said. "She's a lovely lady and it was nice to make a friendly acquaintance on my journey."

"So, you haven't met many other friendly people along the way?" she asked.

"Some here and there, I suppose."

I decided not to mention the night at the hotel in Buffalo when the drug dealer stopped by my room.

"I realize now that it's not necessarily always better somewhere else," I said. "It doesn't seem to matter much where you go; everyone has problems of some sort…"

"That's very true," she said. "You've gained a bit of wisdom during your trip, I see."

And I had Bel to thank for it.

* * *

We stayed at the cabin for the remainder of the day just talking more about things. Kat and I discussed thoughts and feelings that had been on my mind, including our lack of time together.

To her credit, she said that she would work to ensure that our visits were more frequent.

We also spent more romantic time together, which was definitely the highlight of the day for me.

By mid-afternoon, I had eaten half of Bel's apple pie, which tasted amazing, and had eaten the remainder of the cold cuts in the refrigerator.

By early evening, just past sunset, I was ready for something more substantive. Kat had engaged in a number of phone calls and was busy coordinating activities on her notebook computer, which was set up on the dining room table.

"How do you feel about dinner out tonight?" I asked.

She looked up from her email while holding her mobile phone to her ear.

"Um, I just have to finish—"

I nodded. "Sure thing."

Some things never changed.

As I wandered into the living room, I heard her in the background.

"Listen, I'm placing this project in your more than capable hands," she said. "I have other more pressing matters to address."

I felt a swoosh of air around me followed by her arms wrapping around my chest from behind.

"We'll enjoy a nice dinner together," she said.

I smiled. "Sounds great. And I have the perfect café in mind, too."

"Um, I believe it's the *only* café around," she said.

"Too true," I said.

Kat and I went alone, and Bel was ending her shift as we arrived. Since I was planning to leave later that evening, I was grateful to be able to say goodbye to her, as well as thank her for the tasty apple pie that she had baked for me.

I noted that Kat observed us with a curious expression.

"Safe trip home, Caleb," Bel said. "But I better get going. I have to pick up my kids from my parents' house. They're going to an Elks Club function together."

"They sound like veritable socialites for around here," I said.

She shook her head. "You'd think that. Dad always talks about civic involvement, but Mom said he just likes to talk to people. She said that she endures it just to save wear and tear on her ears."

It was refreshing to hear about someone else's life; something that sounded charmingly ordinary.

"Don't worry though; Candace will take excellent care of you again. Hey, be sure to check in with us here if you're ever in this part of the country again," she said.

"You bet I will," I said.

"Incidentally, where do you and Katrina call home?"

"We're in New Haven, Connecticut right now."

She appeared surprised. "Wow, you really were off the beaten track then."

"Yeah," I said. "I'm all about finding the most remote places possible, it seems."

"He has quite a knack for it, in fact," Kat said.

After a quick hug, I watched Bel walk away before reseating myself across from Kat.

"You shameless flirt," she said. "And doing it right here in front of your mate."

I flushed. "What? I wasn't flirting!"

She adopted a sly expression. "You're so cute when you're flustered."

* * *

Back at the cabin, I tossed my two backpacks of belongings into the back of one of the SUVs. Then I turned to look at the mud-splattered moped still leaning against the wall on the front porch.

"So, about my scooter," I said.

"No," Kat said. "No way are we taking that with us."

"I could use it back in New Haven. I don't have a car yet," I said. "Honestly, I've grown sort of attached to that scooter."

She rolled her eyes as a number of other vampires stood nearby observing our exchange. Someone snickered and Kat turned her attention toward them with a baleful gaze.

Everyone fell silent.

"Fine, we'll take it with us," she said. "My team can secure it to the top of one of the SUVs."

Kat turned to the group of vampires.

"Yes, General," they said in unison.

As the scooter was secured, I walked out toward the nearby line of trees and took a deep breath of the cool night air.

I was definitely going to miss the serenity of the place.

Warm arms enveloped me from behind.

"How do I compete with such beauty?" Kat asked.

I leaned my head back against her shoulder. "As if you had any real competition."

Her breath tickled the skin of my neck and she kissed me on my jugular vein.

I turned my face toward hers.

She gazed into my eyes in that piercing fashion that always unnerved me, even while sending a shiver of pleasure down through my body.

"Am I still enough to keep your attention, Caleb?"

My throat felt tight and dry as every fiber of my being wanted nothing less than to kiss her squarely on the lips.

"Of course you keep my attention," I said. "You've always mesmerized me, ever since the first time I laid eyes upon you."

The edges of her mouth turned upward slightly. "That first night in history class."

I swallowed hard. "That, and then the other first time."

She frowned at me.

"You know, the first time that wasn't 'the first' until my memories were returned to me by Dr. Guilhelm," I said.

"That memory was only one day," she said. "And you were so very young."

The memories and emotions of that day flooded through my mind all at once, like a giant wave crashing down upon me; fresh as if only months old. Rather, only remembered for just a few months after nearly a couple of decades of being blocked.

The day that my bastard of a father was killed before my young eyes.

"It was a big day for me," I whispered, my throat practically too tight to speak.

Her features softened and a sympathetic expression formed. "We won't dwell over that day. Our first day was the one in your history class. That's our first day; at least, for who we are now."

"I know. But the other one was also…important."

She took my face in her warm, soft hands and kissed my forehead. "Yes, my love. It always was, and it always will be. And I've never regretted it."

"And that's yet another reason why I could never, ever, be less than smitten with you," I said.

I never wanted to ever feel differently about her, either.

I looked up into her eyes. "Look, I know you're unhappy with me right now, but do you think there's a chance you'll go back to feeling the way you felt about me before I left?"

She stared into my eyes in a piercing manner. "Oh, you silly man," she said, shaking her head. "I never stopped."

She took me into her arms, tightly hugging me against her. I embraced her with all the strength in my arms, conveying everything that I couldn't quite say in the way it deserved to be said.

"I love you, Kat."

I felt her hand reach up and massage the back of my head and neck.

"I love you so very much, too, Caleb," she said.

Our lips met in a passionate kiss.

I wanted that kiss to last forever.

Finally, I relaxed my arms. She pulled away from me slightly and stared down into my eyes. Then she tapped me on the end of my nose with tip of her forefinger.

"Ready to go?" she asked.

"Not really," I replied. "I'd much rather just stay here and set up house with you."

She chuckled. "Here? In this little cabin in the middle of nowhere?"

"I could get used to it. It's peaceful enough."

"Yeah, I can see that," she conceded while taking a long sweeping look around her. "But if we stayed, the world won't just forget about us."

I inhaled a deep breath and slowly let it out. "Probably not. The world seems to interfere with us a lot lately."

She gave me a sympathetic look. "I know."

"There's absolutely nothing we can do about it, is there?" I asked.

An edgy expression formed on her face. "Oh, I may not be able to make the world stop interfering with us, but I can sure as hell make it regret doing so."

I smiled. "I'm okay with that."

She took me by the hand and led me toward the front door. "Come on, then. Let's go make the world regret they ever set eyes on us."

As I held the hand of the woman I loved, perhaps the fiercest woman I'd ever known, I couldn't have agreed more.

Part III

NEW REALITIES

CHAPTER 17

Caleb

It had only been a week since Kat and I had returned from Tar Hollow, but I already wished that we were still there.

Though Kat was warming to me more and more with each passing day, everyone else was still rather put out with me.

Roman wasted no time letting me know how much he disapproved of my leaving in the first place.

"You're a real dickhead, Caleb," he said. "And that was a real dickhead move, too. Let's face it, for someone like you—"

"For a dickhead, you mean?" I asked.

"Exactly," he said. "At least you stayed true to your convictions at the time. You made a tough decision and took a chance."

"Thanks."

"Of course, you're also a putz."

I ignored that. "I'm going down to the basement to work out," I said, anxious to be anywhere else.

Suffice to say, some things hadn't changed. My college home still wasn't the most relaxing of refuges.

Hell, relaxing refuge aside, my house didn't even feel the

same.

It's wasn't quite complete. Something was missing.

Or, rather, someone.

Paige was gone. She'd removed most of her clothes from her bedroom, though some random articles of clothing still hung in her closet. A handful of discarded personal effects lay scattered atop her dresser, including some perfumes and gaudy-looking fashion jewelry.

However, she was nowhere to be seen. And when I'd last phoned her, the number was no longer in service.

Even more unsettling was that not even Kat had an updated contact number for her.

I called Ethan, but he said that he hadn't actually seen her. He conceded that, during his most recent phone conversation with her, she had pointedly refused to talk about me.

"I don't suppose you'd share that number she called from?" I asked.

"It wasn't on the caller ID, and she didn't bother leaving one for me," he replied. "Caleb, she'll probably turn up when she's ready."

"I hope that I haven't complicated things between you and her," I said. "I mean, she wouldn't have gone off the radar if it wasn't for me."

"Yes, well, it's a good thing that I'm busy here in Atlanta with the hospital," he said. "Or I might consider coming up there to see to you myself. I'm still a little surprised over what you did."

I winced. "Yeah, I probably deserve that. Listen, I can't apologize enough for everything, Ethan."

"Do you want to try to make it up to me?" he asked.

"Really? Absolutely," I said. "How?"

"Good," he said. "First, don't ever do it again."

I should have seen that coming.

"Anything else?" I asked.

"Yes. Keep some ice handy in the fridge, just in case," he said.

I frowned. "Ice? In case of what?"

"In case I change my mind and decide to show up to punch you in the face," he said dryly.

I swallowed. "I'll bear that in mind."

Yeah, people weren't especially happy with me at the moment.

About the only person who didn't give me some sort of crap about skipping town was Chance. When we met up at Yalehoos one afternoon after Kat and I returned to New Haven, Chance applauded my effort.

"Way to go, Caleb," she said. "You finally showed everyone. You finally took control of your own life."

"Yeah, and that's worked out swimmingly for me," I said.

"Well, maybe the appreciation for it comes later when your psyche fully metabolizes the experience," she said.

"Thank you, Dr. Freud," I said.

"Seriously, Caleb. I'm proud of you."

I supposed what Chance said had some validity, or perhaps I was just trying to put a positive spin on things.

Then again, maybe it had been a growth experience for me.

And yet, I still felt a little guilty about it.

But there was still one major unresolved leftover matter.

Paige.

* * *

I spent the first week, following my return, reconnecting with Kat. However, given Paige's continued absence, I spent the second week simply trying to reestablish some sort of balance in my life.

One thing was certain; waking up beside Kat was an excellent way to start my day.

"Good morning, sleepy head," she said with a warm smile as she wriggled closer to me.

"Mm, good morning," I said.

I briefly kissed her as I reached out to rest my hand atop her cool hip.

"You must have just slipped into bed," I said.

"Ah, but I was here when you woke up, wasn't I?"

It was the fourth time that week, in fact.

"You don't have to pretend that you're an up-all-night sort of person, you know," I said.

"I know," she said. "But I'm trying to normalize our relationship."

I arched my eyebrows.

"Daylight notwithstanding, that is," she added.

It was a perfectly understandable exception.

"Does that include a more normalized Thanksgiving?" I asked.

Her wan look spoke volumes.

"I'm working on that," she said.

"Don't tell me you're heading back to London before Thanksgiving," I said. "It's only days away now. And besides, I'll have a few days off from college, too."

"I know, my love," she said, lightly running her fingertips through my hair. "I'll work on that."

Her nails felt like heaven on my scalp.

"Well, I suppose I could always just have Thanksgiving in New Haven," I said.

"Really?" she asked.

"Yeah, if I had to," I said. "Maybe some of my friends who aren't going home for the holidays might want to pitch in together. We could have a dinner here at the house."

"That's very mature of you," she said.

"Everyone could bring a dish. There's bound to be some of us who won't be going home. At the very least, I'd bet that Chance would jump at any opportunity to avoid dinner with her family," I said.

Kat fixed me with a gaze that I couldn't begin to define, except to say that it wasn't good...at all.

"On second thought, I think I'll call Alton today and see what can be arranged," she said.

"Um, okay," I said. "Only if you're sure—"

"Shut up."

I already felt more encouraged about Thanksgiving plans.

"Do you think we can find Paige by then?" I asked.

"Given recent events, probably not."

"But—"

"I've warned you before that your actions have repercussions," she said. "That's never truer than when you play with a vampire's feelings."

I couldn't help feeling there was a double meaning there.

"Don't you remember the dinner chat that you and I had together soon after I revealed to you that I was a vampire? I told you that small decisions today take on larger impact and meaning tomorrow."

"You remember that?" I asked. "How in hell can you quote a conversation that we had over dinner more than a year ago?"

She tapped the tip of my nose. "My powers of recollection have improved remarkably over the past five centuries. Oh, and I'm a woman. We rarely forget what we tell men."

"Seriously?" I asked.

My eyebrows rose as she rolled out of bed, though I certainly appreciated the view of her shapely, beautiful butt.

She turned to look at me over her shoulder. "Oh yes. Rest assured, I'm serious about many things."

I decided not to press the topic.

While Kat showered, I pulled aside the curtains on the nearby window for some natural light and sorted through my backpack and various folders of assignments to prepare for classes that morning.

It seemed my professors had an endless supply of creative ways to keep me busy. Memories of my own brief experience as a college history professor resurfaced.

I missed my teaching position and wished that I could return to it. Those were some of the best days of my life.

"Ow!"

The bathroom door slammed shut.

"*Caleb*," growled Kat.

"What?" I said, turning to stare back at the closed bathroom door.

Then I remembered the parted curtains and noticed the morning light filtering in onto the floor from between the opened blinds.

I quickly closed both the blinds and the curtains.

"Sorry," I said, walking over to open the bathroom door.

Kat stood before me wearing nothing but a towel.

Then her towel dropped to the floor.

"Bad Caleb," she said with an arched brow. "No morning playtime for you."

"Maybe just an abbreviated playtime?" I asked.

She rested her hands atop her bare hips.

"No," she said. "Now go downstairs while I get dressed."

"Aw, crap," I said. "You know that drives me crazy when you do that."

The edges of her mouth upturned slightly. "Yes, as a matter of fact, I do."

As I sullenly went downstairs, silently vowing never again to open the bedroom curtains during daytime when she was around, I heard Roman whistling in the kitchen.

"There you are, slacker," he said.

I joined him at the kitchen counter where he was mixing fruit into two steaming bowls of oatmeal.

"What's the latest?" I asked.

"You're running late," he said. "Again."

"Aren't you ever gonna cut me a little slack?" I asked.

He pushed one of the bowls toward me. "Nope. And neither should you. We've got a schedule to keep here, you know."

I stirred the oatmeal in my bowl. "I'm taking advantage of time with Kat while she's still here."

"Nice to see that someone can keep you from skipping

town," he murmured.

"I think that's enough, Roman," Kat said from the bottom of the stairs. "You've been riding him for an entire week. I think he appreciates his mistake by now."

"Yes, ma'am," he said. "Sorry, ma'am."

Kat walked over to give me a brief kiss.

"Hey, I was thinking, what about you and me—" I asked.

"I'll be juggling conference calls and email for most of the day, but I'll see you this evening when you return home," she said. "That being said, you can call or text me if you need anything before then."

She poured a mug of hot coffee and walked in the direction of the den without saying anything further.

"And the obligations continue," I said.

"Yep. Always," Roman agreed.

After breakfast, Roman and I headed out for campus and I was soon lost in the hustle and bustle of classes. I had to wait around until late afternoon to meet with Dr. Gowan about my dissertation, so I hung out in the main library for part of the day.

While there, I received a text from Kat to meet her at Witches Brew after my meeting was finished.

By early evening, I finished my meeting, complete with a listing of new materials to research. As I tried to delve further into the background of Dr. Oliver Simonson, there were fewer primary source materials to draw upon.

I felt as if my dissertation topic was becoming an effort in futility.

Worse yet, I still didn't have any specific idea as to what revelations Alton expected me to discover. For the most part, it seemed as if Simonson was just a scientist who had become so immersed in his work that he progressively withdrew from visibility.

His published papers became less frequent as his work proceeded. It was as if he disappeared from his world.

I felt that, at the rate I was going, I'd end up much the

same way.

As I exited the elevator at the ground floor of the building, I noticed that the lobby was deserted.

"Roman?" I asked.

He was nowhere to be found.

I tried texting him, but received no response.

That was really strange.

I texted Kat. *Just left Dr. Gowan's office. Roman is nowhere to be seen.*

She replied: *Proceed directly to Witches Brew. I'm here and will locate Roman. Be careful.*

My day just got weirder.

I walked outside, paying close attention to my surroundings. Roman was gone.

I took a deep breath and strode down the sidewalk in the direction of Witches Brew. Fortunately, it was on Grove Street and in close walking proximity.

There weren't many people out and about on campus. It was close enough to the Thanksgiving holiday that many students were skipping out early on their vacation.

What few passersby I saw quickly made their way to nearby parking lots or into other buildings. New Haven was definitely a much colder place outdoors by mid-November, particularly at night.

Fortunately, the sidewalk I was walking on went directly through the scenic heart of campus and was well lit by lamps.

As I entered through a small grove of trees and hedges, I noticed a young woman, wearing matching black leather pants and jacket, walking in my direction.

I watched her out of the corner of my eye as she passed by me, but she kept walking. Her footsteps continued in the distance.

Then they abruptly stopped and I turned to look back over my shoulder at her.

It appeared that she had stopped to talk on her cell phone.

"Watch where you're going, you twat," said someone

with an English accent.

I turned to face forward. A young man stood before me. His faded leather jacket and jeans gave him an edgy appearance.

"My mistake," I said, giving him a wide berth to walk past him.

"You can say that again," he said.

I stopped to give him a hard sidelong look.

That's when he grinned and I noticed his extended fangs.

CHAPTER 18

Caleb

"Don't press something you might later regret," I warned.

"Oh, I'm tickety-boo," he said. "And you Yanks are such wankers. Who are you to threaten me?"

I reached to the small of my back where I kept one of my combat knives sheathed.

"Sweet Fanny Adams!" said a woman with an English accent from behind me.

I turned in time to see the young woman wearing the leather outfit with an expression of mock surprise on her face.

"I think he means to cut you down, Dane," she added.

"Listen, mate," said the man. "Don't be pissing around with me."

I backed up to keep both of them in view, my hand still grasping the hilt of my knife.

"You've made quite the impression on him, I think," she said.

"Nah, not this one. He's flat barmy," the man said.

"Who the hell are you people?" I demanded.

"Cheeky. You're absolutely gormless, aren't you?" she asked.

"Disappointing, really," said the male vampire. "He's not worth the trouble of killing."

"Well, I think he's somewhat dishy," said the woman. "He has potential, I suppose."

"*Really?*" the man asked. "Where's your standards, sis?"

"Still, orders are orders," she said with an exaggerated shrug.

"Rightly so," he said.

Both of them turned toward me and sneered in a menacing manner.

A moment of irony flashed in my mind. There I was, on the way to meet my vampire mate for dinner, and I was about to become dinner for two vampires.

I dropped my backpack to the ground and finally extracted the knife hidden at the small of my back while reaching inside my jacket with my left hand to grasp one of my UV flashlights.

I was very scared, but I also felt angry, fed up with people trying to kill or take advantage of me.

If I was about to die, I damned sure intended for them to regret trying.

Hell, I might even take one of them out.

"Well now, it looks like the chin wag is over," said the man. "Oh, but what Roman would give to see the look on your face right now. I told him it'd be priceless."

Roman?

Was Roman part of this?

All of a sudden I felt betrayed.

It pissed me off.

"You want trouble?" I asked. "Try it."

"*Stop.*"

I turned to see Kat standing not far behind me, leaning against a tree trunk.

Relief surged through me even as my heart raced.

Finally, the cavalry.

I looked at my two opponents with a satisfied expression.

"Oh, don't look so pleased with yourself," the male vampire said. "You'd already be dead if I wanted you so."

Kat walked over to stand beside me.

"Caleb, meet Dane and Lyra," Kat said. "They're your new handlers."

"What?"

I traded looks between the two vampires and Kat.

Dane extended his hand to shake. "No hard feelings, eh?"

I grudgingly shook his hand.

"Bit of a weak handshake there," Dane said. "I thought someone said that you worked out?"

I pointedly ignored him and turned to shake Lyra's hand.

She folded her arms before her and stared at my outstretched hand with an arched brow, so I dropped my arm to my side.

"We really need to talk about this, Kat," I said.

She looked at me. "Look, Paige simply can't be located at the moment, so Alton sent them to help us out. We need nighttime coverage for you."

"But—"

The entire prospect sucked; pun intended.

"What do you two think of your new charge so far?" Kat asked, focusing her attention on the two vampires.

Lyra looked me up and down. "Him? Boring. He definitely screams bookworm."

Dane laughed. "Oh, darling, you're off to a great start, aren't you?"

She hiked her hands atop her hips and gave him a go-to-hell look. "Hey, he's a job. I'm not here to make new friends."

"And Dane?" Kat asked.

He adopted a semi-serious expression and thoughtfully rubbed at his chin.

"Aside from a possible fixation to knife people who piss him off, he looks a mix of smart but clumsy," he said. "That being said, in the end, I'd guess he's quite a tosser."

A sense of indignation rose like a storm inside me.

"What an asshole," I said. "Kat, there's no way."

Her look of amusement didn't do much to encourage me.

"As he's my mate, I'll have to disagree on your latter assertion," she said to Dane. "Though I'll admit that he has his moments, particularly recently."

"Hey," I said.

"What? I'm only being honest."

"Thanks loads," I said, folding my arms before me.

"Despite that, give him time. He'll quickly grow on you," Kat said.

"On my nerves, perhaps," Dane muttered.

I barely restrained myself from displaying my middle finger to him. There had to be better options than these two sarcastic vampires.

How far down the bottom of the barrel were Alton's available options anyway?

"How about if we all go to dinner so that we can get better acquainted?" Kat asked. "My treat."

"And would spirits be included, General?" Dane asked.

"Certainly," she replied.

"Then I'm all yours," Dane said. "Coming, sis?"

"Anything's better than standing around here," she said.

I felt sorely tempted to disagree.

* * *

After a dinner punctuated by a combination of small talk with me and shop talk with Kat, we made it back to the house. I was hardly feeling enthusiastic about the two English vampires.

And I had learned little more about them other than that they were siblings and that Alton thought highly of their abilities.

"How did it go?" Roman asked, rising from the couch.

Dane tossed his leather jacket over the back of a nearby

recliner. "I've had easier nightmares. Though it went better for me than it will for you. I think your stock fell mightily tonight, old beam."

Roman frowned. "Whaddya talking about?"

Dane pointed toward me. "You should've seen the look on his face when I mentioned your name tonight during our grand introductions."

Roman's face went blank as he stared at me.

"Think about it, mate," Dane said. "He thought you'd bailed on him and given him up. Gads but you're a bit thick for an ex-Seal."

"Would anyone care for a beer?" Kat asked.

"Yes, thanks," Dane replied.

"Definitely," Lyra said.

"Please," I said.

"I think I need one now, too," Roman said.

He looked at me. "How could you possibly think that, Caleb? After everything?"

Kat offered bottles of beers to everyone, except for me.

I didn't know what to say to Roman. What was I supposed to think in the heat of the moment?

"Hey, you were gone. Then when he said—"

"Man, I don't even know you anymore," Roman said to me while twisting the cap off his beer.

I took a deep breath and let it out slowly.

Kat flicked the cap off her beer using her thumbnail and took a swig.

I looked at her inquiringly.

"You had two at the restaurant already," she replied to my silent query.

I shook my head, but then she handed me her opened bottle of beer.

I took a swig of beer and picked up my backpack before heading upstairs.

It felt like an evening from hell.

"Goodnight, everyone," I said.

"I'll be up later," Kat said.

Nobody else said anything.

Not that I cared at the moment.

* * *

I sat at the desk in my bedroom, checking emails while finishing my beer. I had hoped to see something from Paige, but she was still incommunicado.

I wasn't overly surprised; even at the best of times she only checked her email about once a month. She was mostly a texter; not that I had valid a mobile number for her anymore.

I couldn't send a text message to her if I had to.

It made me feel like crap.

In fact, since returning from Tar Hollow, it felt as if other portions of my life had also sort of turned to crap.

Yet, aside from assorted irritated personalities, Paige was the only person actually absent from my life.

That had to say something about her importance, didn't it?

And I had totally screwed things up with her.

I took another swig of beer and reached into my backpack to retrieve my earbuds, which I plugged into my phone.

After queuing up "Flaws" by Bastille, I started writing out a list of assignments that I needed to work on.

Afterward, I jotted down some research sources that I needed to track down.

By the time I had finished that, I felt tired so I took a shower.

While rinsing my hair beneath the hot water, I felt a shift of cool air around me.

When I opened my eyes, Kat stood before me, looking at me with a sympathetic expression.

Her body was stunningly beautiful.

She reached out to massage my upper shoulders and neck and I felt like melting before her.

As soon as she kissed me, I felt like other things, as well.

"Rough night?" she asked.

"Crappy night, if you must know."

"I think that you hurt Roman's feelings," she said.

"Yeah, well, you might've come to the same conclusion that I did if you had been there," I said.

"I was there," she said. "I saw and heard everything."

"Oh."

"You don't like Dane and Lyra, do you?" she asked.

"Dane seems like a real jerk," I replied. "And Lyra...hell, she's hard to read, but I'm pretty sure I don't like her, either."

"Hm. They both said similar things about you," she said.

"Screw them," I said while rinsing my head under the hot water.

"Funny. Dane said that about you, too," she said.

"Figures."

I wiped the water from my eyes and looked into hers.

She traced the edge of my chin with her fingertip.

"In retrospect, I suppose that your introduction to them could've been handled differently," she said.

"So, why did you do it that way then?" I asked.

She inhaled a deep breath and slowly exhaled.

"I wanted to see what you'd do," she said.

"Why the test?"

"You were away for only a week," she replied. "But you seemed quite different when I finally found you; as if something important had changed inside of you while you were away."

"I still don't understand what that has to do with them," I said.

"You're edgier now," she said. "The Caleb who left New Haven wouldn't have confronted two vampires so aggressively."

"I thought that was it for me," I said. "It made me feel angry."

She took my face between her warm palms and kissed me.

"Exactly," she said. "You're angrier since you've

returned."

"Maybe."

"Why?"

I leaned against the ceramic tiles of the shower and let the hot water wash over both of us.

"Paige is gone, people are mad at me for leaving," I said. "And any day now, you're leaving town again for God knows how long. I don't even know if I'll see you for Thanksgiving."

"Oh, Caleb, don't be angry," she said. "Things will improve eventually."

"Yeah, well, it's sort of hard for me to take the optimistic road right at the moment," I said.

She hugged me. "Hey, I talked to Alton today and we worked out arrangements for Thanksgiving."

"Really? That's something positive."

"How do you feel about spending the holiday in the Mediterranean?"

"Not Slovenia," I said. "And please not another vampire summit."

"No, nothing like that," she assured me. "We just need to meet with a special vampire influencer in the area while we're there. Alton and I believe that we can shore up another ally relatively easily."

I considered the selection of locale.

"I'm intrigued," I said. "Tell me more."

"We'll spend a few days there," she said. "The hotel is close to the sea and has an amazing view. And the beaches will be very romantic at night."

Admittedly, it sounded tempting.

"Just us?" I asked.

"Alton, you, me, and maybe we can talk Ethan into meeting us there, too," she said. "Then you two could talk and lighten things up between you."

"That's if he's not being with Paige somewhere," I said.

Her expression turned somber. "I understand that's not likely."

"What have you heard?" I asked.

"Oh, Caleb," she said. "You could make a lesser woman jealous with your complex female friendships."

"Hey, Paige is like a sister to me."

She gave me a wan look. "Well, at least that concept has stuck with one of you."

How was I supposed to respond that?

She handed me the bottle of shower gel.

"Here, soap me up," she said, turning around to face the wall. "And maybe massage it in a little bit while you're at it. I've had a long day, too."

I smiled and started with her shoulders and back, kneading my fingers against her tense muscles.

She moaned with pleasure.

* * *

The next morning, before I left with Roman for classes, Kat told me that she would be packing to return to London that night.

"Already?" I asked.

"Alton needs for me to meet with a Belgian vampire leader and then brief our team," she said.

"Why can't he do it?" I asked.

"Because he's in Belarus."

"Belarus?"

I started to say something more, but didn't really know how to proceed, nor was I curious enough to want to pursue the matter further.

Vampire politics were getting more and more convoluted.

"Where's my two newest fanged handlers?" I asked.

"They're upstairs in their rooms," she replied. "And please try to be polite. They're highly qualified and they've already earned Alton's trust, which you know isn't easy to acquire."

"Fine, fine. I'll try to be civil," I said. "But they do understand that I have nighttime things to do, don't they?"

She gave me a wan look. "They've been briefed on your need for research, as well as some social time away from the house."

That made me feel somewhat better.

However, I still didn't like them.

"Please try to get along," she said.

I kissed her. "Yep."

Then I headed out the door, accompanied by an unusually quiet Roman. He was yet someone else I had to try to patch things up with.

Sometimes relationships seemed like more trouble than they were worth.

* * *

My day had been rather uneventful, but mostly I was satisfied just to have a day pass without a major incident.

I texted Kat from the main library again, where I was doing some additional research. Fortunately, she was going to be able to have dinner with me before going to the airport to catch her flight.

She texted me: *I'll send the twins to escort you.*

My thoughts returned to the very old book before me; though it was less a book and more a compilation of years of medical research notes that had been bound together by an early European physician and researcher.

A student aide walked over to me and looked at the various books stacked around me.

"Would you mind if I reshelf some of these?" she asked. "It would help me get out of here earlier this evening."

"Sure," I said, and sorted through the ones that I didn't need anymore.

It was a shame that I couldn't just check most of them out and then review them back at the house, but they were all part of a rare collection that had been bequeathed to the university's foundation. As such, nothing could be removed from the reading room.

Fifteen minutes later, I looked up from where I sat to see Dane and Lyra entering the room and looking less than enthused about it. He wore a long black leather trench coat that appeared to drift away from him as he walked, while she wore a somewhat Goth-looking outfit, complete with dark eyeliner.

"And the vampires have arrived in cliché fashion," I murmured.

They both stopped before the table I sat at, Dane staring down at me while Lyra nibbled on the edge of one of her fingernails.

"It smells musty in here," Dane said.

"These stacks house a rare and very old collection," I said.

"Damn, I split a nail tip," Lyra said, seemingly oblivious to what I had said.

A young guy carrying a short stack of old books eyed her longingly while walking by.

"Ew. Go back to your panel van, freak," she said with a mock look of horror.

The guy quickly averted his gaze and hurried on his way to a nearby table.

"Studying hard or hardly studying?" Dane asked.

"Research," I said. "Or maybe just killing time."

"I can think of a helluva lot better places to kill some time," he said.

"Or kill someone," Lyra added.

I frowned at her.

"What?" she asked.

Dane thoughtfully rubbed at his chin. "Look, I love chit chat as much as the next fellow, but we'd better get going," he said. "The General is expecting us."

A student sitting within earshot of us looked over with a curious expression.

"Oh, I just love those funny nicknames of yours," I said.

Dane looked over at the guy. "Yeah, me and those nicknames," he said, giving the guy a hard look.

193

The student quickly returned his attention to the book before him.

I gathered up my notes into my backpack and then remembered I had stowed a couple of books from the public stacks to take with me to check out.

"I have to stop by the circulation desk on the way out," I said as we exited the reading room. "Have you two known Kat very long?"

Lyra remained silent.

"Not as long as some," Dane replied. "But long enough to know that she doesn't like to be kept waiting."

"I might be an exception to that," I said.

I noticed a glint in his eyes. "Maybe, but then, who would want to keep a lady waiting?"

"Touché," I said.

"Oh, I'm just getting started," he said.

They walked ahead out through the main entrance while I checked out the books I wanted.

I walked outdoors and saw them leaning against the wall near the doors. However, I kept my stride and they followed a few steps behind me.

"Do you walk everywhere?" Dane asked.

"Walking's good for a person," I replied. "Besides, parking's at a premium around here and the fees are outrageous."

He chuckled.

I stopped to let them catch up to me.

"You're amused?" I asked.

"The *parking fees*? I'd wager the tuition alone is absurd," he replied.

As if I had any idea what Alton and Kat were paying for me to be at Yale. It suddenly made me see myself as one of those typical spoiled rich kids.

Crap! Was I one of *them* now?

I turned and started walking again.

"Yeah, absurd," I said.

"Where do you want to go later tonight?" Lyra asked.

I looked over at her with a curious expression, but she gave me a flat look.

"*Dane,*" she clarified.

"I dunno, sis," he replied. "Depends upon what time we're free. Maybe we'll just wander about; get to know the place better."

"Hey, I can recommend a potential place to check out that's fairly close," I said.

"Yeah, I bet you can," Lyra said. "It's probably known for its milkshakes and is chock full of lonely nerds who date their hand, just like that guy back in the library."

"Hey, haven't you heard?" I asked. "Nerds are the new cool."

I glimpsed a fleeting smirk from Dane, but Lyra gave me a flat look.

"So, there's this bar called Yalehoos," I said. "It's one of my favs; great beer selection."

"Thanks for the heads up," said Lyra. "I'll be sure to avoid it."

She was definitely a tough nut to crack.

Though I was making an honest effort on Kat's behalf to be polite, I really didn't like her.

"Now, now, sis," said Dane. "The lad's just trying to be helpful."

I looked up in time to see her give Dane a dirty look.

"*Lad?* I'm not as young—or inexperienced—as I might look," I said.

"And I don't feel a day older than I look," he said.

"So you're siblings, then," I said, changing the subject. "There's got to be a story there."

"But that's neither here nor there," Lyra said.

"Hey, just making small talk," I said. "If you don't mind me saying, you two seem like an unlikely pair to be here with me. Where were you before here?"

"Oh, all over the bloody place," Dane replied.

Lyra snickered.

"Speaking of small talk," said Dane. "And, if you don't

mind *me* saying, word on the street is that your surrogate vampire—that's a really weird thing, by the way—has deserted you."

"Smart girl," Lyra quipped.

I pointedly ignored her.

"So, you're saying people are talking about me on the street?" I asked. "My star must be rising."

I glanced over to see the corners of his mouth edge up slightly.

"Well, street's a bit of an exaggeration. It was really more of a run-down cul-de-sac," he replied. "But there was pavement, as I recall."

"Somebody please kill me," Lyra muttered.

"Yes, please," I said.

Dane chuckled, but Lyra actually appeared affronted. I reveled in my momentary victory and mulled over his earlier reference to Paige.

"Suffice to say, with Paige, it's complicated," I said. "We've had a bit of a falling out."

"Sorry to hear that," Dane said.

I looked over at him to see what appeared to be a look of sincerity.

Then I looked over at Lyra. "I won't *bore* Lyra with the details," I said. "Any more than she already is."

She refused to meet my gaze.

We remained silent for the remainder of our walk to the restaurant to meet Kat.

CHAPTER 19

Caleb

Kat had been gone for days. Since she had returned to London, my relations with Lyra were still rather chilly, but at least I was forming a cautious respect for Dane. To my surprise, our mutual efforts at sarcasm and trading barbs fostered an odd fellowship between us.

As for Roman, I worked to try to mend the hard feelings that had formed, but it was also still a work in progress.

Between breaking in new strangers, strained relations with Roman, and Paige's absence, the house felt oddly empty; certainly not some place that I wanted to spend a lot of my spare time.

As such, I spent more time away from the house, typically at my local haunts. Fortunately, I was surrounded by my college friends, including Chance.

On Thursday, most of the campus was gearing down for the Thanksgiving holiday break. The following Monday and Tuesday were technically class days, but many students planned to leave early for home.

Even most of my friends were leaving town Friday or Saturday, including Chance.

"I can't believe you're actually going home early," I said to her during lunch.

"I know, right?" she said. "Mom wants for us to have a girls retreat since my dad is out of town on a business trip through next Tuesday."

"Well, that's cool."

"Yeah, though I think it's mostly because Mom hates to stay at home by herself," she said. "But at least my dad won't be around getting on my nerves. And it means I get to engage in some wicked retail therapy."

"Sounds like you're in for a good time," I said.

"What are you doing for the weekend?" she asked. "You could always be a third wheel with us, you know. We need someone to help carry shopping bags."

"Thanks, but I'm hoping to fly out of town on Friday," I said.

"Have you already reserved your tickets? If not, you may be screwed," she said.

My mind reeled as I realized that I hadn't actually checked into that yet.

"All taken care of," I lied. "What about you?"

"Train," she said. "And you make it sound like you've got a travel agent in your pocket or something."

"Fortunately, I have access to an amazing guru who has the inside scoop on last minute ticketing."

Her eyes narrowed. "Why do I get the impression that you're referring to Katrina? I'll bet you think she's amazing with everything, don't you?"

"Well, she sort of is," I said with a grin.

She rolled her eyes. "Oh, God, Caleb's in love."

Then her quirky expression changed to something darker.

"What's wrong?" I asked.

"Isn't that guy sitting over at that table your friend who you hang out with a lot?" she asked. "What was his name? Romie?"

I glanced over my shoulder at Roman sitting by himself on the other side of the dining room.

"Oh, yeah. Roman," I said.

198

"Why not ask him to join us?" she asked.

"Nah, he looks like he's in deep thought," I said.

"You have the weirdest sensibilities sometimes, you know? Speaking of weird, where's your sister lately? I haven't seen her around."

"Uh-oh, hater alert," I teased.

"Whatever. Paige is okay, I guess," she said.

"So, where's she been hiding herself lately?"

My mind raced for a viable answer.

"She's gone out of town to see some friends," I said.

"But she's meeting up with you guys for Thanksgiving, right?"

"Yeah, of course," I said. "She'll catch up to us by next week."

Chance stared at me. "Okay, but my bullshit meter feels like it's getting ready to peg. You wouldn't BS me, would you, Caleb?"

I gave her my best innocent look. "Me? Never."

She crunched on the end of a carrot stick. "Just make sure that's true, mister. I don't give second chances very often."

"Okay, I get it," I said. "No second chances."

The remainder of our conversation was far easier to negotiate.

As soon as I left Chance at the student center, I got on the phone to the person who often seemed to pull miracles out of a hat: Alton's assistant, Marla.

"Hey, Marla? Listen, I really need your help with some last-minute Sunset Air tickets for three," I said. "And could we please keep this just between us for the time being?"

* * *

"London? Tomorrow night?" Dane demanded. "I thought we were leaving the day after tomorrow."

"What can I say? Plans changed."

"Why the hell am I just now hearing about this?"

"It was sort of a last minute decision," I said.

He narrowed his eyes at me.

Lyra threw her arms into the air. "Will somebody please decide where the fuck we're supposed to be for more than a week at a time?"

I gave her a sharp look, but Dane held up his hand.

"C'mon, sis," he said. "We're world travelers. And spending some time in our old haunts wouldn't be so bad, would they?"

"Whatever. It all pays the same, I suppose," she said.

Roman, on the other hand, appeared reflective from his seat at the kitchen counter.

"Roman, how would you like a prolonged vacation visiting your family?" I asked. "Of course, if you'd like to go to London you're welcome to, and I can probably get another ticket. But I thought you'd like to——"

"No," he interrupted. "Actually, given everything in recent weeks, I'd relish some time with my family. My dad's complained that they don't see enough of me as it is."

"Good. But I want to keep this under wraps; it's a surprise for Kat."

"Fine by me," Roman said.

Dane nodded, but Lyra appeared less than pleased.

"Well, we had all better start packing then," Dane said.

The next twenty-four hours passed quickly, and before I knew it, we were seated in a comfortable cabin for the lengthy Sunset Air flight to London.

Due to the time change, we landed only a couple of hours prior to sunrise. Thankfully, I had managed to sleep a little bit during the flight.

Upon disembarking from the plane, Kat and Marla stood in the practically deserted receiving area to greet us.

Kat adopted a knowing expression on her face.

"Aw, hell, this was supposed to be a surprise," I said with a stern look at Marla, who merely shrugged.

"To your credit, it was certainly a surprise when I heard about it," Kat said.

I gave her a bland look as she reached out to embrace me.

"Surprise," I murmured.

She gave me a warm kiss.

"So, you're not annoyed that I showed up early?" I asked.

She smiled. "Me? Not in the slightest."

Well, that was gratifying, at least.

"Welcome, Caleb. I'll have your things taken to the hotel," said Marla. "Your uncle Alton has asked that you see him once you've had a chance to rest a bit."

The realization hit me like a speeding comet to the face.

Oh, yeah...my chat with Alton...about my leaving town abruptly.

I swallowed hard.

I had forgotten all about that.

Then I noticed that nobody was speaking and I saw Dane staring at me. On top of that, Lyra looked at me as if I was an alien bug who had jumped out at her.

"Pardon me, Ms. Kendrick, but did you say *Uncle Alton?*" asked Dane.

Marla folded her arms before her with an amused expression on her face.

"Marla, would you please take Caleb to see about their luggage?" Kat asked. "We'll catch up to you in a few minutes."

I looked up at Kat, but knew better than to challenge her when she had that telltale determined expression on her face.

She spared me a momentary wink and reached out to run her fingernails down the back of my back, eliciting a shiver that ran all the way down my spine.

I dutifully followed Marla.

"What's that all about, do you think?" I asked once we reached the escalators.

I noticed that two men wearing business suits, who were standing nearby, fell into step behind us.

"I suspect that Katrina would like to clear the air a bit with Dane and Lyra," she replied. "Speaking of whom, how do you find them?"

"Difficult," I replied. "It's been somewhat of a challenge, really, though Dane's starting to grow on me a bit."

"Ah," she said. "And Lyra?"

"A completely cold-hearted bitch," I replied.

"*Caleb,*" she chastised. "My word, but I'm surprised to hear something like that from the likes of you."

I mildly regretted my frank assessment, but only slightly, for the mere sake of it sounding rude.

"Truth hurts," I said. "Besides, I'm sure you'd hear as much, if not worse, from her."

Marla retrieved her smartphone from her purse.

"Something the matter?" I asked.

"No, just routine checking in," she replied, beginning to text.

"Is Alton still angry with me?" I asked.

She paused in her texting. "I'll let you determine that for yourself, if you don't mind."

A sour feeling formed in the pit of my stomach.

CHAPTER 20

Katrina

I watched Caleb and Marla walk away before turning toward Dane and Lyra. Then I motioned for them to follow me over to a relatively deserted portion of the terminal.

I turned to face them. "Is there a problem?"

Lyra started to speak up, but then folded her arms before her and looked at her brother.

"Really? You're not even baited to touch that one?" he asked his sister. "Honestly, you're a mystery even to me sometimes."

"Shut up," Lyra said.

He shook his head at her before turning his attention to me.

"Problem? Not exactly, General," Dane replied. "Curious? Absol-bloody-lutely."

"Please, do proceed," I said.

"Uncle Alton? As in Alton Bloody *Rutherford*, the nearly millennium-old vampire and our employer?" he asked.

I arched my brow at him and he appeared slightly unnerved.

"By the by, just to be clear, when I said *our employer*, I had me and my sister in mind," he added. "You notwithstanding, General."

"Naturally," I said. "The term is one of endearment for both Alton and Caleb. You might know that Mr. Rutherford is quite fond of Caleb."

"Ah," he said.

He paused, as if internalizing what I had just said.

My smartphone buzzed and I read a text message from Marla that concerned me.

"How are the two of you getting along with Caleb?" I asked.

Dane hesitated before answering.

"Well, General, it's not smashing, but it's coming along," he replied, looking at Lyra. "A bit of work in progress, wouldn't you say, sis?"

I stared at Lyra, unwilling to accept yet another quiet deference to her brother.

"Um, sure," she said, folding her arms before her once more. "It's been a rough start."

"Do you like him?" I asked her.

Her mouth opened and then closed.

"Not so much," she said.

"Thank you for your honesty. While I regret hearing that, it's not essential for your duties," I said. "That is, unless you'd prefer to be reassigned to something else."

Lyra took a deep breath and looked at her brother in silent query.

"Do as you will, darling," he said. "But I'm going to give it a go for a bit longer."

She frowned at him. "Really?"

"What can I say? I'm a classic glutton for punishment," he said.

"You would be," she said before returning her attention to me.

"It's truly your choice," I said. "And there's no hard feelings either way. I only want what's in both of your best interests."

Lyra appeared a little taken aback by my response.

I noticed that Dane's eyebrows rose.

"You know, I'm going to go get a coffee and let you two talk for a few minutes," he said. "Would either of you care for anything?"

"You don't even like coffee," Lyra said.

"I do right now," he said, gesturing toward me.

"No, thank you," I replied.

"Give us a bell when you're ready," he said before quickly walking away from us.

"Your brother is oddly charming," I said. "Bit of a lady killer, too, I'd imagine."

"He certainly thinks so. Oh, he's the dog's bollocks, for sure," she said. "When he's not being a complete wanker."

I spotted a momentary crack in her usually hard shell. Then her expression smoothed over again.

"Tell me, has Caleb been rude to you?" I asked.

"I think we're a bit rude to each other," she replied. "But he doesn't go out of his way, if that's what you mean."

"Lyra, I hope that you won't mind me being forward, but my hands are relatively full working with Mr. Rutherford on international vampire affairs. I don't have the luxury to worry over Caleb's daily security detail, much less his relations with those detailed to protect him," I said. "That being said, would you care to share your view on why the two of you can't seem to get along?"

She looked at me as if I had just challenged her to eat something heinous.

"Oh, but this is hellish," she said, hiking her hands atop her hips.

"Perhaps," I said. "But trust me when I say that there will be no hard feelings from what you tell me."

She took a deep breath and let it out in one long exhale.

"You know how sometimes when you meet someone for the first time, and you're not sure why, but you just don't get a good vibe from them?" she asked.

I nodded. "Okay. The eternal conundrum surrounding first impressions."

"Well, your Caleb just rubbed me the wrong damned

way, ever since we first met," she said. "I dunno. He seemed really full of himself, despite there being something infuriatingly simple about him, too."

"Simple?"

"Yeah, I mean, like he was a deer in the headlights. You know, sort of naive," she said. "And he comes off as the worst sort of nerd."

"Not a fan of nerds?" I asked.

"They're just so awkward, and yet, they're supposed to be all smart and everything. Smart arses, the lot of them," she said. "But then, they don't ever know really anything about the *real world*; just whatever they read in a bunch of books, or whatnot. They're just such twats."

I took a moment to consider what she had told me.

"You were what—twenty-something—when you were turned?" I asked.

"Twenty-two," she said. "Dane and I were turned at the same time, actually."

A somber expression formed on her face. "We were told that it would be a damned shame not to age together as twins."

"So, you really hadn't seen much of the world by then, had you?"

"Well, no, for me not really. It was Dane who had been the street-wise one between us."

"And you and Dane were turned in—"

"1976," she said.

I thought, from reading their files, that they were relatively young as vampires went.

"You know, Caleb's already twenty-seven now," I said. "And he was—still is, at times—relatively naive. He'd had a rough time growing up, you see. He bunkered inside himself for a number of years after that."

She frowned at me. "Excuse me, General, but why are you telling me all of this?"

I took a deep breath and slowly exhaled.

"I don't know," I replied. "I just hoped that you might

see some parallels between the two of you, that's all. We'd better signal your brother now and then rejoin the others."

Lyra retrieved her mobile phone and started texting.

"Please tell him we'll meet up in the parking garage," I said. "Section A-47."

She quietly walked alongside me as we proceeded toward the escalators.

During our descent, she sighed.

"Caleb's quite unlike any mate I've had as a vampire," I said. "I've found him to be both endearing and sincere. And he's very intelligent."

She gave me a sharp, sidelong glance and then stared straight ahead.

"Growing up, I dated a really smart boy while I was in Upper School," she said.

"Oh?"

I felt relieved that Lyra was sharing anything personal at all with me.

"His name was Thomas. He had it all: dishy, popular, athletic. Everybody loved him, even the teachers," she said. "Tickety-boo Thom, his mother used to say. I always hated that.

"Anyway, Thomas used to ask me questions about stupid facts and all sorts of rot. I think he used to enjoy making me feel stupid or something," she said.

"I can't imagine that was easy to endure."

"He used to laugh at me," she continued. " 'Til one day when I'd had about enough and told him to stop. I said that he wasn't treating me right, and I wanted us to stop seeing each other. He actually slapped me, the bugger."

"Thomas sounds like a truly horrible person," I said.

"He was a real bastard in the end," she said. "Dane saw to putting him right, though. Afterwards, Thomas wouldn't even blink an eye at me. Sometimes, I would step in front of him in the hallways at school, just to see him give me a wide berth. It was like my own little private joke to play on him. I wanted him to suffer.

"Later, I found out that he'd gone on to Cambridge," she said. "He'd always talked 'til he was blue in the face about that damned place. I'd bet he fit in nicely there with all the other tossers."

I remained silent as we walked to the parking garage.

"I can see why you might not care for college types," I said.

"Can't stand them," she said.

"Lyra, you realize that Caleb's not anything like Thomas," I said.

"Yeah, maybe not," she said. "But I couldn't help thinking of Thomas when I first met your mate. That sort of first impression is hard for me to get beyond."

Frankly, given everything, it seemed that Caleb and Lyra had a long hard row to hoe together before anything positive came about between them, if ever.

Still, stranger things have happened.

"I won't hold you to your assignment to guard Caleb, if you prefer," I said.

She remained silent for a few moments.

"No, I'll stick with Dane," she said. "For now."

"I appreciate that, and I hope that you might eventually see a different side of Caleb," I said. "Perhaps if you could see him for the kind of man that he truly is, you might find that he's not so bad."

"Yeah, maybe," she said. "I mean, you obviously think highly of him. And I suppose Mr. Rutherford, too, what with calling him uncle and all that."

"He's my mate. I love him. And yes, Mr. Rutherford thinks quite highly of him, as well," I said. "But believe me when I say that I'd never tolerate a moment of behavior from Caleb like you experienced from Thomas."

She chuckled. "I can't begin to imagine that you would. I'd wager he'd never survive the moment."

She was definitely right about that.

"Lyra, I appreciate your sharing with me about your past and Thomas," I said. "And I'll keep your confidence, but it also might help if Caleb understood what you told me."

"I'd really rather you didn't," she said. "I'm not all that comfortable talking about it. I'm surprised that I even told you."

As we exited the elevator to the parking garage level, I turned toward her.

"You are a quiet one," I said. "Why is it then, do you think, that you were able to share with me just now?"

She frowned. "I don't know; an odd whim, I suppose. I respect you, at least."

"I wondered when you two would be along," Dane said, walking out from behind a nearby concrete pillar.

"No coffee?" I asked.

"Nah, changed my mind, after all," he said, looking at his sister. "Everything all right?"

"Tickety-boo, dear brother," Lyra said.

She and I exchanged knowing looks while Dane narrowed his eyes.

"*Tickety-boo?*" he asked with a pained expression.

Lyra snickered.

"Aw, never you mind; I don't want to know," he said, throwing up his arms and marching toward the SUVs that were parked nearby waiting for us.

JAZ PRIMO

CHAPTER 21

Caleb

I waited outside the SUV while Marla sat inside, talking on her phone.

Then I spied Kat walking alongside Lyra while Dane strode well ahead of them.

"What kept you guys?" I asked Dane.

"I haven't the foggiest, but believe me when I say that you don't want to know," he replied. "Now, be a good lad and get in the vehicle."

I opened the passenger door and started to join Marla in her vehicle, but someone whistled. I turned to see Kat point to the SUV parked next in line.

Lyra walked directly toward me and I almost slammed the door shut before she arrived near it.

Instead, I politely held the door open for her as she hopped inside.

She gave me a suspicious look before reaching out to grasp the door handle.

"Thank you," she said quietly.

Something in the way she said that sounded odd.

I made my way to the SUV that Kat was standing beside.

"So, did you have a good visit with Lyra and Dane?" I asked.

She opened the door for me. "Wouldn't you like to know? Now inside with you."

Two vampires sat in the front cab while Kat and I sat in the back seat. A smoked glass barrier rolled up before us to provide us with some privacy.

"Do me a favor, won't you?" she asked.

"Sure," I replied.

"Try to be nicer to Lyra," she said.

"But I just—"

"I know," she said. "I saw that."

"Well, she started—"

"Yes, I realize that might be the case. Just don't give up on trying, okay?" she asked. "I understand that you've both been digging at each other."

I folded my arms before me. "Just giving back as good as I'm getting."

"Really? Ah, well then, how's that working for you?" she asked with a knowing expression.

I started to say something, but decided against it.

"Nice start," she said. "Keep that up and you'll go far, I think."

I looked up at her to catch her sly look. Then she gave me a quick kiss.

"I have confidence in you, my love," she said.

"I hope someone challenged her to do the same," I said.

"I wouldn't be the least bit surprised about that."

Why did I end up feeling as though I was blindly stumbling in on the tail end of something?

* * *

Kat and I went to her hotel room and, to my surprise, I dozed off on the couch for a few hours.

Upon waking, I found a note from Kat asking me to meet her at Alton's office. A wave of dread washed over me.

My meeting with Alton.

Within the hour, I stood before the door to Alton's

office. I looked down the short distance of hallway toward Marla's office, where she and Kat stood watching me.

"Go ahead," Kat whispered while making shooing gestures.

I hesitated before finally knocking.

"Come in," Alton said.

I took a deep breath and entered.

"Hello, Alton," I said.

"Hello, Caleb," he said, standing from his desk chair and walking around to greet me. "How good of you to come."

"I hate to bother you if you're busy," I said.

We shook hands and he motioned to the nearby couch. "Perish the thought. I've been looking forward to us having a chat."

I bet.

I sat down at one end and he chose the opposite end. Then he crossed one leg over the other and stared at me.

"Well, where to—" he began.

"Look, I was completely an idiot for running out like I did, and I realize how utterly disappointed you must be in me," I interrupted.

"I see," he said.

"But things were getting crazy and I was unbelievably stressed, and I didn't know where my place was anymore. Hell, I didn't even know where my future with Kat was headed, or even if we still had one. I mean, I sort of had to find myself and figure everything out," I continued, feeling as if everything was rushing out of me like a geyser.

"But my experiences were really helpful and brought everything further into perspective. I think that I understand exactly where I want to be in life now. I'm totally committed to Kat, and college, and you—"

He held up one hand. "That's a lot to say without taking a breath, especially for a human. Just breathe, Caleb."

I inhaled, the smell of Alton's office filling my lungs.

"Now, let it out slowly," he said. "Don't stop until you finish counting to seven."

I exhaled until I'd pressed nearly every bit of air from my lungs.

"There. Now breathe normally," he said.

He watched me. "Much better."

I leaned my head back against the couch.

"I've been thinking a lot about exactly what I was going to say when we finally met," I said.

"And I think you left very little of it unsaid already," he said wryly.

"Yeah, I know," I said. "I'm sorry. I've just been sort of dreading our meeting."

Realizing what I had just said aloud, I looked over at him staring at me with upraised brows.

"Oh, shit," I said.

I was once again the victim of an overshare.

"Brutally honest, as only I can appreciate," he said good-naturedly.

I closed my eyes and rubbed at my eyelids with my fingertips.

"Caleb, how do you continually manage to find yourself in the most desperate of situations?"

"I dunno. Chalk it up to a lifetime of practice, really," I replied.

He chuckled. "Oh, how I've missed our chats."

I opened my eyes. "Really?"

"Chats, yes," he said. "Reckless jaunts across the globe with complete disregard for your own safety or the feelings of those around you? No."

Any hope of an easy conversation immediately evaporated before his steady gaze.

"I'm very disappointed in what you did," he said.

"So was pretty much everyone else important to me."

"As well they should have been," he said. "Have you already forgotten our conversation following your interview at Yale?"

"What? Of course not," I said.

He gave me a long look. "I think you have."

I fell silent, waiting for him to continue.

He stared at me.

"I mean, we talked about a lot that day," I said.

It was his turn to take a deep breath and let it out slowly.

I did remember that it had also been an emotionally charged conversation. Upon reflection, many things flooded back with my memory of the event.

"I remember you said that I could lead an army," I said.

"Someone who could be a king," he added. "And be worthy of it."

"Yeah, I remember that too now."

His brow furrowed. "Though perhaps I was rash about that."

My heart sank.

"I wished you hadn't said that," I said.

"What would you have me say, Caleb?"

I considered his question at length. "I wish that you hadn't made it sound as if I was just some sort of complete failure. Rash is a hard word that sounds far worse than a mistake when you say it."

"Yes, rash is also a word that can portent repercussions," he said. "Your rash decision to leave jeopardized our position with opposing factions."

"Wh—? How?"

"Think of what position we might have been in had you been captured by someone hostile to our objectives, much less killed," he said. "You're the cherished mate to the second most powerful vampire in our organization. Can you imagine the impact on Katrina?"

There was that, of course.

"And you're important to *me*," he said, leaning toward me. "Though it pains me to have to remind you of that."

I stared into his steely gaze, unable to look away. It felt like being nailed in place.

"I'm very sorry," I said with all the earnestness I could convey. "I realize that I screwed up and I'm—"

My breath caught in my throat.

"I'm truly very sorry," I said.

The tension around his eyes appeared to abate slightly.

"Have you gotten all of that pent-up rebellion out of your system? Are you all sorted out now?" he asked.

"Yes. I'm—it's all over now."

He leaned forward.

"Good," he said, rising from the couch to walk over to a small wet bar. "I'm relieved to hear it, though I'll happily finish sorting you out, if needed."

I deliberately swallowed to clear the tension in my throat.

"Perhaps we can right the ship and proceed onward," he said. "Hm?"

Only then did I release my death grip on the edge of the couch cushion.

"Onward?" I asked.

He retrieved a bottle of Coke, opened it, and walked over to the couch to hand it to me.

"Thank you," I said, grateful for something to moisten my dry throat.

"You're welcome," he said.

The first swallow felt sharply cold and fizzy.

He leaned down closer to me. "Rest assured, Caleb, adopted nephew or not, if you ever do anything like that again, I'll bite you in the neck so hard you'll feel it in your guts," he said.

I choked and coughed uncontrollably.

He reached down to pat me on the back.

"Careful there," he said. "It wouldn't do either of us any good if you drowned in your Coke."

I wiped my mouth on the back of my hand and stared into his eyes. The glint of near amusement reflected back at me made me feel unnerved.

The door to Alton's office swept open to reveal Kat with a concerned expression on her face as Marla peered inside from behind her.

"Who's choking?" Kat demanded.

"The boy's fine," Alton said. "A bit of soda down his

windpipe is all."

Kat walked over to stand before me.

"Okay?" she asked.

"Fine," I gasped. "Just great."

She cast a long, suspicious look at Alton. "How's your chat going?"

He rubbed his palms together. "Oh, I think our meeting of the minds was rather successful, wouldn't you agree, Caleb?"

I nodded vigorously. "Minds met. Everyone's happy," I said, still trying to catch my breath and ease the burning discomfort in my throat.

"I, for one, feel quite happy now," he said.

She folded her arms before her. "Happy? You?"

"Well, quite satisfied, anyway," he amended with a sly smile.

"Mm-hm," she said.

"So, Caleb," he began in a good-natured tone. "Since Marla's here, let's talk about Thanksgiving."

"Fine," I said. "Let's start with where we're spending it."

"Yes, well, that's a surprise," he said. "Trust me, you'll like it."

"Always with the mystery and intrigue," I said.

"Oh, I'm full of surprises," he said. "What would you like to see on the menu?"

I gave him a wary look. "Anything but me."

CHAPTER 22

Caleb

With Alton's stern lecture behind me, I felt as if I had survived a formidable storm. The impact of our conversation continued to resonate with me.

I would have appreciated some quality time with Kat, but she and Alton had an important meeting with a prospective vampire leader.

"You have more meetings than I have classes," I said.

"Don't make me get mean with you," she said. "I would have thought that Alton would be enough for you for one day."

I folded my arms before me. "Not nice."

She spared me a more sympathetic expression. "Caleb, it's important. If we can build a much larger coalition than our enemies, that may forestall more direct actions," she said.

"You mean killing," I said. "As in, you out killing people...while they're trying to kill you."

She stepped closer to me and encircled my waist with one arm. "Meetings can be good things."

"Quality time spent with me could be a better thing," I said, wrapping my arms around her waist and pulling her closer.

"Then you'll have something to look forward to once

our meeting is over."

"I can't wait," I said.

Her lips pressed against mine and I pulled her tightly against me.

Someone cleared their throat.

Kat growled. "Poor timing, Alton."

"I might point out that you're using my office," he said.

She gave me a quick kiss on the lips before gently disengaging from me.

"We'll meet up later, my love," she said. "It should only be two or three hours."

I looked up at Alton.

"Don't worry, I'll find something to do," I said.

"Good," he said. "Or I can happily find something for you."

I hastily exited his office.

I went back to our hotel room, but grew bored watching television. I had been to see most of the closest museums and I was in no mood to do any studying or research.

Most of the things that I wanted to do involved Kat.

Within the hour, I sat idly in a guest chair opposite Marla's desk. Her office was smaller than Alton's and optimized for efficiency.

"You had better hope that Alton doesn't walk by and catch you moping around here," she said.

"Yeah, well, there's nothing much worth doing in the time I have available," I said.

"There are six museums within—"

"Seen them before," I said.

"The London Eye is—"

"Romantic destination for Kat and me," I said.

"Shakespeare's is open—"

"Not hungry."

She gave me a look of annoyance. "Well, try not to be a bother then. Some of us have lots of work to do."

I watched as she shifted a stack of multicolored folders before her.

"Need any help with those?" I asked.

She appeared pleased. "I thought you'd never ask. Here, let me show you what I need."

Helping others was nice, but filing and sorting left a lot to be desired. However, I soon came upon something interesting.

"Hey, why is there a file called Saint James the Less Church?" I asked.

"What? Oh, that's a local church that Mr. Rutherford supports," Marla replied. "They do a great deal of community outreach to the poor and homeless, and they're renowned for their local food pantry."

"Surprising," I said. "I wouldn't have expected that."

"Caleb, don't be impertinent," she said. "Mr. Rutherford happens to be an active practitioner of charity toward the common good. He realizes that there's a practical interest in supporting the community. Woe to the businessman who ignores his local communities."

I had to admit, the revelation was surprising.

Marla's mobile phone buzzed and she picked it up to read a text message.

"Mr. Rutherford's guest has arrived," she said, rising from her seat. "Stay here and continue sorting. I'll return soon."

I had finally fallen into a rather good rhythm when I heard an oddly familiar voice. The man's classic New York accent was noteworthy.

"Ah, Mr. Rutherford," said a man's deep voice. "I've heard so much about you in recent years. During our elevator ride, Ms. Rawlings was telling me how surprised you were over my visit."

"I believe the exact words I used was pleasantly surprised," said Kat.

"Happy to meet you, Mr. Pitt," said Alton. "It's so rarely that we receive you Americans here in London. I find that I'm typically the one flying to North America."

"Nice to meet you, as well, Mr. Rutherford," he said.

"I've seen many parts of the world, but this is my first opportunity to see London, so how could I refuse?"

"Please step into my office so that we might speak further in private," Alton offered. "Ms. Kendrick will see to some refreshments for us."

"Something to drink, perhaps?" Marla asked.

"Type B, if you have it," the familiar voice replied.

So, he was a vampire.

I was certain I'd heard his voice somewhere before, but where? When?

It was maddening to have something on the tip of my tongue, and yet, not quite accessible. I felt like game show contestants must, when they knew the answer, but couldn't seem to retrieve it.

The minutes passed as I sorted through memories and places. I'd met so many new people since beginning my journey at Yale. But his voice was that of a vampire, which most assuredly shortened my list of possibilities.

Then again, I had been surrounded by vampires at the Slovene conference. He might have been one of the many attendees. And yet, that seemed wrong somehow.

"Here you are," Marla said.

I lurched slightly at her sudden appearance beside me.

"Sorry," she said, proffering a mug of tea toward me. "I think you've earned a break. It's tea time, after all."

I gratefully accepted the hot beverage. She placed a small plate of cookies on the edge of her desk before me.

"Help yourself to some biscuits, if you'd like," she said. "I need to check in on our guest now, but I'll return soon."

"Thanks," I said, reaching out to take one of the cookies.

My mind wandered as I nibbled at the cookie while contemplating a host of thoughts, the least of which was why that voice sounded so familiar to me.

Marla reappeared and sat before her desk, only to begin typing on her computer keyboard.

"This is a pretty bland cookie," I said.

"Yes, well, I admit I've had better myself," she said,

typing away on her keyboard. "But they're a local bakery; only opened a couple of months ago. I prefer the one on the other side of town, but Mr. Rutherford said we need to buy local first. It's a bit of a waste, if you ask me. Honestly, so few of us around here actually eat them. Still, Mr. Rutherford's an observer of teatime traditions."

"So they're for decoration then?"

She gave me an unamused look, barely skipping a beat with her rapid typing. "I'll try to look into the matter further. You don't have to finish them, you know."

"Not trying to be critical," I said. "Just another surprise revelation for me, that's all."

She stopped typing and turned to look at me. "Do you really think so little of us here, that we only care for vampire-related things?"

"Well, um, I wasn't trying to be insulting or anything."

"There's something you should know, Caleb; something very important," she said. "Mr. Rutherford realizes that eventually—though who knows when that may be—humans will discover us. He believes that the more we vampires are already integrated into society in productive, nurturing ways, the easier it will be for us to survive, much less thrive."

I nodded. "Yeah, that makes sense. At least, it's a hopeful expectation."

"Most of us enjoy being vampires, but haven't entirely forgotten was it was like being human," she said. "I still remember living with the fear of growing old, though I realize now it was merely vanity. Nobody cherishes the idea of their own venerability; of time passing and then eventually withering away to die."

She had never shared that sober perspective with me before, and I found her words had quite an impact.

"I was so fortunate the day I met Mr. Rutherford," she continued. "He was easily the most articulate and charismatic person I'd ever met. Truth be told, I was somewhat surprised when he hired me..."

She stared at me, but it was as if she was looking through

me.

"Even before he revealed to me his true vampire nature, I'd grown to be in awe of him, impressed with how he valued others, even when he didn't have to," she said. "He has a genuine quality about him; something that's rather unforgettable."

"I get it," I said. "Distinctive qualities resonate about people…"

"Distinctive and admirable," she said.

A vivid recollection struck me like lightning.

"I know now," I said.

"Hm?" she asked. "Know what, dear?"

"I know where I've heard that voice," I said.

"Whose voice?" she asked.

"The vampire meeting with Kat and Alton."

"Are you sure? To my knowledge, he's a new acquaintance to both Mr. Rutherford and Ms. Rawlings," she said. "You must be mistaken."

I shook my head. "No. I need to see Kat. Now."

CHAPTER 23

Caleb

As I scrolled back through my text messages from Chance, a shift of air washed over me, closely followed by the scent of cherry blossoms.

Kat's face appeared beside mine as she squatted down beside me. She appeared unamused.

"You look serious," I said.

"Mm. You do realize this is a very important meeting?" she asked.

"Yes, I do," I said. "But this is important, too."

Her eyebrows arched as Marla quietly closed her office door.

I stared into Kat's penetrating gaze. "The man you're meeting with, I've heard his voice before."

"That's not likely," she said. "He wasn't even at the Slovene conference. In fact, his faction was sitting on the fence to see what happened afterward."

"Fine," I said. "Maybe I've never met him, but I've heard his voice."

"Caleb, I know that you want to feel useful—"

"Fine," I said, throwing my hands up. "Ignore me then. Just forget I said anything at all. Go back to your meeting."

She paused, completely still and saying nothing.

"Where and when?" she asked.

Well, at least she was taking me seriously.

"On the phone with Chance," I said. "It was when I called her a few weeks ago."

She stared at me. "Chance? Why was she talking to him?"

"No, it wasn't Chance," I said. "The guy was talking in the background to her father."

"In the background?" she asked. "Was it over a cellular phone call?"

"Yes, in the background."

"Caleb, do you realize how easily a person's voice can sound distorted via digital communications? And more so during a bad cell phone connection."

"Yeah, sure," I said. "You're probably right, and I misheard everything. Never mind."

She growled at me.

"Hey," I said. "Don't be all growly at me just because I wanted to help out."

I looked up at Marla, who was holding her hand over her mouth, trying to contain a smirk.

"Caleb—"

"Look, I heard the guy's voice in the background," I insisted. "That New York accent is unmistakable."

Kat appeared deep in thought.

"Wait, where precisely was Chance when she was talking to you?" she asked.

"Like I said, she was on her mobile phone," I said.

She gave me a wan look. "I *know* that. Where specifically was she located at the time that she talked to you?"

"Oh," I said. "At her parents' home."

She gave me a long look.

"In Philadelphia," I said.

She frowned.

"Pennsylvania," I added.

Marla stifled a chuckle.

Kat narrowed her eyes at me. "I *know* where Philadelphia

is."

I folded my arms before me. "I was just being specific like you wanted."

She gave one of her infamous don't-get-me-started looks.

"What?" I asked.

She slowly reached out and tapped me on the chin.

"Remember I love him, remember I love him," she quietly chanted.

I swatted at her finger, but found only empty air.

"What did the man say in the background?" she asked. "Think back and remember as specifically as possible. Don't try to manufacture any words that you don't actually recall him saying."

I closed my eyes and thought back on my conversation with Chance. Admittedly, I hadn't been paying that close of attention.

"He wanted to know what he was supposed to do about something," I said. "And he said that it wasn't part of a deal they had apparently made."

When I opened my eyes again, Kat was watching me closely.

"Anything else?" she asked.

I shook my head. "Honestly, I wasn't listening that closely at the time, and it sort of caught me off-guard. I mean, I was more worried about if Chance was okay or not."

"Was she in trouble?" she asked.

"Nah, her father—I think his name is Nick—just wanted her to get off the phone," I said.

Then I recalled something else.

"Chance and I had dinner after that," I said. "And when I asked her about it, she said that the guy and her dad were grilling her about her time on campus. She thinks that it had something to do with her father stalking her or something."

"Stalking her?" she asked. "Why would he do that?"

"I don't know," I replied. "She's told me a few times that he's a major control freak."

"More importantly, if you're correct, why would Chance's father have anything to do with a vampire?" she asked.

"Ms. Rawlings," Marla quietly prompted. "Shall I interrupt Mr. Rutherford to inform him about this?"

"No," she said. "But he should hear this. I'll return to the meeting and tell him that he needs to check with you on something. Then Caleb can recount what he told me."

"Very good," she said, opening her office door.

Kat gave me a reassuring look and a quick kiss on the lips. "Whatever you may think, I don't casually discount what you confide to me," she said before disappearing amidst a flurry of air.

Moments later, I heard heavy footsteps down the hallway and Alton appeared in the door.

"What's going on?" he asked.

"That would be for me to explain," I said, holding up my right forefinger.

He closed the office door behind him and turned toward me, folding his arms before him.

"Why do I get the impression that I'm not going to like what you're about to tell me?" he asked.

"I dunno. Recent history?" I asked.

His steady gaze fell upon me. "Start talking."

* * *

Once Alton had finished speaking with me, he returned to his meeting, but not before giving me an assignment.

"Marla will get you a blank writing tablet," he said. "I want you to write down everything you can remember about what you overheard, as well as everything you have ever learned about Chance's father."

Well, there went my day.

Midday gave way to late afternoon and, by the time I finished writing down everything that I could recall, what should have been a brief meeting with a guest vampire had turned into a marathon meeting.

"Do you think they'll be much longer?" I asked.

"I'm not sure," Marla replied. "Perhaps you should go eat an early dinner or something."

It was true that I had grown somewhat hungry over the ensuing hours.

"I'll be back later," I said. "Maybe have Kat text me when the meeting's over?"

"I will," she said.

I proceeded to Shakespeare's, with two vampire bodyguards in tow, for a quick bite to eat and then returned to our hotel room to take a nap.

When I awoke, it was early evening and I felt both refreshed and pensive.

On a whim, I grabbed my smartphone and searched for something that had piqued my interest.

I exited the hotel room and headed downstairs to the lobby. One of Alton's vampires, a lady wearing smart business attire who I remembered seeing around the office, looked up from where she sat reading a magazine in a lobby chair.

As I approached the hotel's front exit, she rose from her seat.

"Mr. Taylor," she called. "Going out?"

"Yeah, just headed out for a walk," I said.

"Very good," she said. "I'll arrange for your escort."

Oh, yes…my escort; whomever that might be.

I missed the days when I was pleasantly of no interest to the world at large.

Dane and Lyra soon appeared through the doors of the hotel's entrance. In particular, he looked wholly displeased while she appeared merely less than enthused.

"I hear that somebody needs a keeper," Dane said.

"Hey, guys," I said. "I hope that I'm not interrupting anything."

"Well, you are," he said. "Still, it's my job."

I just couldn't win with these two.

"Yeah," I said, turning to lead the way back outside.

I led the way, occasionally glancing at my smartphone to make sure I was following the proper route from the Internet mapping app. Dane and Lyra remained a couple of steps behind me.

"So, where are we headed?" Dane asked.

"I need some exercise," I said.

"You know, I'm told that the hotel has a lovely workout room, complete with treadmills," he said.

"And a sauna," Lyra added.

Not used to her saying much of anything, I glanced back over my shoulder at her.

"Oh, well of course, let's not forget the sauna," Dane said.

"Shut up," she said.

"Sitting about in a steamy room with all sorts of strangers," he said. "Who wouldn't flock to that?"

"Hey, it's no worse than you and your hot tub tarts," she said.

"Now, now, hot tubs are quite chummy," he said. "Particularly when shared with some lovely ladies with whom I'm trying to socialize."

"Or as I call them, strangers. My brother, the cheeky monkey," she said. "And ladies? Slappers, the lot of them."

"To each his own, I say," he said. "You just don't know them like I do."

"Happy to say I won't," she said. "I prefer a different sort."

"Oh, real men's men, as I recall," he said. "Pity that few of them have seen the proper end of a deodorant stick."

"Don't start," she said.

I smiled.

We walked for a few blocks before I stopped to double-check my smartphone for further directions.

"Listen, Caleb, I like a walk just as much as any other bloke," Dane said. "But do you have any idea where you're going?"

"Yes," I replied. "And we're almost there."

Minutes later, we stood before the rustic-looking property of Saint James the Less Church.

"What? You've brought me to a bloody parish church?!" Dane demanded. "Look, mate, you're daft if you think I'm going in there."

"Not that you've seen the insides of one to know what you're missing," Lyra murmured.

"Spare me, Mother Theresa," he said.

He gave her a long look before returning his attention to me.

"Burst into flames when you pass beyond the doors?" I asked.

"Oh, sod off," he said. "Look, I just don't fancy hanging about with that pious lot. Bunch of worthless old duffers for the most part."

"What are duffers?" I asked, noting Lyra's sardonic expression. "Listen, I shouldn't be very long."

"Funny, I didn't take you for the worshipping sort," he said.

"I just heard about it and wanted to check it out," I said.

"Do you want one of us to go inside with you?" Lyra asked.

I looked at her and noticed a tentative look of sincerity.

"No," I said. "But thank you."

Her expression turned bored again. "Have a nice chin wag then," she said. "We'll wait out here for you."

I walked through the main gates and up to the historic-looking church doors.

Inside, I felt as if I was walking into a bastion of antiquity, peppered here and there with modern accents. A bingo signup sheet sat atop an old oak table while a locked wooden box beside it stated *Food Drive Donations.*

Above that, a message board hung against a section of the church's original brick wall. A prominent message cautioned *Please Silence All Mobile Devices.*

The interior was lit in subdued fashion, but it felt

welcoming, if not a bit dated.

I proceeded into the main sanctuary and immediately noted the beautiful stained glass that was inlaid along the brick walls of the sanctuary. Rows of worn wooden pews proceeded along a central aisle leading to the raised front dais.

"I'll be with you in a moment," said a nearby clergyman who was kneeling down to minister to an older lady sitting in one of the pews.

"Oh, no need," I said.

He gave me a peculiar look and returned to the lady before him.

I stared again at the interior of stone and brick buttresses. I wondered what history the old church had seen over the decades. For the most part, it seemed eternal, as if untouched by modern times.

That is, until I laid eyes upon the projection screen hanging at the front of the chapel, just above the pulpit.

My gaze returned to the line of nearly medieval-looking stained glass images.

I wondered if Alton frequented the old church. Somehow, much as Dane had noted about me, I didn't envision Alton as the worshipping type, though we had never discussed religion at length.

A few minutes later, I was preparing to walk out when the clergyman, a fellow who was a few years my senior, approached me with a welcoming expression. The old woman to whom he had been ministering walked up the central aisle toward the front entrance area.

"Welcome to Saint James," the clergyman said. "I'm Thomas, one of the reverends here. How can I be of service?"

"Hi," I replied, reaching out to shake his hand. "I'm Caleb. I was just passing by and wanted to take a peek inside. The stained glass is beautiful."

"I see," he said. "Yes, the architecture is remarkable here. The church was built during the late 1850s, so we do host the occasional curious tourist from time to time. Feel free to take photos of the interior."

"Thanks," I said.

"Certainly. Enjoy your evening," he said.

I watched as he returned to replacing hymnals along each of the pews into their respective holders.

My thoughts returned to Alton and how rapidly things were changing around me and Kat. Things were evolving so fast. I ventured that pretty soon I'd feel much like one of the relic images depicted in the stained glass.

Just a couple of years ago, vampires were merely mystical creatures from movies and novels—pastimes of popular fiction, but little else of substance to me.

Now I felt as if the world around me was something foreign, if not alien in some ways.

How much of what I believed the world to be was misconception, much less outright fantasy?

More to the point, beyond being Kat's mate, it was hard for me to determine exactly where I fit in amongst the ranks of Alton's vampire-centric organization.

"Caleb, wasn't it?" Reverend Thomas asked, suddenly standing beside me.

"Hm?" I asked. "Yes."

"I don't mean to pry, but I couldn't help but notice that you appeared somber, as if perhaps something might be weighing heavily in your thoughts," he said. "Is there anything that I can do to help? If you'd like to talk, I think you'll find that I have quite a sympathetic ear."

He seemed nice enough, but how was I supposed to broach the subject of vampires while standing in a church? One of the cardinal rules of being Kat's mate was never to reveal the truth about vampires to anyone. Rules aside, and given the fantastical nature of such a claim, mentioning vampires to him might result in little more than his referral to a psychologist.

"As I look at these stained glass images, I can't help wondering if people from days gone by understood the world around them. Sometimes I feel as if I don't even know what's real in the world anymore," I said. "Much less knowing exactly where I fit into it."

"Ah, well, that would indeed feel troubling," he said. "Still, you're not alone. As has always been the case with humanity, the world is rapidly changing before our very eyes. Granted, it's moving at a much more accelerated pace in recent years."

"Yes, but in here it feels as though time were suspended," I said. "I can sort of understand why Alton likes it."

"Alton?" he asked.

"Oh, a friend of mine," I said. "It was through him that I learned of your church."

"Well, the church is hardly mine. It belongs to God and those served by its presence in this parish," he said. "Incidentally, would you be referring to Alton Rutherford?"

"Yes," I replied. "I understand that he supports the church, perhaps even worships here."

"Supports, yes," he said. "Mr. Rutherford is a very generous benefactor, though one wouldn't necessarily refer to him as among our regular parishioners."

"Ah," I said.

He studied me for a moment. "Wait, you're an American. You must be Caleb Taylor then," he ventured.

I frowned. "You've heard of me?"

"You're Katrina Rawlings' mate, I presume?" he asked.

My eyes widened.

He held up one hand. "Please, don't be alarmed. I shouldn't have been so forward."

"How did you know—"

"Rest assured, Mr. Rutherford and I go back a long way together," he said. "You have nothing to fear."

I hadn't really taken notice before, but he did have an unusually pale complexion.

"No way," I said.

"I beg your pardon?" he asked.

"Nothing," I said.

He gave me a patient look. "Oh, many years it's been since I've seen that expression used on me. Is it so very strange that I might be a vampire and a reverend?"

I didn't know what to say at that moment.

"No way," I repeated.

"We're all children of God," he said. "Only some of us have been at it longer than others."

I felt dumbfounded, nearly numb.

"How is that even possible?" I asked.

He gestured to the nearest pew. "Please, take a seat."

I weighed the options of leaving versus staying, but my curiosity won out.

I sat down and he sat beside me.

"Caleb, at one time or another most of us wonder what our place in the world is," he said. "It's a challenge to know where we're supposed to fit in. I'm happy to say that I've found my place, and it's quite rewarding."

"Have you served here for very long?" I asked.

"Oh, quite a number of years now," he said. "Time gets away with me just as it does everyone else."

It was hard to wrap my mind around the contrast before me.

"But you're a vampire," I said.

"Being a vampire is what I am," he said. "But it doesn't have to define *who* I am."

I hadn't considered it that way.

"When you think about it, that's really no different with anyone else in this world," he said. "We each have free will to decide who we choose to be in life; those decisions are part of what defines us as beings."

"Yes, but how do you talk to people—minister to people—knowing what you do and what they don't even realize?" I asked.

"I do what any other reverend does," he said. "Only mostly at night."

"Yeah, I can imagine," I said.

Then something occurred to me.

"So, pardon my asking, but being a vampire, do you actually believe there's a God?" I asked.

He looked at me with an amused expression. "Did you happen to notice my outfit? This collar is neither a fashion statement nor a disguise, you know."

"A vampire reverend with a wry sense of humor," I said.

"A keen sense of humor is even more important in the ministry," he said. "And yes, I'd like to believe that there is a God."

"But you don't know," I said.

He shrugged. "Who does, really? Yet, I have faith that He might be there, after all."

"But what if He isn't real?" I asked.

"Better yet, what if everyone's had it wrong and He is really a She?" he countered.

I hadn't even considered that.

"Look, Caleb, the manner in which I choose to conduct my life is helping others," he said. "Even if there is no God, though I'm hopeful there is, at the very least I can feel that I've made a positive difference in people's lives. That has to be worth something, wouldn't you agree?

"And, let's be frank," he continued. "If there really isn't a God, it isn't going to disappoint any of us for very long after we take our last breath, is it?"

I mulled that over for a moment.

"You make some pragmatic, if not compelling, points," I said.

He slowly gazed around the room. "Yes, well, I've had a long time to refine my views on the matter. Mind you, I keep some of my views to myself."

I was tempted to ask him how old he was, but that seemed very forward to ask that of someone who I had just met.

"I appreciate our chat," I said. "Though I still can't say that my initial quandary has been solved."

"Ah, the eternal question as to where you belong," he said.

"Yep," I said, still reeling over the concept that I was talking to a vampire reverend.

"Caleb, I'm sorry, but that's a question that only you can answer for yourself," he said. "Remember that, while your experiences or relationships may guide or influence your decision-making, only you can truly decide the person you want to be."

"I'll bear that in mind," I said. "Well, it's getting late, but thank you for the visit. I appreciate your time."

I started to rise, but then paused and looked back at him, weighing the merits of a further query.

"Yes?" he asked.

"I apologize if this sounds invasive, but as a minister, how do you reconcile your whole blood-drinking thing?" I asked.

"You are ever the curious one, aren't you?" he asked. "Oh, the things you must have already seen to be so matter-of-fact about such topics.

"However, if you must know, I've never taken blood from a parishioner. I've also never killed anyone since becoming a vampire, either."

"Then how—"

"For years, I relied upon the measured—shall we say, charity—of others," he said. "However, I suspect that you're well aware of modern blood bank services, aren't you?"

"Oh, I see," I said. "I meant no offense in asking, of course."

He maintained a pleasant expression. "I can assure you, none taken."

I rose. "Well, I'd better get going now. Um, thank you for your time and it's a pleasure meeting you, Father Thomas."

He shook my hand again. "Yes, a pleasure visiting with you, Caleb. And please be sure to stop by again for another chat. I'm here to help, and it may be comforting to be able to speak with someone who understands your unique challenges."

"Thank you," I said. "Um, about our chat—"

"As with all our parishioners, our discussions remain confidential," he said. "It's just between us and God."

He accompanied me to the front of the sanctuary.

"Please give my best to Mr. Rutherford," he said.

"I will."

As I walked toward the entrance, I spied the box for food bank donations. I reached into my pocket and pulled out a sole ten-pound note, which I folded and stuffed into the narrow slot at the top.

When I turned to look back, Father Thomas smiled and inclined his head toward me.

I opened the front door and nearly walked into a young couple who were entering.

"Oh, sorry," said the man.

I held the door open for them.

"Thank you," said the young woman.

"Father Thomas, we're so sorry about running late for our counseling session," the man said. "We had a flat on the way."

"No apologies necessary. I'm here all night, you know," Thomas said.

"And what a night. It's getting to be almost pea soup out there," the woman said.

"Well then, you hang up your coats while I brew us a nice hot cup of tea before we begin," Thomas said.

I shook my head as I closed the door behind me and stepped into the night.

Suddenly, the world had become a much stranger place than I gave it credit for.

As I stepped out onto the sidewalk, I failed to see either Dane or Lyra nearby. I also noted that an eerie fog had set in.

"Oh, *that* pea soup," I said while removing my smartphone from my jacket pocket. "Great. Just great."

I texted Dane, *Where the hell are you guys?*

CHAPTER 24

Caleb

The ominous fog thickened fast and a light mist fell.

London wasn't a quiet city, and yet, the conditions seemed to mute the sounds of traffic as if they were happening in another part of the world.

I considered the warmth and relative safety of the church before proceeding up the sidewalk in the direction of the hotel.

A vehicle passed by and was quickly enveloped into the mist. Moments later, the muted sounds of heavy footsteps came from behind me.

My phone buzzed and I looked down to see a text reply from Dane.

Thought you'd taken holy orders. Relax.

As I returned my phone to my pocket, the footsteps grew louder and I reached into my jacket with my free hand to grasp one of the UV flashlights.

I reached for one of my combat knives and turned to face the figure approaching me.

I first glimpsed a long black leather coat before my eyes focused on Kat's face and long red hair. She pursed her lips with amusement.

"Wondered what you'd do," she said.

I relaxed, inwardly relieved to see her.

She stopped before me and bent down to give me a warm kiss, sending a wave of happiness through me.

"Surprised to see me?" she asked.

"Actually, yes. But it's a very happy revelation," I replied. "Where's Dane and Lyra?"

"I gave them the night off," she said. "Shall we hail a lift back to the hotel?"

"Let's stroll for a bit," I said.

"As you wish, my love," she said. She reached down to grasp my hand and walked alongside me.

Despite the foreboding setting, there was an oddly romantic feel to walking beside her in the mist and fog.

"Did your meeting go well?" I asked.

She didn't answer me immediately.

"It was interesting," she said. "Alton and I are delving into some things more cautiously, given your unusual knowledge of our guest. But let's not talk about that now."

Part of me wondered why she sounded so hedgy. However, another part of me really didn't care. I was happy to finally spend some quality time with her.

We walked in silence for a time while holding hands. The mist lightened up but the fog remained dense. Despite the slight chill, it felt like being encapsulated inside our own private bubble of reality.

"I was rather surprised to hear that you were visiting a church," she said. "I didn't think you were especially religious."

"Not especially," I said. "I was curious."

"I see," she said.

"Father Brookins was very welcoming," I said.

She looked at me. "So, you met Thomas, then. He's an interesting fellow."

"He's a vampire," I said.

"Oh, I know. Though you'd hardly suspect it," she said. "What are the odds that you would wander into a church and find the only vampire clergyman in London?"

"I learned about Saint James the Less from a file I was sorting for Marla," I said. "Though I didn't know anything about him until going there firsthand."

"Thomas doesn't like to embrace his nature," she said. "He's unusual, even for a vampire."

"I like him," I said.

"Are you going back to see him again?" she asked.

"I dunno," I said. "Maybe. It depends."

"Anything that you want to discuss?" she asked. "Are you having a crisis of faith?"

"Not especially."

Then something strange struck me.

"Have you ever?"

"Crisis of faith?" she asked. "Yes, but it was a long time ago. And I've moved well beyond it over the years."

"Years?"

She squeezed my hand. "All right, then, more accurately centuries. There's no need to accentuate my protracted existence, if you please."

"Oh, please," I said. "It makes you seem so much more exotic."

"You mean ancient," she said.

I grinned. "Cradle robber."

She yanked my hand and pulled me against her. I felt her teeth playfully nip at my neck and I laughed.

Then she kissed me there.

"I love and adore you," I said, taking her into my arms and kissing her.

"I'm very happy to hear that," she said between kisses.

I spied a coffee shop across the street.

"Hey, I've got an idea," I said. "Perfect for a nibbler like you."

Minutes later, we sat at a small corner table sipping hot tea. She picked at an orange-frosted scone while I ate a hot sandwich and crisps with a frosted chocolate cupcake for dessert.

She smiled at me. "I think you're the nibbler here."

"Fog makes me hungry," I said.

"Breathing makes you hungry," she teased.

We spent more than two hours just sitting and chatting about nothing and everything. It felt like the times we had spent together when we first started dating more than a year ago.

It was the best of times.

By the time we left the shop, it had started raining outside.

"How do you feel about either a taxi or the tube?" I asked.

"Good idea," she said, retrieving her phone from her pocket. "Try hailing a cab."

I stepped out to the curb and raised my hand while looking up and down the street, but I didn't see any available taxis in the vicinity.

"I think we'd better plan to find the nearest tube access," I said.

As I dropped my hand, a pair of dark SUVs sped down the street and came to a screeching halt before us.

I turned to look at Kat and she winked at me.

"They just happened to be nearby?" I asked.

She stepped forward and opened the rear passenger door of the lead SUV for us.

"You don't think I'd leave us stranded out on such a foreboding night?" she countered, gently ushering me into the back seat.

"Where to, General?" asked the driver.

"Home," she replied.

As we proceeded, I stared out the window at the nearly deserted streets.

"What about Thanksgiving?" I asked.

"As we planned, it'll be in the Mediterranean," she replied.

"When do we leave?"

"Tomorrow night," she replied. "Looking forward to it?"

I almost hesitated to answer with my desired reply, but

then braved it.

"Yes, though I'd like it better if Paige were there," I said.

"I know. I passed along word to Ethan," she said. "I also left messages with some of her older contact points."

I looked at her with a hopeful expression.

"I can't make any guarantees, Caleb," she said. "She's unpredictable, though I wouldn't get my hopes up if I were you given how things went between you two back in Ohio."

It made me sad to think that Paige might not be part of our upcoming holidays. She felt like family to me now, and the holidays were all about family. Even Ethan felt like extended family.

Before I realized it, our SUV pulled up in front of the hotel. During our short walk and elevator ride to our room, my thoughts wandered back to Paige.

God, how I miss her.

As I lay in bed beside Kat, I reflected on the events of the day, including Alton's stern counseling with me that morning.

Alton saw so much promise in me. Yet, none of that mattered if I wasn't devoted to fulfilling those expectations.

Before falling asleep, I recalled something Father Brookins had said during our meeting.

Remember that, while your experiences or relationships may guide or influence your decision-making, only you can truly decide the person you want to be...

* * *

When I awoke, I felt strangely more settled about my life, though I couldn't point to any specific reason why. Maybe I was merely looking forward to Thanksgiving.

It was, after all, my favorite holiday.

Kat was busily packing two suitcases for herself. Fortunately, most of my things were still packed from my arrival two days prior.

"Kat, one question," I asked.

"Just one?" she countered. "Will wonders never cease?"

I gave her a bland look. "Fun-ny."

She appeared a little too pleased with herself.

"Where precisely are we going for Thanksgiving?" I asked. "Alton seems to like the whole surprise aspect, but today's the day we leave and I'm dying of curiosity."

"But Alton wanted to surprise you," she said. "We're even leaving during the day so that we arrive before sunset. I hope that you appreciate his efforts."

"Do you know our destination?" I asked.

"Of course," she replied.

I folded my arms before me. "I thought mates don't keep secrets from each other."

"It's not a secret. It's a surprise."

I gave her a flat look.

She placed her hands atop her hips. "Caleb Taylor, you're going to be surprised and like it."

I shook my head and carried my suitcases to the front door.

Two hours later, we boarded a Sunset Air flight for points unknown. Kat and I shared a luxurious private cabin with Alton, but he remained tight-lipped about our destination.

Almost five hours later, we landed and I eagerly disembarked the flight, only to stand inside a closed hangar. Two men wearing business suits stood nearby and Alton motioned to them.

"These gentlemen will escort you outdoors," he said.

Kat stood to Alton's right, watching me.

The taller of the two men reached out to shake my hand. "Pleasure to meet you, Mr. Taylor. I'm Wes Chamberlain, daytime security coordinator."

"Nice to meet you," I said.

"If you would permit me, we'll proceed toward that exit," he said, gesturing toward the nearest metal door.

As we exited the hangar, bright sunshine beamed down upon us. I raised my hand to shield my eyes as both the view and scent of the ocean assailed me.

Then I realized that the airport appeared to be placed in the midst of the bay.

"This is—," I said. "Wow."

"Mr. Taylor," prompted one of the guards. "It's my distinct pleasure to welcome you to the British territory of Gibraltar.

*　*　*

Gibraltar was beautiful.

Alton had outdone himself; something I let both he and Kat know the moment I returned inside the hangar.

The temperatures were in the mid-sixties and the abundant sunshine was an added bonus compared to the pea-soup fog of London.

"Enjoy the sunshine, my love. However, the windows to our suite aren't UV-coated, so please mind the curtains during the day," Kat reminded me.

It was the least I could do.

Our first day there was the day before Thanksgiving, and was one of the most relaxing that I had experienced in weeks. I toured part of the island with a local resident—a charming young lady named Clarissa—who had been hired by Alton. I was so happy that I didn't even mind the security detail that accompanied us.

Fortunately, Clarissa never even asked about them.

That evening, Kat and I spent quality time enjoying Gibraltar's diversions. It was definitely a popular tourist destination, teeming with a vibrant night life that frequented its restaurants, clubs, and numerous festive outdoor settings.

The next day was Thanksgiving. As Kat and I were out very late the previous evening, I slept in the next morning. I also saved my appetite for what Alton promised would be a savory and traditional Thanksgiving menu.

The evening was designated as a formal dinner. Kat and I attired in formal eveningwear; she in an elegant silk dress and me in a dinner tuxedo.

Kat's hair was pinned up into place high above her shoulders, revealing the pale skin of her neck.

She looked ravishing.

Our setting befitted something from a fairy tale with our dinner being served upon a banquet table on the roof of our luxury hotel.

The evening felt remarkably warm thanks to strategically placed heaters. However, even receiving a chill would have been worth it; the view was breathtaking.

As an added surprise, Alton arrived looking dapper in his tuxedo, but also accompanied by his human mate, Dorianne Rousseau or, rather, Dori as she preferred to be called. She looked stunning in her white satin evening dress, and her hair was done up in a manner that completed the look of some fabled princess.

She and I embraced and she gave me a friendly kiss on the cheek.

"Caleb, it's wonderful to see you again," she said. "It feels like forever, in fact."

"Dori, you look spectacular," I said. "And it does feel like forever since Slovenia."

As a special agent with Interpol, her help had been absolutely instrumental in our survival at the vampire conference in Slovenia over the summer.

"Well, shall we take our seats?" Alton asked, gesturing to the elegantly laid dining table placed in the center of the open roof.

I noted the six empty chairs to our party of four and looked at Kat, who merely shrugged to my silent query.

"Are we waiting for two others?" Dori asked.

She was one of the most observant people I knew, especially for a human, but certainly even compared to most vampires I knew.

"Ethan said that he might come," Alton said. "Though I haven't heard back from him in a day or so. And as for Paige…"

A pang of disappointment washed through me. I wanted so very much for both of them to attend.

Kat reached out to lightly touch my shoulder.

"I'm sorry," she said.

"The night is still young," Dori spoke up. "But I think neither of them would want us to miss out on such a grand event."

She flashed me a supportive look; one that I could scarcely discount.

"It certainly looks amazing," I said.

"Indeed," Alton agreed. "As host, I'll place everyone."

As if such a thing were even in question.

Alton sat at the head of the table, with Dori seated at the opposite end in the hostess position, while Kat and I sat beside each other to Alton's right.

It was then that I noticed the discreet placement of a handful of vampire guards stationed around the roof, accentuating the fact that holiday dinners had changed significantly for me these days. Not even the continued tensions between opposing vampire factions took a day off.

A series of waiters proceeded around us as Alton was presented with a bottle of vintage wine for his approval. Our first course consisted of savory baked bread and salad accented with fruits and nuts of the Mediterranean region.

"This is really wonderful, Alton," I said. "Thank you for arranging this for us."

"My pleasure, dear boy," he said. "As fate may have it, our little trip paired quite nicely with a meeting that we had today with—"

"Dear, I'll have no shop talk at Thanksgiving dinner," Dori admonished. "After all, this is Caleb's and our family night."

"What? Oh, certainly, my dear," Alton said.

I grinned at her with appreciation, to which she inclined her head toward me.

"I'm so happy that you could attend, Dori," Kat said, raising her wine glass in homage. "You're working veritable magic already this evening. Wouldn't you agree, Alton?"

Alton appeared momentarily flustered as he raised his glass in kind. "Um, quite so."

I adored Dori.

The main course of our meal soon arrived, and I looked down at my platter-sized plate, arrayed with thick slices of roasted turkey, herb dressing, garlic mashed potatoes, grilled mixed vegetables, cranberry sauce, and a portion of sweet potatoes in a glaze.

More fresh bread was brought to the table as a server topped hot gravy upon my meat, stuffing, and mashed potatoes.

I glanced aside to note that Kat's plate had everything except the turkey, though I noted what appeared to be fresh fruit compote in place of it.

"Oh, this is amazing," I said, breathing in the fresh scent of my food.

"I'm happy that it meets with your approval," Alton said.

"Truly, it's perfect," I said. "Thank you, Alton."

He smiled at me. "My pleasure. Happy Thanksgiving."

The food tasted so wonderful and flavorful that I completely lost awareness of the otherwise scenic view around me.

"Caleb, what are you most thankful for?" Dori asked.

"Food aside, of course," Kat added.

Everyone laughed as I gave her a bland look.

"Each of you," I said, glancing at the two empty chairs across from me and feeling a pang of sadness. "It's definitely the people in my life that matter most."

"Well said, Caleb," Dori said. "I feel much the same."

After I finished cleaning my plate of any remaining morsel of food, I leaned back in my chair.

"Everything tasted wonderful," I said. "And yet, I can't wait to see what's for dessert."

"Oh, I scarcely have room left for that," Dori said, sitting back from her plate, which was still nearly a third full of food.

"Do you hear that?" Alton asked.

I looked at him. "Hear what?"

A helicopter quickly rose above the top of the roof behind Alton, hovering in place.

"What the he—" I started to say.

Everything seemed to erupt all at once.

Black-clad figures leapt from an open door at the side of the helicopter onto the roof.

Our guards immediately responded with gunfire. My world spun as Kat grabbed my arm and rolled me onto the decorative rug beneath us.

I raised my head in time to hear gunfire erupting around me and see Kat moving in a blur toward the nearest attackers.

Another helicopter appeared out of my peripheral vision. More black-clad attackers sprang onto the rooftop, some firing automatic weapons, while others bore swords.

Dori threw her plate at an oncoming attacker and engaged him with a table knife, though the figure slammed her back onto the roof's hard surface.

I scrambled to my feet, grabbing at the upturned dining chair beside me. As Dori's attacker pointed his assault rifle at her, I swung the chair into an arc, slamming it against him and knocking him aside. His rifle fired wildly as rounds impacted the dining table beside me.

Dori was upon him like a feral cat, repeatedly stabbing him in the neck with her table knife.

A metal door slammed open behind me, followed by fresh gunfire, which I desperately hoped was ours. I turned just in time to see Alton's security detail engaging in the foray.

Out of my peripheral vision, a figure rushed toward me, and I spun to confront a sword-wielding attacker.

Luckily, my clumsiness kicked in at a timely moment and I tripped, falling backward onto the roof's surface. As my assailant adjusted his attack, I swiftly kicked at his kneecap and he fell to one side while howling in pain.

I reached out to wrestle the sword from his hands and we battled for control. Unfortunately, he was a vampire and I felt his strength quickly overtake my own.

"Caleb!" Kat screamed from somewhere nearby.

That's when Dori appeared, firing a captured rifle directly at the vampire's head, which exploded in blood and gore before me.

She swiveled her body to fire at other attackers near us while I wrestled the sword from the dead vampire's grip.

Gunfire, shouting, and the sounds of battle surrounded me.

"Caleb, behind you!" Dori shouted.

I pivoted with sword at the ready, slamming the blade upward into the gut of an attacker who was swinging his blade downward at me. The attacker's blade cut into the roof's surface, very nearly slicing into my foot.

Dori fired two rounds, each impacting the attacker's head and neck.

I tried to extract my sword from the vampire's stomach as he toppled off to one side.

Looking up, I glimpsed Kat engaged in a swordfight against two attackers simultaneously.

Things were frantic, though it appeared that we had more forces on the roof than did our attackers.

My orientation faltered as another helicopter rose from above the roof line to my right.

"Guards! Concentrate fire on the chopper!" Dori shouted.

A hail of gunfire impacted along the length of the helicopter as its door opened, hitting some of the attackers standing inside. The helicopter quickly veered away as two assailants fell from the open doorway and disappeared amidst screaming.

Then I caught sight of Alton, a sword in each hand, engaged in hand-to-hand combat with two attackers. His swords moved in a blur.

An assailant slammed into Alton, knocking him backward.

"No!" I yelled, running toward them.

Alton's attacker held onto Alton's tuxedo jacket, pulling him beyond the roof's edge.

I threw myself against the concrete parapet, grabbing after Alton as he disappeared from view before me.

I clumsily grasped his wrist, even as his weight pulled me further over the side with him.

CHAPTER 25

Caleb

A moment of vertigo washed over me. I felt myself sliding over the roof's edge, clinging to Alton's wrist.

One of my legs managed to catch onto the parapet. Pain instantly ripped through my shoulder from the yank of Alton's body weight.

I heard yelling and saw Alton's attacker plummeting downward even as I felt Alton's hand grasping my own.

Alton looked into my eyes with a horrified wide-eyed look that I'd never seen on him before.

"Hang on," I said between clenched teeth.

The problem was that I didn't have the strength to pull him up.

He seemed to grasp the situation rather quickly and his eyes turned steely.

"Caleb, you have to let me go," he said flatly.

"N-no," I stammered, straining to hold onto him. "I won't."

"You must," he urged. "You'll die if you don't."

My eyes clouded with tears as I realized that he was definitely right about that. I felt my leg slowly losing its grasp on the parapet above.

They say that in times of danger, your life flashes before

your eyes, but it wasn't true for me. I only felt pain through increasingly blurry vision.

"You're family," I rasped. "I can't lose you."

"But Katrina can't lose *you*," he said. "Let go. It's okay, Caleb. It's my time."

No, it wasn't okay. It couldn't be his time!

Not even close.

Not ever.

I loved Alton like the father I had always wanted.

Suddenly, I understood the advice that Father Brookins had given to me. I instantly realized that I knew the person I wanted to be.

Alton let go of me and my sweaty hand began losing its grip on his wrist.

"No!" I yelled, frantically struggling to tighten my grip.

Someone screamed from the roof above.

That's when my leg slipped over the edge of the roof and I felt my body drop.

My descent stopped abruptly and I was hoisted upward.

"Alton! Hold on!" Dori yelled from above.

Alton's gaze turned hopeful and his grip instantly tightened around my wrist.

"Hang in there, dear boy," he encouraged.

"I have you!" Kat yelled; her voice nearly a howl.

A high-pitched sound erupted in my ears as I nearly blacked out from the unbearable pain shooting through my shoulder, back, and neck.

The next thing I knew, I was lying on the roof staring up into Kat's horrified expression.

She pulled me into a tight embrace and I sucked in air through my teeth.

"Oh, Caleb, oh, Caleb, oh, Caleb," she chanted. "Are you insane?!"

"Couldn't lose Alton," I managed to say as I held onto her with my relatively uninjured arm.

The sounds of chaos were all around us, including the growing wails of sirens from below.

I heard Dori crying and glimpsed her and Alton holding each other as if for dear life.

"I know, I know," Alton said to her. "We're okay now."

Kat pivoted me into her arms and I lay against her body. Alton's gaze fell upon me and he stared at me in a penetrating fashion.

He disengaged from Dori and moved toward me.

He cradled my face between his hands. "Thank you, my dear boy," he said. "I will *never* forget what you did…or what you said."

I nodded dumbly.

"And, I promise you, you have a family for as long as you live," he said.

Then he rose and took Dori in his arms in a warm embrace.

"I love you, Kat," I said.

"I love you, you lunatic of a man," she replied, gripping me tightly in her arms. "But don't ever do something like that again."

I didn't have time to reply before one of Alton's guards squatted down beside us.

"General, we managed to capture one of the attackers," he said.

"Caleb, are you—" she asked.

"Go," I said. "I'll be fine."

"You need medical attention," she said.

"Don't worry. I'll see to him," Dori said, staring down at us.

Kat gently disengaged from me and stood beside Alton.

"Show us," she said.

They accompanied the guard to the other side of the roof.

Dori squatted to help me stand while I favored my injured shoulder.

We negotiated our way through dead bodies and other carnage and debris. A growing sense of numbness set in as we entered the stairwell leading from the roof.

Numerous individuals dodged by us, heading upstairs, so we kept to one side of the stairwell.

As we proceeded onto one of the mid-floor landings, someone ran squarely into me and hugged my body, sending renewed discomfort shooting through my shoulder.

It was Paige!

"We just got here and I heard—" she said. "Is Red—"

"No, she's okay," I said. "We're all okay. Well, I mean, except for some of Alton's vamp—"

"All right, kiddo," she said. "Hush."

"Paige, listen, I'm so sorry—"

"Yeah-yeah, shut up now," she said, hugging me tightly. "You're ruining my moment."

I wrapped my good arm around her and looked over her shoulder at Ethan, staring at me with a concerned expression.

"Well, at least you're alive," he said. "I'll examine you soon. For now, I'd better go up and see if anyone else needs aid."

"Hello?! Having a moment here!" Paige exclaimed.

Ethan sped past us, headed upstairs.

Dori let out a nervous sigh and chuckled.

My shoulder was throbbing with pain, but pain be damned, I was so freaking happy to hold Paige in my arms.

CHAPTER 26

Caleb

My life felt like an endless roller coaster, complete with loops and inversions. And I was damned lucky that I hadn't fallen out of the cart yet, though that was certainly due to the people in my life who served as my buzz bars.

"...extremely lucky that he didn't break anything, much less require surgery," Ethan said.

"He's damned lucky he's still alive," Kat added.

Over the past twenty-four hours, she had spent equal parts holding me close to tell me she loved me and alternatively chastising me for my heroic stunt on the roof of the hotel to save Alton's life.

That experience seemed like something out of a surreal dream; or, rather, a painful nightmare.

I became aware that the room had fallen silent.

"Caleb?" Ethan asked.

My attention returned to the present and I looked down at my arm, which was cradled in a shoulder harness.

"Earth to kiddo," Paige said, snapping her fingers in front of me.

"Yeah-yeah, I'm fine," I said.

I swatted at her hand using my good arm, but she swept her hand out of the way before I made contact. A twinge of pain shot through my injured shoulder and I sucked in air through gritted teeth.

Kat patted me on the back.

Having returned to London, we sat in Alton's office discussing the implications of the failed attack in Gibraltar.

We still didn't know who specifically had instigated it. The surviving attacker who had been taken prisoner was a vampire mercenary who had been contracted via a third-party liaison.

I scanned the faces around the room in series. Alton sat before his desk while Ethan and Marla commanded the two chairs before him. I sat between Kat and Paige on the couch.

Dane and Lyra sat together in two of the chairs at the nearby conference table. Both had seemed overly subdued when they learned about the Thanksgiving attack.

"It was a bold attack, I'll give them that," Alton said.

"Whoever *they* are," Marla said.

"I'll be giving them a number of things once we identify them," Kat said, her voice flat.

I looked at her face and nearly shivered at her cold, stony expression.

"Katrina and I have discussed how we plan to move forward," Alton said. "Dane and Lyra will return to New Haven to continue assisting with Caleb's security detail."

"Hey, I'm back now, you know," Paige said.

Alton's cool expression fell upon her. "Pray tell, I had noticed that, actually. Nevertheless, their presence will permit additional latitude for field work as the opportunities present themselves."

"I could stand with a bit of field work, actually," Dane said.

"Funny," Lyra muttered. "I thought you were pretty much averse to work."

He gave her a dirty look.

"Dane," Alton said. "I'm confident that you shall have marching orders soon enough."

Dane inclined his head in deference.

"What about you, Ethan?" Kat asked.

"I plan to spend a couple of weeks in New Haven," Ethan said. "However, I'll need to return to Atlanta after that. I have surgeries scheduled through mid-December."

I admired how dedicated he was to helping others, but I wished that he could spend more time with us in New Haven. From the expression on Paige's face, I was willing to bet that she felt much the same way.

I leaned over toward her, nearly touching her shoulder with mine.

"You know, if you wanted to go back to Atlanta with Ethan—"

"Shut up or I'll bite you," she said. "You're not getting rid of me again that quickly."

"Ah-ha, so you missed me," I said.

"Get real," she said. "I just can't wait to begin harassing your little ass for pulling that cross-country stunt of yours."

"You're all heart," I said.

"It's all about channeling my inner bitch and working through the angst," she said.

"Hey, I thought all was forgiven," I said.

"Nah, just on hiatus," she said. "This will be much more therapeutic for me."

I gave her a long look.

"As I was about to say," Alton continued. "Katrina and I will keep each of you informed about developments. That being said, none of you are to engage anyone, except in the defense of either Caleb or your own welfare, without first clearing it with either Katrina or me. Understood?"

There was a variety of mumbled assents in the room.

Kat cleared her throat and I looked sidelong at her.

"You, in particular, are to do absolutely *nothing* risky, and especially without approval," she said.

"So, you'd approve if I asked?"

"No," she replied.

"The exception being, of course, unless I have to defend myself."

JAZ PRIMO

Her eyebrows arched. "As if that was ever in question."

"Any further questions?" Alton asked. "If not, your return flight is leaving in just under three hours. I suggest that everyone finish packing or finalizing any last-minute details between now and then."

I reached out to grasp Kat's hand in mine.

She looked at me with a concerned expression.

"Want to help me finish packing back at the hotel?" I asked, playfully wriggling my eyebrows.

"Oh, packing?" she countered. "Well, I'm all about that then."

I smiled in anticipation.

* * *

Hours later, at the airport, Ethan checked his and Paige's luggage at the counter while Kat had a final discussion with Paige, Dane, and Lyra.

Alton, looking more serious than usual, guided me across the terminal to an unoccupied space away from the others, as well as from prying ears.

"Everything okay?" I asked.

"Caleb, do you remember our little chat when you arrived here in London a few days ago?"

How could I forget? It wasn't every day that a vampire threatened to bite you in the neck for bad behavior.

"Don't worry. My days of cutting town without permission are over," I said. "Your admonition was more than memorable enough for me."

"I meant every word," he said. "Stay safe, and focus on your dissertation research. Your project results are important for far more than merely acquiring your doctorate."

"Any chance you'd like to tell me why?" I asked. "I mean, if it's so important, why not put together one of your expert teams for it? Isn't it better suited for private investigators? I'm just a junior history professor who got laid off barely a year into his career."

His expression softened somewhat. "My dear boy," he said. "You're so much more than that. And, besides, I already hired some of the best investigators on the market to look into your topic. They each hit dead ends."

My eyes widened. "Then what do you expect for me to do that they couldn't?"

"In the short time I've known you, you've managed to uncover clandestine London spy cells, international vampire conspiracies, and foreign government corruption," he replied. "That's far more than a coincidence. You have an unusual way of looking at the world and that may be just what I've been waiting for."

I shrugged. "I'll give it my best."

"I know you will," he said. "And besides, even if you turn up little more than others have, at the very least you'll have completed the dissertation required to earn your doctorate. That's something you've wanted for some time now."

"Yeah, that's true."

"Hey, kiddo," Paige called from where she stood next to Kat. "Get a move on! We're boarding."

I reached out to shake Alton's hand.

"Take care of yourself," I said. "And maybe Kat, too, if you can manage it."

He took my hand and pulled me into a fraternal embrace. "You know I will. And, Caleb, one more thing."

"Yeah?"

He hugged me for a moment longer.

"Thank you for what you did, saving me on the roof of that hotel," he said. "Your actions told me everything about who you are, and I couldn't be more proud of you than I have been since that night."

"In the end, it was Kat that saved both of us," I said.

"Quite true," he conceded. "But it was your arm that I was suspended from. For that, I'm grateful."

"It was my pleasure," I said. "I'm always happy to lend a hand."

He pulled a pained expression over my pun.

"You really do mean the world to me, Alton," I said. "You're like the fath—, I mean uncle, that I always wished I'd had."

I almost felt embarrassed over my Freudian slip.

We separated from our embrace, but he held me a moment longer by the shoulders as he stared down into my eyes.

"Listen to me," he said. "From now on, no matter what transpires, you'll never want for family again. You have Kat, Paige, and I suspect, even Ethan. But, more to the point, you're part of my family now. As far as I'm concerned, you're a Rutherford, and I'll never abandon you. That's my vow to you."

That touched me so very deeply. It struck at the fiber of everything that I thought had been lost since my mother's passing from cancer some years prior.

My throat felt tight all of the sudden and my eyes began to water. I reached up to rub at them with my fingertips.

"Thank you," I said. "That means more to me than you could know."

"You're welcome. And you may be surprised over what I know," he said. "Now, go board your flight. I'll be in touch again soon to check in on your research progress."

I nodded and turned to walk across the terminal toward Kat. She stared intently at me, a concerned look on her face.

Then I stopped and turned back to look at Alton as an onerous inspiration surfaced.

"By the way, thanks for the surprise Thanksgiving trip to Gibraltar and all," I said. "But do you think that maybe next we could just do a boring Christmas at my house?"

He shook his head and playfully wagged his upraised index finger at me. "Board your plane, you scalawag."

I grinned as the edges of his mouth upturned slightly.

"And I'll consider it," he added.

* * *

The others had already boarded the flight as I held Kat in my arms just outside the entrance to the ramp leading to the aircraft.

"Did you and Alton have a good chat?" she asked. "It looked serious from my vantage point."

"Yeah, he wants me to be careful and focus on my research," I replied.

"Good advice," she said. "Please don't do anything that puts you in harm's way, my love. I can't bear a repeat of what you did on that hotel roof."

I hugged her tighter. "I know. I'm sorry. But Alton means so much to me now."

She sighed. "I know. I love him, too. But I—I love you even more. I *need* you as much as I need air and blood."

"I need you, too. I love you, Kat."

She brought so much happiness, love, and companionship into my life, fulfilling me more than anyone I could imagine.

We held each other a moment longer before separating from our embrace.

I gave her a long, warm kiss while grasping her hands in mine.

I didn't want to leave her.

"These separations are getting harder," I said.

She lightly ran her fingernails across my cheek. "I know," she said. "I feel it, too."

I swallowed to try to alleviate the growing tightness in my throat.

"There's going to come a day, and it's coming very soon, when I won't be able to endure this anymore," I said.

She gave me a sympathetic look. "As a matter of fact, I'm almost there myself."

"*Final boarding call for flight—*"

"Dammit, there's never enough time," I said.

"I know, my love."

I gave her a final kiss before turning and stepping onto

the boarding bridge. I glanced back over my shoulder at her a final time and saw her glassy-eyed expression.

She gave me a cute little wave and tried to smile.

Alton stood beside her, wrapping a supportive arm across her shoulders and nodding at me in a reassuring manner.

As I stepped across the threshold into the cabin of the aircraft, it took everything I could muster not to turn around and run back to Kat.

In that moment— a moment of near-clarity—I believed that I fully understood the power and magnetism of true love.

ABOUT THE AUTHOR

Jaz Primo: Delving into flights of fancy and realms of imagination; eagerly sharing with you.

Jaz lives in the Great American Midwest where he writes paranormal romance, urban fantasy, and young adult literature. He's a history aficionado, Doctor Who fanatic, "pun-master", an all-around fan of vampires, and a caregiver to the world's most endearing cat.

You can easily find Jaz Primo online at the following locations:

Website: http://jazprimo.com

Twitter: @jazprimo

Sunrise at Sunset: Revamped
Sunset Vampire Series, Book 1
(Second Edition)
by Jaz Primo

The Sunset Vampire Series achieved Third Place in the Reviewer's Choice Award for Best Paranormal Series of 2012 (Paranormal Romance Guild).

This new, second edition of the original, has new never-seen-before material, *Revamped* includes a forward by Jaz explaining how this version improves over the original. Additional bonus material includes a new bonus chapter that bridges events between the first novel and the sequel, *A Bloody London Sunset*.

When is a bloodthirsty predator the best protection against a psychotic killer?
When the predator is both a vampire...and the woman you love.

Caleb is bravely overcoming a dark past while having no memory of the beautiful vampire that saved him. Despite a promise to stay away, Katrina is compelled to return to him.
However, a vengeful rival from her past has dire plans for both of them.

Available in trade paperback and all major eBook formats!

Go to http://jazprimo.com/books for purchasing links!

Winner of the Paranormal Romance Guild's Reviewer's Choice Award for Best Young Adult Novel of 2012!

Gwen Reaper
A Young Adult Paranormal Romance
by Jaz Primo

Boy meets beautiful and mysterious, yet reclusive, girl who harbors a potentially-lethal secret.

"A thing of beauty is a joy forever: its loveliness increases; it will never pass into nothingness." John Keats, English romantic poet.
I never thought that my first exposure to real beauty would be tinged with the threat of oblivion...
~ ~ ~ ~ ~

When high school junior Scott Blackstone is forced to move from his childhood home in Springfield, Illinois to small-town Custer, South Dakota, he expects nothing less than to languish in complete disappointment. Instead, he discovers a beautiful and mysterious seventeen-year-old girl named Gwen, who captivates him from his initial, adrenaline-laced sight of her on the shores of Stockade Lake. Scott's pursuit of the elusive Gwen sweeps him into the midst of a potentially lethal family heritage that was birthed in hope, only to be passed into a legacy of guilt and death.

Scott engages in a journey of discovery, tinged with both angst and danger. Like many dire legends throughout history, he is unprepared for the untimely revelation that both love and despair are often two sides of the same coin.

Gwen Reaper
(A Young Adult Paranormal Romance)
is available in trade paperback and all
major eBook formats!

Go to http://jazprimo.com/books for purchasing links!

A Bloody London Sunset
Sunset Vampire Series, Book 2
by Jaz Primo

In *A Bloody London Sunset*, a timid spirit rises to assert himself, a forbidden love sparks, and a forgotten past threatens to topple the power of love.

Katrina Rawlings is a vampire who has finally rediscovered happiness for the first time in centuries. But unwanted complications erupt with a vengeance. Decisions of necessity combined with dark memories from a forgotten past threaten her relationship with the love of her life. When a sacrifice must be made, can she endure her decision?
Caleb Taylor's life is finally back on track. He has rebounded from a near mortal injury, both physically and emotionally. Yet, his reality is shaken by the suggestion of a betrayal of trust from the woman he loves. Can the power of love overcome the power of a lie?
Paige Turner is a century old vampire who fearlessly revels in a simple existence pursuing blood, dancing, and sex. Simple needs, and all met in the same manner: hot, fast, and without regrets. But a spontaneous visit leads to heartfelt sacrifice, and unexpected complications strike fear to the core of her soul. Will she survive the revelations?
In the exciting second novel in the Sunset Vampire Series, a trust is betrayed, bonds of friendship are strained, relationships may end, and a tenuous neutrality among the world's vampire population is threatened. With stakes so high, some will not survive A Bloody London Sunset!

Go to http://jazprimo.com/books for purchasing links!

Summit at Sunset
Sunset Vampire Series, **Book 3**
by Jaz Primo

Does the fate of one innocent human soul outweigh the needs of the entire vampire race?
The third, and most exciting, novel in the *Sunset Vampire Series* has finally arrived!

Powerful vampire Katrina Rawlings and her human mate, Caleb Taylor, are once more drawn into dangerous circumstances. Representatives of the most powerful and influential vampires from around the world converge upon a scenic mountain retreat located in Slovenia's Upper Bohinj Valley for a summit of historic proportion. Mystery leads to treachery, and events quickly spiral out of control. With the fates of both vampires and humans in jeopardy, Katrina desperately struggles to reconcile the balance of worldwide vampire power against honoring her commitment to the love of her life. Unwilling to be rendered helpless, Caleb initiates a desperate gamble that leads to a mortal decision. Meanwhile, the sexy and sassy vampire, Paige Turner, spearheads her own mission involving both surprising revelations of heart and grave circumstances for those around her.

In *Summit at Sunset*, unlikely alliances will be sought, eternal bonds of friendship will be tested, unrequited love will be unleashed, blood will be shed, and one pivotal person's fate will collide with destiny.

Available in trade paperback and all major eBook formats!

Go to http://jazprimo.com/books for purchasing links!

Wicked Sunset
Sunset Vampire Series, Book 4
by Jaz Primo

After exploring urban fantasy with *Bringer of Fire*, and young adult romance with the award-winning *Gwen Reaper*, author Jaz Primo returns to his beloved and extremely popular *Sunset Vampire* series with the eagerly-awaited fourth novel, *Wicked Sunset*.

Security, more than ever, is an illusion.

The world's vampires are on a terrifying course of destruction, putting everyone in mortal danger. Katrina has a confrontation with dire consequences. Caleb, surrounded by darkness, and facing challenges at every turn, makes a surprising decision- that has even more surprising results.
Even his relationship with Katrina, something he could always believe in, may be changed forever. But if Caleb can finally come into his own, he may be able to claim a legacy he never dared imagine.

Available in trade paperback and all major eBook formats!

Go to http://jazprimo.com/books for purchasing links!

Sunset Rising
Sunset Vampire Series, **Book 5**
by Jaz Primo

A Quick Note from Jaz:

Now that you've finished reading *Sunset Rising*, would you please post a quick recommendation for my *Sunset Vampire* series on your website, blog, or Facebook page to help spread the word about my works to others? How about a quick tweet or share my novel cover images on Pinterest?

While you're online, please post a quick review on Goodreads.com, Amazon, Barnes & Noble, Shelfari.com, or any other book review outlets available on the web.

Thanks so much for your kind support and assistance!

All the best,
Jaz Primo

Keep an eye out for book #6, Sunset Burning, coming out in late 2016!

Bringer of Fire
Logan Bringer Urban Fantasy Series, Book 1
by Jaz Primo

The twenty-first century has arrived, but the world is a darker place where international superpowers tenuously jockey for both political and economic supremacy. It's a time when the rights and interests of the individual carry little weight. But a medical breakthrough spontaneously blossoms telekinetic abilities within the body of one man, altering humanity's evolution and threatening to tip the world's balance of power. That man is Logan Bringer.

When humankind's greatest achievement leads to a race for its control, some will bring political and economic powers to bear.

Others unleash an array of assassins and weaponry.

However, when Logan's family is directly threatened, he unleashes himself.

He is...the *Bringer of Fire*.

Available in trade paperback and all major eBook formats!

Go to http://jazprimo.com/books for purchasing links!